Anything But a Gentleman

By the same author

A Most Unusual Governess

Anything But a Gentleman

AMANDA GRANGE

ROBERT HALE · LONDON

© Amanda Grange 2001
First published in Great Britain 2001

ISBN 0 7090 6906 5

Robert Hale Limited
Clerkenwell House
Clerkenwell Green
London EC1R 0HT

2 4 6 8 10 9 7 5 3 1

Typeset in 11/15½pt Revival Roman
Derek Doyle & Associates in Liverpool.
Printed in Great Britain by
St Edmundsbury Press, Bury St Edmunds, Suffolk.
Bound by Woolnough Bookbinding Limited

CHAPTER ONE

'*A* new tenant?' Marianne Travis, seated on her beautiful grey mare, looked out from her vantage point on Seaton Hill, across the neighbouring Billingsdale estate. It was the February of 1793, and the Billingsdale estate had been without a settled master for over a year. 'Good. Then something will be done about the mantraps.'

'I shouldn't go counting on it, miss.' Tom Gunther, groom to the Travis family for fifty years, spoke in his customary slow way. 'The gennulman, might not want to take an interest in the estate. He might want to leave it all to the manager.'

'Do you know who he is, Tom? The gentleman?'

'Lord Ravensford, Miss Marianne, if what they say in the village is true.'

'It usually is,' said Marianne with a smile.

'Yes, miss. It is at that.'

'It will be Better, in a way, having Lord Ravensford as a neighbour,' said Marianne. 'Better than the Billingsdales. Mr Billingsdale has lived in London for so long that he has lost all interest in his estate. When I wrote to him and told him that his manager had laid mantraps in the woods he simply wrote back saying he had every confidence in the man. But if Lord Ravensford is the new tenant, then perhaps I will be able to persuade him to have the traps removed.'

Tom nodded. 'Terrible cruel, those traps are,' he said.

A chill breeze blew suddenly across the snow-covered hill and Marianne shivered. 'It's cold. We should be heading for home.'

She suited her actions to her words and turned her horse's head. Tom, wheeling his mount, followed her down the hill, northwards, towards Seaton Hall.

She's a credit to my teaching, he thought ruminatively as they made their way along the border between Travis and Billingsdale land. And indeed Marianne did cut a graceful figure as she rode side-saddle on the back of her grey mare. A beaver hat was perched on her glossy black ringlets, which fell halfway down her back. A dark-blue riding habit, with its white silk lapel *à la Minerve*, set off her trim figure, and Moroccan leather boots, blue to match her habit, encased her neatly turned ankles.

Just as they reached the bottom of the hill, however, Marianne came to a halt.

'Is anything wrong?' asked Tom, as he stopped behind her.

'I thought I heard something.'

Tom, a little hard of hearing, had heard nothing.

'There it is again. A cry.'

This time Tom heard it, too. A human wail. A human in great pain.

'The mantraps!' Marianne looked at Tom in dismay. 'Someone's been caught!'

She wheeled her horse and set off at a gallop. Tom rode after her. She jumped the stream that separated the two estates and galloped on, across the white fields and into the woodland, where she was forced to pick her way more carefully. The stark branches of the trees caught at her habit and she had to duck in order not to lose her hat.

'I reckon it was from over there,' said Tom, drawing level with her as she paused, unsure which way to go. He nodded north-eastwards.

Marianne listened.

The cry came again. Turning her mare's head slightly she rode slowly between the bare trees until at last she caught sight of a man writhing on the ground.

'Don't you go any further, miss,' said Tom, slipping off his horse. 'It won't be a pretty sight.'

'You'll need help,' said Marianne, dismounting. Despite the lack of a block she accomplished the movement with a minimum of fuss, and steeled herself for what she knew she would find.

Since Mr Billingsdale's estate manager had taken to trapping the woods it was not the first time she had found a poacher caught in one of the cruel traps: when the winter was hard, many of the villagers had no choice but to catch a rabbit or two in order to stay alive. Even so, she could not prevent a shudder as she approached the man.

Tom was already beside him, examining the vicious trap.

'You'll have to pull it open, whilst I help him to free his leg,' Marianne said. 'Thank goodness the trap's an old one. The jaws are bent. With any luck it will not have broken his leg.'

Tom nodded.

Marianne turned to the stranger, whose face was contorted with pain. 'We're here to help,' she reassured him.

He was a short, stocky man and appeared to be about fifty years of age. His head was balding and he had a dark moustache. Despite his agony, he was trying desperately to free himself.

Marianne and Tom applied themselves to the difficult business of helping him, and at last he was freed; but at a price. The savage jaws of the trap had badly damaged his leg, and blood ran down his calf.

'Easy now,' said Tom, as he helped the man to rise.

The man gave a sharp intake of breath as he tried to put his injured foot to the ground. 'Ah!' he gasped, as beads of sweat stood out on his forehead.

'Who are you? Where are you from?' asked Marianne, but he was almost unconscious with pain and could not reply. 'Do you know him, Tom?' she asked, turning to her groom.

'No, miss. He's not local, that's for sure.'

'Local or not, he needs a doctor, and as we don't know where he's from we had better take him back to the Hall.' She looked northwards to where the roof of Seaton Hall could just be seen. 'He can't walk. Somehow we have to get him on to your horse.'

Tom nodded. It would be a difficult business. But difficult though it was, it must be done.

'First thing tomorrow morning I intend to call on Lord Ravensford,' said Marianne, as the feat was at last accomplished. 'We will set out at nine o'clock, Tom. And I will see what I can do about putting a stop to this terrible business, once and for all.'

'Oh, no, you don't, Miss Marianne,' declared Trudie in outraged terms later that afternoon when Marianne revealed her intention of speaking to Lord Ravensford on the following morning. 'Going to call on a gentleman, and you an unmarried young lady? Your mother would turn in her grave!'

Marianne gave a tired smile as she sank down on to the *chaise-longue* in the pretty sitting-room, back at the Hall.

She could not be angry with Trudie, although she would not have allowed such familiarity from anyone else. Trudie had always been much more than a housekeeper in the Travis household, she had been a valued and trusted friend. Ever since Marianne's mother had died she had looked after the little girl, providing the motherly attention that Marianne's father, however loving, had not been able to give her.

'No,' she said. 'Mama would understand. It has to be done, Trudie. You've seen what the traps can do to a man. Lord Ravensford must be persuaded to order their removal.'

'But not by you,' declared Trudie. 'There's no need for you to go persuading him nor to go chasing around the countryside rescuing waifs and strays. Especially when you don't know anything about them. Who is this man? That's what I'd like to know. He could be a burglar, come to steal the silver, or an escaped convict, come to murder us all in our beds!'

'I don't think he would find it easy with his leg in bandages,' said Marianne, as she leaned back with a tired smile.

'That's not the point, Miss Marianne, and well you know it. He could be anyone or any*thing*! And yet you bring him here and put him in a guest room and bandage his leg, for all the world as though it was his due.'

'You know his leg needed dressing,' said Marianne. 'Dr Moffat's instructions were plain. It is only fortunate that his leg was not broken.'

'And that's another thing! Paying the doctor out of your own pocket!' said Trudie, shaking her head in exasperation. 'Ah, well,' she went on in a gentler tone, 'I may as well save my breath. Nothing I can say is going to change you. You're too much like your mama, Miss Marianne; she was forever doctoring waifs and strays as well.'

Marianne smiled as she remembered her dearly loved mother.

Trudie gave her an affectionate look and then her tone became brisk once more. 'But as to visiting Lord Ravensford,' she continued, tucking the end of a neatly rolled bandage beneath one of its folds to secure it, 'that's another matter. With the rector's sister away there's no one to go with you as your chaperon—'

'I will be taking Tom.'

'Tom!' snorted Trudie. 'What kind of a chaperon is he for a young lady? No, Miss Marianne, it won't do. Best leave this business alone.'

Marianne stood up wearily and walked over to the fireplace, where a cheery blaze brightened the gloomy afternoon. 'It's no

good, Trudie, I can't let matters rest. You saw the man's leg. It
can't go on.'

Trudie dropped the rolled bandage into a willow basket on top
of a dozen others. 'Then wait until the rector's sister returns from
visiting her aunt. Or better yet, wait for the Cosgrove ball. Lord
Ravensford'll be there, and Mr Cosgrove can introduce you. After
that – well, there'll be no harm in mentioning it then.'

Marianne turned round to face Trudie. 'The rector's sister will
be away for another week. And as for the Cosgroves' ball, that's
nearly two weeks away. No, Trudie, I can't wait. If I do, another
man may be caught in the traps. I must go tomorrow as arranged.'

'Then I'm coming with you,' Trudie declared.

'No.' Marianne was firm. 'You will have to stay here. Now that
we have so few servants there is no one else I can leave in charge.
Don't worry, Tom will see that no harm comes to me. Besides,
Lord Ravensford is a gentleman. He is not likely to take advantage
of a perfectly respectable neighbour.'

'Just as you say, Miss Marianne,' said Trudie, reluctantly giving
in. 'But if he gives you a minute's trouble,' she added darkly as she
turned away, 'he'll feel the force of my rolling pin!'

Marianne guided her horse and cart along the snowy lanes towards
the Billingsdales' house. The weather was better than she had
expected, and she was relieved to find that the ground was not too
slippery. She often went about in the pretty little cart which,
despite its rustic appearance, was light and easy to handle. It was
just as well, for this morning she had had no choice but to use it
as her mare had been taken ill in the night. Tom was in the stables
now, looking after the animal, and Marianne was managing the cart
alone.

She gave a sigh as she thought of Trudie's protests at the idea of
her visiting Lord Ravensford without even Tom by her side, but
Marianne had never once contemplated putting off her visit. She

needed to persuade Lord Ravensford to have the traps removed as soon as possible, and that meant visiting him straight away.

She rounded a corner, controlling the horse with an expertise born of long practice. She had reached a particularly pretty part of the lane, where arched trees met overhead and, putting all her unpleasant thoughts aside, she gave herself up to enjoying the beauty of the winter scene. With the sun catching the frosty coating on the trees' bare branches and sending out gleams from the thick blanket of snow that covered the earth it was a lovely sight.

Fir trees now began to grow down to the road, their thickly needled branches contrasting with the stark limbs of the deciduous trees Marianne had just passed. Although beautiful, they cast a heavy patch of shadow on the lane and the ice beneath them was unmelted. Marianne gave her full attention to the horse and cart. It was a good thing she did because, as she turned another corner, she felt the cart begin to slide. The horse slipped, the cart slewed across the road – straight into the path of a man on horseback who had just come round the bend. His horse reared; there was a loud whinnying from both animals; and the man, with a curse, was thrown to the ground.

As soon as she had brought the cart to a safe halt Marianne stepped down, shedding the stone hot water bottles that had kept her warm despite the coldness of the day, and taking care that she, too, did not go sliding across the ice.

'Let me help you,' she said, offering him her hand as he struggled to his feet.

'Thank you, but you've done quite enough,' he said angrily. 'What the devil do you think you were doing, sliding across the road like that? You could have got someone killed.'

'You surely can't think I did it on purpose?' returned Marianne. 'My horse lost its footing and the cart skidded; something that wouldn't have mattered if you hadn't been riding at such breakneck speed. With so much ice about you were asking for a fall.'

11

He stopped in the middle of dusting off his many-caped great-coat, turning gold-brown eyes towards her. His face was arresting. High cheekbones gave it structure, whilst a firm jaw gave it character and strength. Framing all was dark hair, tied in a black ribbon bow at the nape of his neck.

'I didn't expect to run into a cart blocking the road,' he returned curtly. He caught the reins of his horse, which had wandered several yards away, and checked the animal over. 'Nothing broken, thank God. I suggest, in future, that you hire a groom to handle your horse, Miss . . ?' he said, swinging one leg over the animal's back and mounting effortlessly.

Marianne, nettled by his implication that she could not handle her horse, did not give him the satisfaction of her name, and replied with acerbity, 'And I suggest that you hire a groom to handle yours. And now, since you are obviously unhurt, I will thank you to take your horse and be on your way. I am about to resume my journey, and would not like to be accused of unseating you again.'

To her surprise, his look of anger began to dissolve and he laughed, showing a gleam of white teeth. 'Wit as well as beauty,' he said with a mocking smile. '*Touché*!' He touched his three-cornered hat. Then, still laughing, he spurred his horse and the animal sprang away.

Marianne let out a sigh when he was out of sight, relieved that he hadn't been hurt. One invalid in the house was enough. If he had been knocked unconscious she would have had to put him in the cart and take him home with her as well!

At the thought of taking him home with her a strange shiver washed over her and, giving herself a shake, she told herself she had been standing too long in the cold. Turning her attention back to Hercules, the carthorse, she gathered up the reins and finally succeeded, by a mixture of pushing and pulling, both of the horse and the cart, in getting it straight again. It would have been so much easier if Tom had been with her, she thought, as she climbed up on to the box: skilled though she was, there was no denying that, with all the ice about, she would have preferred to let him drive. Still, there was no use repining. She would just have to take extra care until she reached the Manor.

She settled herself comfortably on the box, arranging her cloak about her and putting her feet once again on the stone hot water bottles, before telling Hercules to 'Walk on.' Carefully manoeuvring the cart over the icy patch she guided it along the lane. The way became broader, and she was soon passing a patchwork quilt of fields on her right. They sparkled and gleamed in the sunshine, setting her thoughts wandering again, this time down different channels.

The fields, looking so pretty under their covering of snow, had once belonged to Marianne's family, and it gave her a pang to think that they had recently been sold to Mr Billingsdale. Though Mr Billingsdale no longer took an interest in his estate his men of business worked to keep it profitable. They had snapped up the fields, which had been a bargain, because Marianne's father had had to sell off a parcel of land in a hurry to pay off her brother's gambling debts.

Marianne shook her head. Even now she could not believe it. She had always loved and admired Kit, and had not believed it when her father had told her that her older brother had run up huge gambling debts; especially when he said that Kit needed money urgently to pay them off. It had seemed so unlike Kit. So much so, that at first she had refused to believe it.

But then Kit had admitted it himself, and if he had admitted it, it must be true. Even so, it was not like him. It must be, as rumour said, that he had been led astray. He had certainly been seen in town in the company of Luke Somerville, and Luke Somerville was, by all accounts, exceedingly wild.

Marianne sighed. Whatever the truth of the matter she wished it had not happened. She missed Kit. And now that he had fled, in shame or disgrace, she did not know when she might see him again.

She was now nearing Billingsdale Manor. She could see it in the distance, away to her right. In another minute she would have to turn off the road and follow the long drive up to the house.

She slowed Hercules as she came to the gateposts. They made an imposing entrance. She carefully guided both horse and cart through the narrow opening and then made her way up the drive. The drive was long but fortunately straight, so that it was an easy matter to negotiate it, and some five minutes later she arrived at the house, cold and tired, but glad that she had come. If she went home with her mission accomplished she would rest easier, knowing the woods would once again be made safe.

She slowed her horse at the bottom of a flight of imposing steps, expecting a groom to rush out at any minute, but none came. She frowned. The house was occupied, Tom had told her; but what if he was wrong? What if there was no one at home?

There was only one way to find out. Looping the reins over the front of the cart she stepped down carefully. She smoothed the full skirt of her blue carriage dress and resettled her plumed hat on her glossy black ringlets before arranging her cloak around her and then mounting the imposing flight of steps. Still no one came to greet her. She hesitated for a moment and then knocked on the door. She heard the sound echo inside the house, but the door did not open. She glanced back at Hercules, who was standing dejectedly with his head hanging down. The poor horse was cold, and she did not want to leave him standing – certainly not for any length of time – but she was loath to go with her errand undone. She hesitated again but then tried the door. It swung open. She went slowly into the hall, looking around for signs of habitation. There were none.

She was just about to leave when she thought she heard a sound

14

coming from the direction of the drawing-room. Squaring her shoulders she walked bravely forward. Just as she reached it the door opened and she stepped back in alarm; to feel a flush of annoyance a moment later as she saw the gentleman she had earlier unseated.

'Well, well,' he said with a slow smile, 'what have we here? The beauty who travels the earth in her cart, as the goddesses travel the stars in their chariots? Have you come to apologize for unseating me, my sweet, or is it more – personal – business this time?'

He drew closer to her as he spoke, until he was so close that his long, lean body was almost touching hers. She tilted her head back so that she could see his eyes, instead of being forced to look at his strong shoulders, which would otherwise have been the extent of her view. She took in his mocking smile and saw that he was looking down at her with anticipation. She swallowed as she saw his regular teeth, noticing that they were extremely white. But it was not only his wolfish smile and gleaming teeth that unsettled her, it was the strange aura he seemed to generate. It threatened to rob her of rational thought. She felt her legs going weak. She tried to step back but she was held fast by some force she had never met with before.

Nonsense, she told herself hazily, trying to fasten her mind on his words, as they were easier to understand than his aura of power. He's talking nonsense. The beauty who travels the earth in her cart? He must have escaped from Bedlam!

'Come, don't be shy,' he said. His gold eyes fastened on her own as one long, strong finger traced the line of her cheekbone. 'There is no need, my dear.'

'I. . . .' She gulped. 'I don't know what you're talking about.' She tried to free herself from his spell. Not only did he somehow seem to be taking the strength from her legs, he also seemed to be taking the breath from her body. Her reply came out in a gasp.

'No?' He looked down at her with a tantalizing smile.

He has mistaken me for someone else, thought Marianne; either that or he has run mad!

But somehow, he did not have the look of a madman. His wild black hair was neatly tied at the nape of his neck, and his clothes were not unkempt, as she felt sure they would be if he was not quite sane. But if he was not a madman, then who. . . ?

Of course! She stirred in relief. Lord Ravensford's secretary! That's who he must be. Come to open up the house before his master arrived. It would explain a lot, even if it would not explain everything – his strange behaviour, for one.

She made a determined effort to break his spell and stepped back, out of reach. Once away from him her head began to clear, and she continued, 'I have come to see Lord Ravensford on a matter of some urgency. Pray tell him I wish to speak with him.' She thought it wiser to ignore what had just happened. She was alone with this strangely disturbing man and was by no means sure she could control the situation if she made any mention of it. 'Oh, and whilst you are about it, my horse is outside,' she went on with unusual arrogance. Her tone was meant to remind him of his station in life, in the hope that he would remember hers. 'He will need attention. Kindly arrange for one of the grooms to see to him.'

Instead of looking abashed at her tone he continued as bold as ever. He ran his eyes over her face as though she hadn't spoken, tracing the gentian-blue eyes that formed such a striking contrast to her black ringlets, her straight nose and the line of her cheek; before dropping them to her body, where they lingered on her subtle curves. She had the feeling he was undressing her in his mind, removing first her cloak and then her carriage dress and leaving her in nothing but her chemise. And then not even that. . . .

She blushed, and he smiled; a wolfish smile.

Then, making her a low bow he said, 'I will see to it right away.

16

Please, go in and make yourself comfortable. The house has only just been opened, but there is a good fire in the drawing-room. I will rejoin you directly. And then we will discuss your – business – my sweet.'

Marianne hesitated. Should she really stay? His behaviour was odd, decidedly so. However, strange as his behaviour may be, it wasn't threatening and, feeling that as soon as Lord Ravensford arrived he would dismiss his secretary, Marianne decided to stay. With a brief nod she went through into the drawing-room

The drawing-room was large and elegantly proportioned. It was decorated in delicate shades of pale green and had white mouldings adorning the walls. A *confidante*, together with a sofa, a number of x-frame stools and a variety of gilded chairs, were scattered about in a pleasing if haphazard manner. To her left was an Adam fireplace, containing a blazing fire, and directly ahead of her large windows gave splendid views over the garden, which was covered in sparkling white snow.

Marianne went over to the fire. Its cheery blaze soon began to thaw her out and she undid the strings of her cloak. Before many more minutes had passed she decided to remove it: she would feel the benefit of it then when she faced her journey home. She laid it carefully over the back of one of the chairs.

And then the secretary returned. To her consternation, however, his behaviour showed no sign of improvement. In fact, it became even worse!

Walking straight over to her he took her hands. 'Now, my dear.' He rubbed her hands with his long, strong fingers – to restore her circulation? she wondered, looking up at him uncertainly. Perhaps. She was certainly becoming warmer! And not just because he was rubbing her hands. His mocking expression had the peculiar effect of heating her insides. 'Let us waste no more time,' he said. 'I can guess what has brought you here—'

'You can?' she asked in surprise.

'Of course.' He let go of her hands and, with one powerful finger, lifted her chin. 'There is only one reason a young woman would visit a man without a chaperon, especially when they have not been introduced, and that is to offer him the . . . comfort and companionship, shall we say? . . . a beautiful woman can give. And I am very pleased you're here. I'm sure we can come to some arrangement which will be – beneficial – to us both.' He gave her another wolfish smile.

Marianne blinked. 'Do you mean to say. . . ?' She took a step back as she tried to take it in. 'Am I to understand that you think I have come here to offer you *myself*?' She didn't know whether to be outraged or utter a contemptuous laugh. He could not possibly have thought she was that sort of woman! Bedlam *was* the place for him after all.

'But of course, sweetheart.' He was amused. 'And I am very glad you did. It's been a long time since I've been offered such tempting wares. I'm looking forward to the pleasure you'll give.' His eyes ran over her figure as he spoke, lingering on the tantalizing curves that were revealed by the smooth fabric of her carriage-dress. Then his eyes snapped nakedly back to her own. 'And receive.'

'This' – she had meant to declare it, but for some reason her voice came out in a whisper – 'this is the grossest insult.' She steadied herself, and then with a steely glance she said forcefully, 'Lord Ravensford will hear of this, make no mistake.'

'He already has.' He took in her sparkling eyes and heightened colour with a look of admiration. 'Who else do you think you are talking to, my sweet?'

'Your *sweet*?' she demanded, before regaining her wits. 'Lord Ravensford?' she asked. She looked him up and down, taking in the broad shoulders and firm body encased in, admittedly, expensive clothes. But then she said contemptuously, 'You are not Lord Ravensford.'

It was his turn to look surprised. 'And what makes you say that? As far as I'm aware, you've never met him. No, I'm sure you haven't. I would have remembered such eyes, such lips. But better put it to the test, perhaps.' And drawing her to him in a movement so assured she had no chance of stopping him he covered her mouth with his own.

The action was alarming, forcing Marianne into a passionate situation that was completely unknown to her. But before she had time to push him away his tongue traced the line of her lips, and she felt them part instinctively to allow him in. As his tongue invaded her mouth the feelings it woke within her reverberated throughout her entire body. It was so delicious a sensation that against all reason her alarm melted, and was replaced by a feeling so earthy and powerful it temporarily drove all thoughts of modesty out of her mind. Her hands rose of their own accord and rested against his lapels. There was an instant of possession as his tongue explored her mouth, touching her own and tantalizing her with a new explosion of sensations; and then he pulled away.

'Passion as well as wit and beauty,' he said, laughing gently down into her eyes. 'A prize indeed. And now I am sure: you and Lord Ravensford have definitely never met.'

Marianne took a deep breath. She must steady herself. She could not let this man take control of the situation like this. 'I don't need to meet him.' Even though she had taken a deep breath, her response came out raggedly, and it was an effort to stand up straight. Her head was still spinning from what had just happened and her legs were weak. Even so, she must not let him know what an effect he had had on her. She had no way of understanding him or her own response to him, and she felt her only hope of dealing with the strange and unsettling events was to act as though nothing untoward had happened. She summoned the last remnants of her dignity to her aid. 'Lord Ravensford is, by all accounts, a gentleman,' she said. 'Whereas you are anything *but* a gentleman. You are some jumped-up servant who thinks he can pose as his master, no doubt. But you are mistaken, and you will regret your impudence when Lord Ravensford arrives.'

'What will it take to convince you that I *am* Ravensford? And that I have the means to make you the most generous recompense for your favours?' He took her hands once again and lifted them to his lips.

She could feel the heat of his mouth even through her gloves and had the desire to pull her hands away. Though not because the sensation was unpleasant, but because, disturbingly, it was quite the opposite.

'Nothing you can say will convince me that you are Lord Ravensford, for the simple reason that you are not.' She struggled to remove her hands from his, but he would not let them go. 'Lord Ravensford would never treat one of his neighbours in this insulting fashion, and—'

'Neighbours?' he asked with a frown.

'Yes, sir. *Neighbours.*'

The amused light left his eyes, and they became searching. 'But you are alone,' he said, letting go of her hands.

'We do not feel in need of chaperons in the country,' she retorted, ignoring Trudie's warning words as they echoed in her head. 'The people in this neighbourhood are gentlefolk, not barbarians, and are not in the habit of insulting young ladies, even if they do not have a chaperon in tow. If you intend to stay here – whoever you are – I suggest you don't forget it.'

And then, anger and confusion having temporarily driven the reason for her visit out of her mind, she turned on her heel and, sweeping up her cloak, she crossed to the door. She had no intention of staying to be insulted, whoever the gentleman turned out to be.

'It seems I have made a grave mistake.' He was having to adjust rapidly to the fact that the delectable young lady in front of him

20

was not a lightskirt who had come to offer herself to him as he had supposed – and could be forgiven for supposing, he told himself, considering the fact that she had been travelling in a cart rather than a carriage, and that she was paying a call on an unmarried gentleman to whom she had not been introduced; to say nothing of the fact that she had arrived without a chaperon – 'You must let me make amends.'

She did not falter. 'No.'

But he was not prepared to take 'no' for an answer. Reaching the door before her, he planted himself firmly in front of it, forcing her to confront him and forcing her, for the first time, to really look at him.

She had not realized quite how tall he was. He was at least six inches taller than she herself, which made him a little over six feet, and his shoulders were broad. His body was well toned – which she found surprisingly at odds with his fashionable clothes, until she realized that it must have become well toned through riding and fencing, occupations that were as fashionable as his outfit. She took in his clothes: a tight-fitting pair of breeches which disappeared into top-turned boots – she could not help but notice the length of his legs – a high-collared shirt and a cutaway coat, beneath which was a striped silk waistcoat. Then she turned her eyes up to his face. His gaze was fixed on her, but his look was not admiring as it had been earlier: to her annoyance she discovered it was appraising.

'You don't like me very much, do you?' he asked, reading her expression.

Something about him challenged her. 'Correction,' she said. She was now fully back in control of herself. 'I don't like you at all. Now kindly let me pass.'

He did not move. He was still planted in the doorway, arms folded across his broad chest. 'Not until you give me a good reason for leaving so soon.'

She almost gasped. Surely he could not be serious? Was it not obvious? There were so many reasons she hardly knew where to begin! 'Only one?' she demanded.

An amused look flitted across his face. 'As many as you like. Pray don't stint yourself.'

She smarted at the mockery in his tone. It left her in no mood to mince her words. 'Very well. I am leaving because you have manhandled me in the most dreadful manner—'

'If it had been so dreadful, your lips wouldn't have parted under mine,' he remarked with a wicked smile.

'—and because I find you rude, arrogant and unscrupulous,' she went on, stung by his remark, and deciding that, as she could not answer it, she would do best to ignore it.

'Oh, do you?' he said. But this time there was an undercurrent to his words. The mockery was still there but there was an edge to his voice, as though he did not like what he was hearing. 'And is that all?' he asked, quiet but dangerous.

'No, it is not,' she replied. She was determined not to let him control this situation as he had controlled the earlier part of their encounter. 'I find you boorish, and . . . and shallow.'

'Shallow?' he asked with a lift of one eyebrow. Then repeated, more softly, 'Shallow.' The anger left his face, and the mocking look was back in his eyes. 'It's the first time I have ever been described as shallow.'

'There is a first time for everything,' she said. She cast him a look that dared him to make a joke out of her use of a cliché. And then, as he refused to move, she swept round him and out the door.

'It can't have been very serious,' he remarked, as she set foot over the threshold.

She stopped; then almost walked on.

'Your business,' he said.

She hesitated. Then turned. Slowly. And took him in. There

was no more mockery in his eyes. He looked, for a moment, as though he might be someone to whom she could talk.

'You said you wanted to see me on a matter of some urgency,' he said.

A perplexed look crossed her face. She would rather sweep out of the room, reclaim her cart and head for home, putting the whole disastrous visit behind her. But the matter of the mantraps had not been resolved, and it was a matter of such importance that she knew she should swallow her pride and stay; at least long enough to put her case before him and hopefully persuade him to speak to Lord Ravensford about having the traps removed. For she did not believe for one minute that he was who he claimed to be.

'I did. That is, I do.'

He nodded. The mockery had left him altogether, not just his eyes. 'If I have offended you, I apologize,' he said, seeming to remember that she was a guest. 'I have no wish to be on bad terms with my neighbours. Will you not let me offer you a glass of Canary wine, and tell me what has brought you here, on icy roads and in all this snow?'

She gave a sigh. She could wish the circumstances were different; that the butler had shown her in and that Lord Ravensford, a kindly old man, had listened sympathetically to her plea. But the circumstances were not different. The man in front of her may be Lord Ravensford, as he claimed, or Lord Ravensford's secretary, as she suspected, but whatever the truth of the matter, she could not refuse the opportunity of having the mantraps removed.

'Very well. That would be . . . most welcome.'

Having decided to stay, she walked over to the duck-egg blue sofa and sat stiffly on the edge of her seat, her cloak folded in her lap. She might have agreed to stay, but that did not mean she wanted to make herself comfortable. As soon as her business was over she would be on her way.

He pulled the bell rope that hung next to the fireplace, and after a few minutes – awkward minutes for Marianne, though not, she suspected, for him, as he continued to look at her with an amused smile playing round his lips – a butler appeared.

'Canary wine, if you please, Figgs.'

'Very good, My Lord,' the butler said, before departing to bring refreshments.

The 'my lord' startled Marianne, and she looked at the man opposite her with mingled feelings of surprise and dismay. So he *was* Lord Ravensford. Which in some ways made her feel better – she had not been insulted by a common secretary, at least – but in some ways made her feel far worse. She flushed. She had been kissed by Lord Ravensford. She closed her eyes briefly. She must try to forget it. Otherwise it would make her future meetings with him acutely embarrassing; if not to say impossible. And, worse still, he had mistaken her for a lightskirt. She flushed more deeply. If only she could have held him entirely responsible it would not have been so bad, but her honesty forced her to acknowledge that she had hardly arrived in the manner he might have expected of Miss Travis of Seaton Hall.

'Yes.' He seemed to read some of the subtle play of emotions crossing her face. 'I am Ravensford – even though my behaviour may have led you to believe otherwise.'

Marianne sighed. 'I suppose I should load you down with further reproaches, but what's done is done. Besides, I have a matter of much more importance to discuss.'

Figgs returned with the Canary wine, and after pouring Marianne a glass Lord Ravensford took a brandy for himself and then said, 'I'm listening.'

He didn't know how it was, but there was something about her that made him want to listen to her; and it went without saying, he thought, as he looked at her intriguing face and figure, that he wanted to *look* at her. A pity she was not a lightskirt. He allowed himself to forget for a moment that she was gently raised and contemplate the pleasures they could have shared. Her response to his kiss had been ardent. Tentative at first and innocent, but afterwards full of a surprising, if untutored, passion. It would have been a pleasure to have taken her to his bed.

'I will come straight to the point.' Marianne was fortunately unaware of his thoughts, and had decided that in such a serious matter a direct approach was best. 'When my groom and I were out riding yesterday, we discovered a mantrap.'

He sat up, resting his hands on his knees as he leant forwards. 'A mantrap?' His whole demeanour had changed, becoming sharp and fully attentive. 'That's a terrible thing,' he said with a frown. He sat back a little. 'But I don't see what it has to do with me.'

'The mantrap was on your land.'

'On my land, you say?' he asked her in surprise.

'Yes. Or rather on Billingsdale land. I know the villagers should not be poaching, but when the winter is hard they often have no choice if they want to stay alive. Usually the landowners here-abouts turn a blind eye to poaching at this time of year, particularly when there is snow on the ground, but Mr Billingsdale's manager is determined there will be no poaching on Billingsdale land. The traps are cruel, and can break a man's leg – surely too high a price to pay for stealing a rabbit in order to stay alive; especially as most of the men have families to feed. I have written to Mr Billingsdale about it but he will not interest himself in the matter. He has every faith in his manager, he says. And so I have come to see you. You are the new tenant, after all; it is in your power to do something about it.'

Lord Ravensford's eyes narrowed, and he put his hands together, steepling his long, strong fingers. 'You are sure about this? Under the snow it's difficult to see anything clearly. Could you not be mistaken?'

Marianne shook her head. 'We – my groom and I – discovered a man caught in one only yesterday.'

'Yesterday, you say?' His tone was penetrating, and an intent look had come into his eye. 'Who was it? One of the local men?'

'No. My groom and I freed him, but neither of us recognized him. He is definitely not from these parts.'

'He will need medical attention,' said Lord Ravensford, getting up and going towards the bell.

'He has already had it. I called the doctor as soon as I got him back to the house.'

'Am I to understand – you have taken this man in?' His gaze was very direct, and she noticed again how unusual his eyes were, of a brown so bright as to be almost gold.

'Yes.'

'And he is not known in these parts, you say?'

'No. But as I told Trudie, we are in no danger from him,' she said, misunderstanding his interest. 'His leg has been badly damaged and although he can hobble around it will be some time before he can walk easily again.'

'That was good of you,' he said slowly. 'To take him in. Particularly if he is a stranger in these parts.' Then, as if recollecting himself, he added, 'But not very wise.'

'I couldn't leave him out in the snow,' replied Marianne simply. 'He was badly hurt, and in too much pain to tell us who he was or where he came from, otherwise I would have arranged for him to have been taken home, so in the end I thought it best to take him back to the Hall. But I am concerned. There are other traps, you see. Tom has seen them.' She raised her eyes to him appealingly. 'I don't want those traps on my – on neighbouring land,' she said. 'Will you remove them for me?'

He gave her a mocking smile, his eyes roving over her gentian-blue eyes and her delightfully rosy lips. 'When you look at me like that, I can deny you nothing,' he said with a quirk of his mouth.

'Are you never serious, Lord Ravensford?' she asked in exasperation; but a smile tugged at the corner of her own mouth nonetheless.

'Not often.' He paused. 'But I promise you I will be serious over this, Miss. . . ?'

'Travis.'

His face froze. There was a moment of unnatural silence. And then he said, 'Miss Travis.' His smile this time was not mocking. In fact, it seemed forced.

'Well, My Lord?' asked Marianne, too concerned about the traps to notice his strange expression and response. 'Will you order their removal?'

He let out his breath. 'Mantraps are an abomination. Yes, I will. I will give orders that they are to be cleared immediately. You are right: the winter is hard. A little poaching is to be expected.'

Marianne breathed a sigh of relief. 'Thank you. I knew I could make you see reason. I am only sorry to have troubled you before you have even unpacked.'

'It was no trouble.'

She looked at him suspiciously, but for once there seemed to be no hidden meaning in his words. 'Well, now that is settled I will not keep you. I must be getting back to Seaton Hall.'

She stood up.

'I will see you again before long, I hope?' he asked, as he, too, stood up; all six feet and more of him.

She hesitated. 'Perhaps,' she replied.

'With that it seems I must be content.' He made a low bow then rang for Figgs, and she was escorted from the room.

'So that's Kit's sister.' Figgs's voice was speculative as he returned to the drawing-room, having shown Marianne out.

'It is.' Lord Ravensford, standing by the window, was watching Marianne as she drove away in her rustic cart. She made a lovely figure, sitting erect as she skilfully handled the reins, her cloak reflecting the blue-grey of the sky and her black ringlets cascading down her back.

'And you weren't tempted to tell her? asked Figgs.

'What? That I am a friend of her brother's, and that I am here to give Kit any support he needs in his venture to rescue Adèle, his beloved, from the revolution in France? That her brother did not need money to pay gambling debts as she supposes, but that he needed it to mount the rescue attempt, and that even now he is on the other side of the Channel, facing God knows what perils in order to bring Adèle safely back to England?' he asked with a wry smile.

'Any of that. Or all of it,' Figgs said. He had lost the deferential look of a servant and was now talking to Lord Ravensford with the air of a comrade-in-arms.

Lord Ravensford's eyes lingered on Marianne until she was out of sight. 'No,' he said, reluctantly turning away from the window and giving his full attention to Figgs. 'I gave Kit my word that I would not tell her anything: he does not want her to worry. Even so, I wish I'd known who she was from the outset. I should have guessed, I suppose, but I hadn't imagined her to be anything like that. Somehow I'd got the impression that Kit's sister was a large-boned, mannish woman—'

'Because Kit told you she'd be able help her father with the estate whilst he was away,' Figgs suggested.

'Probably so,' Lord Ravensford agreed. 'I certainly never imagined such an intriguing beauty, with such a delightful figure or such gentian-blue eyes. But that's no excuse. I should have guessed who she was, or at least guessed who she might be. Particularly once she revealed we were neighbours. Then, if not before, I should have had the idea at the forefront of my mind. It isn't like me to get so carried away.'

'What's done is done,' said Figgs practically.

Lord Ravensford frowned, settling himself in a Sheraton chair. Figgs sat down opposite him.

'Perhaps,' Lord Ravensford said. 'But it's unfortunate all the same. I'd planned things quite differently. I was going to be charming and respectable at our first meeting. I have promised Kit I'll keep an eye on his little sister whilst he is away,' he said. 'And since I've arrived I've been even more determined to help her. I know Kit said that she would be able to help her father with running the estate whilst he was in France, but according to the local gossip Mr Travis has turned into something of a recluse since Kit's departure. He has taken it hard and has retreated to his room, where he nurses his grievances. He rarely comes out, and Marianne has been left to run the estate by herself. I wanted her to feel she had a friend in me; someone she could turn to if she needed any help, so that if the burden of running things at Seaton Hall became too great she wouldn't have to feel she was alone.'

Figgs nodded. 'As we have to be here anyway, to be a back up for Kit, so to speak, it makes sense for you to keep an eye on Marianne. We don't want Kit returning home to find her on the brink of exhaustion from looking after the estate – he has enough troubles.' He looked around the room thoughtfully. 'It's lucky we were able to rent this place. It's ideal: right next door to Kit's home, and with its own coves and beaches so that if we're needed we can put a small boat out to sea without attracting too much attention. And, once Kit's rescued Adèle, we can help him to land.'

Luke nodded. 'Yes. It was fortunate Mr Billingsdale was looking for a tenant. This place makes an excellent base. But that doesn't solve the problem of Marianne. As things stand, she doesn't like me. She doesn't even trust me – though I can't say I blame her,' he said, angry with himself at having so misjudged the situation. 'Even so, if she neither likes nor trusts me she won't turn to me for help if she needs it.'

'Oh, well, it could have been worse,' said Figgs with a shrug. 'At least you didn't tell her to call you Luke.'

Luke gave a wolfish smile, which widened into sardonic laughter. 'That would have put the cat among the pigeons, would it not?' He sobered suddenly. 'It goes without saying that she must never learn who I am. If she discovers that the Earl of Ravensford and Luke Somerville are one and the same person, she'll refuse to trust me altogether. With all the rumours that are flying round she will blame me for leading Kit into temptation and will fight me at every turn. Marianne is no milk-and-water miss: she would not forgive me if she thought I had injured her brother.'

'You could always tell her you didn't lead Kit into temptation,' Figgs said practically.

'And you think she would believe me?' asked Luke with a lift of one eyebrow. 'No. Of course not. Not unless I could prove it. Which I can't – at least, not unless I tell her the truth, which would mean telling her that Kit has gone to France. And that is something I have promised not to do.'

'It's just a pity Kit couldn't tell his family what he's really up to,' said Figgs.

'He didn't want to worry them. Besides, his father wouldn't have given him the money to fund the expedition if he had known what it was for. On the contrary, Mr Travis would have done everything in his power to stand in Kit's way. Which is why Kit had to make up the story about needing the money to cover gambling debts.'

'The old man would have objected, then? Doesn't he approve of Adèle?' asked Figgs curiously.

'Oh, he likes her well enough: in fact, as Adèle is his god-daughter, he likes her very well. But Kit is his heir, and his only son. He wouldn't have wanted him to take any risks!'

'Kit is happy to take them,' shrugged Figgs.

Luke nodded. As he did so he was conscious of a twist inside. It wasn't that he was envious of Kit, but it was something close. He realized that Kit, who, at twenty-five, was three years his junior, had found something in life that he himself had been denied. Kit had found a woman he would willingly risk his life for, whereas he himself had found nothing but idle distractions: barques of frailty and bits of muslin with whom he had had a string of unsatisfactory affairs.

It's no wonder Kit's determined to marry Adèle, he thought. If I found a woman I'd risk my life for, I'd marry, too. But it's hardly likely.

'I don't like deceiving Marianne – or Miss Travis, as I must try and remember to call her, at least to her face; although it will be hard, when I am so used to hearing Kit talking about her as Marianne.' He rose and went over to the mantelpiece. Then, standing with his back to it, he turned his eyes towards the window, through which he had seen Marianne leave the house. 'I never liked the idea of deceiving Kit's sister, and now that I've met her I like it even less. However, to spare her the worry and anxiety she will feel if she knows that Kit is risking his life in an attempt to rescue Adèle from France, it's something I have to do.'

Figgs nodded slowly.

'There is one thing, though,' said Luke thoughtfully. 'Marianne told me she has taken in a man whose leg has been caught in a trap: a stranger, not someone from around these parts. Fortunately, he wasn't too badly hurt. But the thought crossed my mind that it could be Henri.'

'Ah. That would be useful,' said Figgs. 'If it is him, he may be able to win her trust even if you can't. And it would explain why he didn't join us last night as arranged. But how will you discover if it is Henri?'

Luke turned his eyes back to his friend. 'Because I intend to go over to Seaton Hall and find out. In the meantime, we need to get things moving here. Has the luggage arrived?'

'Yes. It came yesterday.'

'And the servants?'

'They should be here this afternoon.'

'Good. The house needs putting in order. We might as well be comfortable: after all, we will be here for some time.'

CHAPTER TWO

*A*s Marianne made her way home she was glad she had drunk a glass of Canary wine. The day had turned colder, and now that her stone hot water bottles had lost their heat the wine's warmth was the only thing that made the journey comfortable.

As she traversed the country lanes she could not help thinking over her meeting with Lord Ravensford. Although in the end it had gone well it had nearly proved disastrous – because she had ignored Trudie's advice and gone out without a chaperon.

Without a chaperon, and in a horse and cart.

Her thoughts went to the Travis carriage, which was tucked away in a corner of the stables. Her family no longer boasted the number of servants needed to polish its brasses and buff its squabs, as their fortunes had been adversely affected by the turbulence in France, but even so, despite its dilapidation, Marianne would have liked to take it. Without Tom to drive it, however, it had been impossible.

Her second choice would have been to go on horseback. If she had done so, it would have given Lord Ravensford a better clue to her station in life. But as Dapple had been taken ill, that, too, had been impossible. Really, it was most unfortunate that Dapple had been taken sick, and that Tom had had to remain behind to nurse the mare.

For the first time Marianne realized how she must look, not to her neighbours, who knew that her means were straitened and who were used to her ways, but to a stranger. It was one thing for her to tool about the countryside in a rustic cart with no chaperon at her side when the only people she was likely to meet were the Cosgroves or the Reverend Mr Stock, but when there was a new person in the neighbourhood? She had to acknowledge that she had been rash. So much so that Lord Ravensford could almost be forgiven for thinking her a lightskirt.

Almost, but not quite.

She turned Hercules in at the gate of Seaton Hall, glad that her journey was nearly over. There would be a big fire waiting for her in the kitchen – the other rooms were seldom used unless there was company, it being more economical that way – and Trudie would be on hand to hear all about her success.

Of her ill treatment at Lord Ravensford's hands she decided to say nothing. It would only lead to a scolding and an 'I told you so' – in addition to making Trudie impossible if Lord Ravensford should ever visit Seaton Hall.

Marianne drove the cart round to the stables. Leaving it in Jack's willing hands, she went to see how Dapple was doing. She was relieved to discover the mare was much better, and that Tom expected a speedy recovery. Then, having satisfied herself that her mare was making good progress, she went into the Hall.

The first thing she noticed on entering the hall was a delicious smell; then she heard the sound of a heated argument coming from the back of the house. Curiously, she made her way towards the kitchen. As she opened the kitchen door a strange sight met her eyes. There, brandishing her rolling pin, was Trudie, glaring at the man who, only the day before, had been caught in the jaws of the mantrap. And both of them had fire in their eyes.

'Miss Marianne! Thank the Lord!' said Trudie, as she turned towards the door.

34

'Ah! *Mademoiselle*! I beseech you—' began the small man, turning imploringly towards Marianne. Before Trudie cut him off.

'I won't have it, Miss Marianne, I told him plain. Coming into my kitchen and messing with my things. That's the best chicken he's had, messing about with it and cutting it up and doing the Lord knows what with it; how I'm to cook our dinner now I really don't know.'

'What . . ?' began Marianne, looking from one to the other of them, pleased to see that the stranger was well enough to be up, but unable to work out what had happened.

Trudie, however, was for the moment too incensed to speak. 'Goo,' she declared finally, glaring fiercely at the little man, 'that's what he's done with it. He said so himself. He's turned the chicken into goo.'

'*Ragout*!' ejaculated the little man, exaggerating the shape of the word with his lips and making a sumptuous gesture with his hands, as though kissing an imaginary plate of food. '*Ragout*! I have turned it into *ragout*! Ah, *mademoiselle*.' he said, appealing to Marianne again, 'I want only to help. To repay you for your kindness. But what can I do? I am only a poor Frenchman, with nothing to give the kind lady who has taken him in. But then I think, I can cook. Cooking is what I know. In France I am the superb chef! I cook for the lords and the ladies.' His face fell. 'But now there are no lords and ladies. Now there are only *citizens*.' He spat the word. 'And what do citizens eat? Heh? Do they eat the wonderful meals, slaved over by the anxious cook? *Non*! They eat bread, and tear with their teeth at the pieces of meat.'

'French,' said Marianne, taking off her gloves and hat and placing them on the end of the kitchen table. '*Monsieur*, you are French?'

'*Mais oui, mademoiselle*. And I am proud of it. I love my country. But this, it is not a good time to be French. And I say to my brother – I say it when I can stand it no longer, the blood and the pain and the fear – I say, I will go to England. I will make a new life for myself. I will get on a boat and cross the Channel and then I will walk to London. And then . . . who knows? Per'aps I will cook for the lords and ladies, per'aps I will even cook for the king. *Oui?* But now I cannot walk to London. I cannot walk anywhere.' He looked sorrowfully down at his leg. 'The young *mademoiselle*, she has been kind to me,' he said with a Gallic shrug, 'but why should she look after me? Heh? No reason. Unless I do something for her. Unless I show her that Henri can be useful. Unless I show her that Henri can cook!'

Marianne looked at Trudie. 'It does smell very good,' she said.

'A-ha!' The Frenchman beamed at Trudie in triumph, then whisked a ladle seemingly out of nowhere and proceeded to stir the savoury dish that was bubbling on the stove. Scooping up some of the liquid he blew on it and, ignoring Trudie's indignant grimace, offered it to Marianne. She sipped at the sauce, and her face lit up.

'A-ha! It is good, *non?*' he demanded.

'It is good, *yes*,' laughed Marianne. 'It really is,' she said, turning to Trudie. 'And it would be such a help to have another pair of hands about the place. You know it yourself. You could leave all the cooking to Henri.' She knew that here she was playing her strong suit because Trudie, much as she might have protested about Henri's meddling, did not enjoy cooking. 'And, as long as he feels up to it, it will keep him occupied until his leg mends.'

Trudie snorted. 'And a good thing too. A foreigner, getting under my feet every day – I dare say you'd be too soft to turn him out.'

'It *is* a good ragout,' Marianne tempted her.

Trudie fought a visible battle. She was not fond of cooking, but she loved to eat.

'*Madame*—' began Henri, turning appealing eyes on Trudie.

'*Mademoiselle*,' said Trudie fiercely, then, a minute later, getting flustered, saying, 'that is, missus to you.'

'*Mademoiselle* Missus,' said Henri obligingly, holding out the ladle to her. 'See for yourself.'

Trudie sniffed aloofly, but sidled closer. Then, deigning to bend her head and taste a little of the sauce, she said, 'Not bad.' And then, truthfulness overcoming her ruffled feathers, she said, 'In fact, good.'

'Ahhh,' sighed Henri, with the contentment of the true artist, 'you like it, yes?'

'I do.'

'Then it is settled?' Henri glanced at Marianne hopefully.

She nodded. 'It is. Henri, you are welcome to stay.'

Life became easier with another pair of hands. Although Henri's leg had been badly injured in the trap he was able to work sitting at the big kitchen table. It was here he peeled and chopped the vegetables, and by means of a chair which Tom had heightened for him by nailing pieces of wood on to the bottom of its legs, he was able to sit at the stove and stir his soups.

Marianne was upstairs a few days later, sorting through the linen and thinking how fortunate they had been to find Henri, the tempting aromas for that day's dinner already drifting up from the kitchen, when she heard a clattering of hooves outside and, looking out of the window, saw Lord Ravensford riding towards the house.

A minute or two later, Trudie appeared.

'You've a visitor, miss,' she said, with an interested expression, adding, 'You didn't tell me how handsome Lord Ravensford was.'

'Perhaps I didn't notice,' replied Marianne coolly.

Strangely enough, she wouldn't have minded Trudie's teasing if she had really been unaware of Lord Ravensford's handsome, if predatory, features, and if she had not been so disturbed by the feelings he had awoken inside her. Then she could have replied with good humour, perhaps even with some banter of her own.

But the fact that Lord Ravensford had had an unsettling effect on her, and that he had invaded her dreams in the most provocative manner, made her unwilling to enter into the subject.

'Your white gown's clean,' said Trudie, ignoring Marianne's remark. 'I pressed it with the flat iron yesterday. You've always looked lovely in white.'

'I see no reason to change just because Lord Ravensford has called,' said Marianne, feeling suddenly awkward. 'I believe this gown will do.'

Trudie said no more. The yellow striped gown Marianne was wearing could not in the ordinary way be faulted, even though it was rather old. Its low bodice was filled in with a lace fichu and its wide satin sash showed off Marianne's trim waist. Its pleated hemline was attractive, providing a pleasing decoration round the full skirt and its sleeves, ending with a froth of lace just above Marianne's elbow, showed off the delicate smoothness of her arms. All in all, she looked very presentable – although Trudie still thought she looked better in the white. However, she knew that Marianne was not one to be led, so she said no more.

With Trudie's eyes on her, Marianne did no more than push a stray ringlet back into place before going downstairs.

Lord Ravensford was standing by the window as she went into the drawing-room, looking out towards the coast, but he turned round as soon as she entered the room. Trudie followed close behind and retired to a corner, where she proceeded to apply herself to some plain sewing.

'Lord Ravensford,' said Marianne. 'I did not expect to see you.'

'You are not disappointed, I hope?' he asked.

Marianne was not sure how to reply. For all his light air she sensed there was something more serious underneath it; something which, for some reason he did not want to show. There had been a hint of it at their previous meeting, but today it seemed more marked.

'Won't you sit down?'

She sat down herself, on an old and handsome gilded sofa, and he followed suit. As she watched him settle himself she thought that he was not, somehow, like the other men she had met. He made her feel somehow awkward, and aware of her heart beating. Was it because of his dark good looks? she wondered. But then dismissed the notion. Her brother was good-looking, and she had never had any difficulty in talking to him; nor to any of his friends, some of whom had looked like Greek gods, and had set the young girls she had come out with fluttering and giggling and hiding behind their fans. No, she decided, it was not because of his looks – although she could not deny that his gold-brown eyes had a curiously melting effect on her, or that his high cheekbones, straight nose and firm jaw were very attractive – it was something else.

'. . . don't you think?'

With a start, Marianne realized she had not been listening. She had been so lost in her thoughts that she had not been paying attention, and she felt a flush spring to her cheeks.

'You seem distracted,' he said with an amused smile.

'I am.' But she could not tell him what had been distracting her. 'I. . . .'

'I was saying I hoped you had a safe journey home, and that you were not too much inconvenienced by the snow.'

'I . . . yes . . . no. That is, yes, I had a safe journey home, and no, I was not too much inconvenienced by the snow.' She smiled suddenly, aware of the absurdity of her reply.

He smiled in return, and this time it seemed a genuine smile, not the amused smile with which he had reacted to her state of abstraction. 'I'm glad. I have come to tell you that I have dealt with the matter of the mantraps. I've had the men out clearing the woods, and so far they've found five. It isn't easy in this weather. There is still snow on the ground and we may have missed some, but once there is a thaw we will know if we have found them all.'

39

'Doesn't the estate manager know how many he laid?'

His eyes darkened, becoming the colour of liquid gold. 'He does, but he refuses to tell me. He gave me to understand that he was employed by Mr Billingsdale and that what he did on the estate was his business, not mine.'

'But you had the traps cleared anyway?' asked Marianne anxiously.

'Yes. Those things are an abomination. How anyone can want to trap their fellow man is beyond me, particularly in such a cruel manner. But then, there is a lot of cruelty in the world I fear.'

'You are thinking of France,' said Marianne.

He nodded. Then, realizing that the horrors of the French Revolution were not a fitting subject for a lady's drawing-room, he returned to the subject of the mantraps; hardly a fitting subject either, but one in which Marianne was concerned. 'I am still worried there may be some traps left. Which is why I have come to ask you if I can speak to the man you found. I would like to ask him if he noticed any others, and if so, where they are.'

Marianne nodded. 'Of course.' She went over to the bell.

She was unaware of how gracefully she moved, or how beautifully the folds of her skirt draped themselves over her rounded hips and legs. But Luke was aware of it.

Too aware.

'Will you tell Mr Billingsdale that his manager refused to help you?' asked Marianne as she sat down again. 'I only ask because generally he does not like to be disturbed, and I don't think you will get much help from that quarter.'

'The day I need Billingsdale to help me deal with a surly manager is the day I return to town for good,' he said with a wry smile. 'No, Jakes has refused for now, but once he sees I mean to take an active interest in the running of the estate he will soon change his tune.'

Marianne felt an unexpected surge of relief. 'I'm pleased to know you care. It isn't good for a neighbourhood to have an absent landowner. The land can often be neglected; either that, or overused. I've been worried for some time that the trees are being cut and none replanted – but then, of course, it's no longer my concern.'

'No longer?' he queried.

She rubbed her hands together, as they felt suddenly cold. 'The woods used to be a part of this estate,' she explained. 'They—' She stopped. She had been about to tell him that they had been sold off to cover her brother's gambling debts, but prevented herself just in time. She hardly knew Lord Ravensford, and it would be disloyal to her brother to say any such thing. Despite everything, she still loved Kit very much and, against all odds, she hoped he would one day return to take his rightful place as the master of Seaton Hall. 'I sometimes forget, and take too great an interest in them.'

'It must be difficult for you, running an estate of this size.'

Marianne felt unexpectedly touched. She had done her best to look after the estate in Kit's absence, but it had been a heavy burden, and she was surprised at how grateful she felt to him for his understanding. Still, she did not want him to feel sorry for her, and said calmly, 'I am happy to do what I can to help Papa.'

At that moment the door opened, and Tom came in.

'Tom, can you ask Henri to join us?' she asked.

Tom looked surprised, but saying, 'Yes, Miss Marianne,' went to fetch him.

'Henri?' queried Lord Ravensford, with a satisfied air that Marianne did not understand. 'He is French?'

'Yes. He was running away from the Revolution, trying to make his way to London – he's a chef,' she explained.

'I must ask him if he has any tips for my Mrs Hill,' said Lord Ravensford with a smile.

A few minutes later, Henri entered the room. He had made it

clear he wanted to give as little trouble as possible, and once Tom had made him a makeshift crutch he had found he could get around quite easily, so that Marianne had called him to the drawing-room instead of taking Lord Ravensford to the kitchen. Lord Ravensford had already seen one example of her unconventionality, when she had visited him without a chaperon before she had been introduced to him, and she did not want him to think her behaviour was completely beyond the pale by taking him into the kitchen to talk to the servants.

'You must be Henri,' said Lord Ravensford, as Henri hobbled into the room.

'Yes, milord.' said Henri.

For a moment Marianne had the curious feeling that the two men knew each other. But then she dismissed the notion as absurd.

'Henri,' she explained, 'Lord Ravensford wants to ask you about the traps.'

'Ah.' Henri was grave.

'He wants to have them removed, and so far has found five, but he wants to know if you saw any more that he might not have found.'

'Ah! Yes. *Mais oui*,' said Henri. 'At least, I 'ave seen two traps, and maybe they 'ave not yet been discovered.'

Although the ground had been covered with snow he had noticed iron traps sticking out of the soft white covering in two different places, he said. He described the places to Lord Ravensford as well as he could, and when Lord Ravensford had learnt everything Henri could tell him he thanked Marianne for her hospitality and took his leave, saying, as he was about to go out of the door, 'You are going to the Cosgroves' ball are you not?'

'Yes.' She flushed, although why she should flush at the thought of the ball she did not know.

'May I have the honour of the first dance?'

She smiled with pleasure. 'You may.'

His eyes brightened. Then he bowed, and went out to his horse.

'*Alors!*' exclaimed Henri, who had not yet returned to the kitchen. 'I remember another one. Milord! Milord!'

He hobbled over to Lord Ravensford, who turned to meet him half way.

'Well done, Henri,' said Lord Ravensford under his breath. 'It was a stroke of good fortune to be able to place yourself in the house. You can help make Marianne's life easier. Your leg isn't too badly hurt, I hope? It was damn bad luck, getting caught in a trap.'

'I will not be dancing any time soon,' shrugged Henri. 'But you and I, Luke, we 'ave suffered worse.'

'Keep an eye on her, Henri, and if she needs any help then send me word. I will do everything I can to lighten her load.'

Henri looked at him with a twinkle in his eye. 'She is delightful, Marianne, is she not?'

'She is,' said Luke with a twinkle of his own. 'But she is also Kit's sister, and I never mix business with pleasure.'

Henri shrugged his shoulders in a typically Gallic gesture. 'It is a pity, all the same. That 'air, those eyes . . . they make the task of 'elping 'er a treat, *non?*'

Luke gave a wolfish smile. 'Too much of a treat.'

And with that he threw his leg over his horse and rode away.

CHAPTER THREE

To her surprise, Marianne found herself looking forward to the Cosgroves' ball. Usually she disliked going out on winter evenings, but this evening it seemed foolish to worry about icy roads and draughty carriages. Not that it had anything to do with Lord Ravensford, she told herself. No matter how interesting she found him she could never think of marriage; not with all her responsibilities to the estate; and—

She stopped, startled. Marriage indeed! What was she thinking of? She must indeed be in need of more company, as Trudie was fond of telling her, if her thoughts were leaping to marriage simply because a bachelor had moved into the neighbourhood.

'It's a good thing you're a slender nymph,' said Trudie, recalling her thoughts to the present as she helped Marianne into her silk ballgown. It was of soft cream, perfectly suiting Marianne's complexion and setting off the colour of her gentian-blue eyes. 'When I used to help your mama dress it was always panniers and wigs and goodness knows what. Now the fashions are any old how, and it's do as you will and come as you please.' She gave a snort, not attempting to hide her opinion on the modern fashions, which in her opinion were not a patch on the opulent styles of yesteryear.

The line of Marianne's gown was simple. Its close-fitting bodice, ornamented with three small ribbon bows one above the other, showed off her trim waist, and the full skirt, with the merest hint of a bustle, was decorated with a large bow at the back. A slight train flowed becomingly behind her.

'And now for your pearls,' said Trudie, fastening the simple necklace round Marianne's neck.

Marianne surveyed herself in the cheval glass. Her dark hair, brushed until it shone, had been arranged into a mass of ringlets that surrounded her face and fell halfway down her back. It was decorated with an ivory plume that picked up the colour of the lace which edged her scooped neckline and spilled from her three-quarter-length sleeves.

She turned to see herself from the back and as she did so the full skirt swirled around her ankles, making a delightful swishing sound – reminding Marianne that it was an age since she had last dressed up and attended a ball.

'Well, I say it as shouldn't,' said Trudie mistily, 'you look as pretty as a picture. Your mama'd be proud.'

'You spoil me,' smiled Marianne.

'Someone has to,' returned Trudie. She knew how heavy a load Marianne had had to carry since her brother had left home and her papa had retreated into his sorrows. 'You've grown too serious of late, Miss Marianne. You need a bit of fun. But mind, you be home by midnight.'

'Or the carriage will turn into a pumpkin,' Marianne teased.

'It better not,' said Trudie with relish, 'or Henri will make it into soup!'

'I must just go in and see Papa before I go,' said Marianne, picking up her fan and gloves.

Trudie stood aside and Marianne made her way to her father's bedroom. She knocked on the door and went in.

The room was sombre, with heavy oak furniture adding to the air of gloom. Dark-red drapes round the four poster bed matched dark-red drapes at the windows. She thought again how much she would like to change them. But her papa, knocked first of all by the death of his wife and then by the disgrace of his son, had retreated into his own little world and would not now hear of any change.

'I have come to say goodnight, Papa,' she said brightly, going over to the man who sat slumped in his chair by the window.

'Is it bedtime already?' he asked querulously, clutching at the blanket that covered his knees.

'No, Papa,' she said, kissing him on the forehead. 'But I won't be home until late. I am going to the Cosgroves' ball, and I know you will not like to be disturbed when I get in.'

'A ball, you say, my dear?' he asked tremulously. 'Are you sure that's wise?'

'Quite sure, Papa.' She spoke briskly, to try and counteract the air of stagnation that hung about the room.

'Miss Marianne looks beautiful tonight, does she not, My Lord?' prompted Lowe, her father's valet, as her father made no comment on her appearance.

'Marianne always looks very well,' he said, without, however, taking any notice of her dress. 'But you had better not go, Marianne. The roads are treacherous and there may be robbers and—'

'I will be quite all right, Papa. I will have Tom to look after me. And tomorrow I will come and tell you all about it,' said Marianne, cutting across his fretful protests. Then, giving him a last kiss, she made her way down to the hall and, donning her long gloves and travelling cloak, went out to the waiting carriage.

Once she was comfortably settled, Tom took up the reins of the carriage, which had been specially polished for the occasion, and called to the horses, 'Walk on.'

It took a good half an hour to reach the Cosgroves' house, but with a hot brick for her feet and a little silver flask for her hands, to say nothing of her cloak and muff, Marianne hardly felt the cold. She was enjoying being Miss Travis for once, and resolved that for this evening at least she would put all her duties out of her mind.

When they were nearly there the carriage took a slight detour – Miss Stock, the rector's sister, was to accompany Marianne as her chaperon – before finally pulling up in front of Mr and Mrs Cosgrove's house. The house was ablaze with light. Flambeaux flickered outside, whilst chandeliers sparkled from within. As Marianne walked up the stone steps that led to the front door, followed by the good Miss Stock, she could hear the sound of chatter drifting into the night. She felt a wave of excitement. It was months since she had been to a ball, and she was looking forward to it.

'Miss Travis! And Miss Stock.'

The Cosgroves gave both ladies a warm welcome, and Marianne was soon at home. Having lived in the neighbourhood all her life she knew most of the people present, and was quickly introduced to everyone else.

'Let me introduce you to Mr and Mrs Hershey,' said Jennifer, Mr and Mrs Cosgrove's bouncing sixteen-year-old daughter, who was delighting in the fact that her parents had finally allowed her to attend a ball.

Mr and Mrs Hershey were charming.

'And over there is Mr Windham,' said Jennifer, as Mr and Mrs Hershey engaged Miss Stock in conversation. She gave an awed giggle. 'Isn't he divine?'

Mr Windham looked over in their direction at that moment and Marianne could see why Jennifer was so impressed. Mr Windham was just the sort of gentleman to provoke a girlish fancy. His features were regular and his face was handsome, if bland.

'But tell me, have you met Lord Ravensford yet?' asked Jennifer, as Mr Windham turned his attention back to his own party.

'Yes.' Marianne was amused at the excitement in Jennifer's voice.

'Is he as wildly attractive as everyone says he is?'

'Everyone?' asked Marianne. She used a teasing tone to cover up the fact that she was uncomfortable talking about Lord Ravensford. She was not sure what her feelings were towards him, and she was unwilling to talk about him until she had decided. On the one hand he had been very rude to her at their first meeting but on the other, he had seen to the matter of the mantraps, and he had taken care, whilst in her own home, to be polite; although even at his politest there was something distinctly unsettling about him. And then there was the fact that he had kissed her. . . .

'Well, the Lenton girls, at least,' said Jennifer, blissfully unaware of Marianne's thoughts. 'I'm just glad they aren't here tonight, otherwise they would be simpering and flirting in the most dreadful way.' Then, remembering her duties as a hostess, she led Marianne over to a long table covered in a snowy white cloth and offered her a glass of fruit punch.

'But is he?' asked Jennifer, returning to her earlier theme. 'Lord Ravensford. Is he as handsome as Mr Windham?'

Marianne glanced at Mr Windham again, and was disconcerted to find he was looking at her. But he quickly looked away.

'His features are not so perfect,' said Marianne. 'But I don't think it would be possible to grow tired of looking at Lord Ravensford's face, in the way it would be with Mr Windham's.'

'But here *is* Lord Ravensford!' exclaimed Jennifer, going bright red as he crossed the room towards them. She gave a long sigh. 'Oh! He looks like a dream.'

Marianne felt her heart begin to beat more quickly: he did indeed look like a dream. His wild dark hair was pulled back from his face, accentuating the masculine line of his cheek and jaw, before being tied in a black ribbon bow at the nape of his neck. His dark green tailcoat, cut away to reveal a heavily embroidered gold waistcoat, clung effortlessly to his broad shoulders, and his knee breeches fitted his long legs like a second skin. White silk stockings revealed the firmness of his lower leg and then disappeared into black pumps.

Marianne opened her fan and began to waft it to and fro, creating a cooling breeze: not only was her heart beating more quickly at the sight of Lord Ravensford, but she could feel herself growing hot. She did not know why, but Lord Ravensford seemed to have this effect on her, wakening her body and making it stir. She was not sure whether she liked the feeling. It was unsettling; disturbing; but she felt that, before she had experienced it, she had only been half alive.

His eyes met hers with amusement, as though he knew exactly what she was thinking, and she found herself blushing. Really! She was behaving like a debutante, instead of a twenty-three year old who ran a country estate.

Giving a sardonic smile, as though satisfied with the effect he had had on her, he turned his attention to Jennifer.

'May I introduce Miss Cosgrove?' said Marianne.

'Miss Cosgrove,' he said politely.

'Lord Ravensford!' Jennifer gave a long sigh.

He smiled, but there was no mockery in the smile, Marianne was pleased to see; no double edge, as there was when he smiled at her. It was a kindly smile; the sort of smile a brother might bestow on a younger sister.

'Miss Travis,' he said, turning to her once more. 'I have come to remind you of your promise. You owe me the first dance.'

Marianne accepted his hand, feeling her skin tingle through her glove and, as the musicians struck up the chords for one of her favourite country dances, they took their places on the floor.

The Cosgroves' house was lacking a ballroom, but the double doors between the dining-room and drawing-room had been thrown open to make a tolerably large room – large enough for fifteen couples, which was all that was needed on the present occasion – and the dancing began.

Lord Ravensford proved to be a good dancer. After years of having her feet trodden on, and her dresses torn, it was a pleasure for Marianne to dance with a man who was in control of his body. And that was one of the things that set him apart from the other men, she realized, his degree of control. There was a tension about him, as though he was controlling himself all the time; as though he could not afford to reveal his true self; and it deepened her feeling that there was something mysterious about him.

'I thought you would like to know that the mantraps have all been cleared,' he said as they came together, touching hands as part of the dance. 'Now that the snow has melted, it has been possible to check that none remains.'

'Has Jakes given you dire warnings about poachers, now they have gone?' asked Marianne.

'He has. But I told him that a good manager didn't need pieces of iron to do his job for him.' He threw her a wicked smile. 'Jakes was not amused.'

Marianne laughed. 'I should think he wouldn't be. But you must not tease him too much. Good estate managers are hard to find, and Mr Billingsdale won't thank me if I lose Jakes for him.'

'It won't come to that, never fear. Jakes was simply testing my mettle.'

Marianne felt the smallest of shivers, knowing instinctively how strong that mettle was.

They were parted by the dance, walking away from each other before meeting up again further down the line.

'And how are you enjoying your time down in Sussex?' asked Marianne. 'This is rather a dead time of year. I hope you are not too bored?'

His eyes roamed over her face. 'No,' he said with a meaningful smile. 'I have not been bored.'

'Have you relatives in the area?' Marianne asked, conscious of her heart beating quickly, and trying to keep the conversation within normal bounds.

He threw her a curious glance. 'No.'

'I simply wondered whether that was why you had decided to rent an estate in this neighbourhood.'

'Ah. I see.' He gave a careless shrug. 'I wanted a large estate in the south of England, and Billingsdale Manor was the most suitable one I was shown.' His words were polite enough, and his tone good-humoured. Even so, Marianne felt as if a constraint had somehow entered the conversation. It was as if the tension she had earlier felt coming from him had now extended to their conversation. He continued to talk to her, but it was as though he was merely making polite conversation, saying the sort of things he might have said to any young lady at a ball, instead of talking to her about things which mattered to them both. He talked to her about the size of the room, the number of couples, and the assembled guests, determinedly avoiding any more personal subject.

At last the music came to an end. He escorted her back to the side of the room, but any hopes she might have had that their rapport would be re-established were dashed as he immediately asked a delighted Jennifer to dance.

Marianne was unsettled. Why should he be so unwilling to talk about his reasons for staying in the neighbourhood? she wondered. Or was it just that she had read too much into his manner, and the things he had said? She had no time to ponder on it, however, as Jem Cosgrove quickly claimed her hand. There was no formality here tonight. The ladies did not have cards on which they wrote the names of their dancing partners, arranging their evening before the dancing had really begun. Instead they accepted partners from dance to dance, and Marianne, in the spirit of the evening, readily accepted Jem as a partner – despite the fact her gown would suffer!

From there onwards she had no chance to think of Lord Ravensford's constrained manner any further – she was much in demand, and had no chance to sit down. After dancing for almost an hour she was completely worn out. She had not danced so much in months, and she took herself into the sitting-room where, the dining-room being used for the dancing, refreshments had been laid out. The Cosgroves' cook had laid on a lavish spread. Silver dishes covered the snowy white table cloth, and silver candlesticks ensured plenty of light. There were tureens of spiced mulligatawny soup, dishes of boiled fowl, and plates of tongue and ham. Pies and pasties were set on silver salvers, and a pyramid of fruit took pride of place. Marianne was just helping herself to a venison pasty – the pastry, alas, being not as light as Henri's – when she heard a voice at her shoulder and turned to see Mr Windham.

Unaccountably, she felt uncomfortable. Her gaze swept the room, hoping for the reassurance of familiar faces, but there was no one else there. They were quite alone.

'Miss Travis, is it not?' he asked as he helped himself to a slice of veal pie.

Marianne nodded.

'I thought that is what Mr Cosgrove said. A delightful family, the Cosgroves.'

'Yes,' Marianne agreed.

'You were dancing with Jem earlier, I noticed. A fine young man. And his sister a jovial girl.'

Marianne agreed again. The conversation, whilst being unexceptionable, struck her as slightly odd. It seemed forced; not natural; as though it was leading somewhere. But where, she could not guess.

His manner, too, made her feel uneasy, although she could not think why. He was perfectly polite – charming, even – but there was something *smooth* about him, something uncomfortable and unnerving. If she had not been in the middle of eating a pasty she would have excused herself and returned to the dancing. As it was, she had no choice but to remain.

'Have you any brothers or sisters, Miss Travis?' he asked.

He gave her a reassuring smile, but somehow it had the opposite effect and she felt her skin prickle.

'One. A brother.' She spoke unwillingly. She did not know why, but somehow she did not want this man to know about her family.

'Ah. You are fortunate. Me, I have no family. It must be a great comfort to have a brother. He is here tonight?'

'No.' Marianne's answer was brief.

'A pity. I would have liked to have had the honour of meeting him. He is in London, perhaps?'

'I – yes.' Marianne frowned. She did not actually know where Kit was, and she wondered why she had just lied. She was usually a very truthful person, but somehow she didn't want to tell this man anything about her brother.

'He is there long?'

The questions, whilst trivial, seemed somehow pointed, and Marianne had just decided that she would excuse herself, no matter how odd it may seem, when Lord Ravensford entered the room.

She felt a tide of relief wash over her.

Lord Ravensford had his own depths but somehow they were intriguing rather than murky, like Mr Windham's.

'Ah! There you are, Miss Travis,' he said, going over to Marianne. 'I have been looking for you everywhere. You have not forgotten your promise to dance the minuet with me, I hope?'

And without giving Marianne the chance to object he took her plate from her, put it down on the table, and steered her out of the room.

The tension in his hand conveyed itself to her through her long glove. She could not deny the fact that she was grateful to him for rescuing her from Mr Windham, but even so she did not take kindly to being treated in such a way. She was about to wrest her arm free when he opened one of the small doors leading off from the hall, and to her surprise he steered her into a small room. Because she had visited the house many times she knew, even before she entered the room, that it was Mr Cosgrove's study, but she suspected that Lord Ravensford had simply picked a door at random.

He dropped her arm, but before she could speak he said, curtly, 'I want you to keep away from Windham, Marianne. Do you understand?'

He had shed his careless air like a sloughed skin, and the effect was electrifying. Marianne could not protest at his use of her name, she could not even remember that she ought to protest, because the atmosphere had become charged with a force so powerful it drove all normal considerations from her mind. Instead of railing against him she found herself fighting a flood of new and unwanted images that had invaded her mind: images of him kissing her hands before pulling her into his arms and kissing her passionately on the lips.

She stood stock still for a moment, overcome by the highly charged atmosphere and her own ungovernable imagination. Where had such images come from? And how had they taken control of her? She shook her head angrily, driving the pictures away. This man had taken charge of her; had steered her out of one room and into another; had told her what she could and could not do, had laid down the law by telling her who she could and could not speak to, and all she could do was imagine his mouth on hers?

It was ridiculous.

'I will decide what I do,' she said, quickly regaining control of herself and redirecting the anger she had built up against herself towards him. 'If I choose to speak to Mr Windham I will do so.

Perhaps it is your custom to cut people you dislike, but it is not mine.' She ignored the part of her that said she had been about to do exactly that, too angry to be fair. 'Mr Windham is a guest at this ball and I would not dream of insulting him, or the Cosgroves either, by refusing to make a little polite conversation.'

'Polite conversation?' he asked. 'Was that all it was?' His eyes were darker now that he was angry, she noticed. In fact, his whole body had changed. It seemed to have grown, and his presence filled the room. 'Tell me,' he demanded, 'what was your conversation about?'

For one moment she nearly told him. So strong was his presence, and so unsettled was she by Mr Windham's pointed questions, that she longed to talk to him about it – though why she should think of talking to Lord Ravensford, when Mr Cosgrove was older and wiser, and an old family friend into the bargain, she did not know. But she was angry with Lord Ravensford for thinking he could order her life, and the moment passed.

'Your manners haven't improved,' she told him, angered by his high-handed attitude. 'I will talk to whomever I choose.'

'Marianne.' He used her name again, and crossing over to her in one stride he gripped her by the arms, looking intently down into her eyes. 'This is too important a matter to trifle with. I want to know what he said.'

His eyes bored down into her. He was so close to her that she was made forcefully aware of everything about him: his angular cheekbones, golden eyes and exciting lips. Her own parted in unknowing invitation and she gazed up at him. She had never felt like this before. She had never lost control of herself. But now she seemed to be melting. The Miss Travis who ran her family's estate and who spent her life on her duties seemed to be liquefying, dropping away, until all that was left at the centre was Marianne. Marianne, who wanted to forget her duties and be free again; Marianne who, innocent though she was, knew there was a world beyond the one she had already experienced and wanted Lord Ravensford to take her there, leading her by the hand. No one had ever made her feel as he made her feel. Not once in her three London seasons had she met a man who made her pulses race, or even made them stir. But Lord Ravensford, newly arrived in the country, made her forget everything else – everything except the fact that she was a woman and he was a man.

It can't be allowed to continue, she thought. Lord Ravensford might have an enormous effect on her body, but he was overbearing and dictatorial, and must be made to realize that he could not order her about.

She wondered briefly what he had against Mr Windham: he had been very adamant that she must not speak to him. She knew instinctively that it was not jealousy – Lord Ravensford, she felt, was, without being conceited, too sure of his own powers ever to be jealous of Mr Windham, or any other man – but she could think of no other possible reason for his reaction. True, she had not liked Mr Windham either, but she would hardly have ordered someone else to keep away from him. No, there must be some reason for it, she thought, as she looked deep into Lord Ravensford's eyes.

And then she saw them change. The gold light burned out of them and he let go of her arms, taking a step back.

'You are right,' he said in clipped tones. 'I have lost my manners completely.'

He gave her one more searching look and then, making her a curt bow, he strode towards the door.

He was almost out of it when Marianne called, 'Lord Ravensford?'

He turned round.

Marianne hesitated. Was it wise to talk to him? But he seemed to know Mr Windham, and she needed the answer to some questions about the man. 'About Mr Windham. . . .'

His eyes remained hard. 'Yes?'

'I . . . didn't like the man. I was trying to free myself from him when you arrived.'

'Then why. . . ?'

'Because I don't take kindly to being ordered about. I am not a child. I have a mind of my own and I use it. I will not allow you or anyone else to tell me who I can and cannot talk to. But all the same, there was something about Mr Windham I very much disliked.'

His eyes were shrewd, and there was an unmistakable glimmer of respect in them. 'Your instincts are good. You told me, at our first meeting, that I was anything but a gentleman – and no, don't tell me again,' he said with a wicked smile, 'because I am not about to disagree. You are right. I am not a gentleman. I was born a gentleman and have been raised as one, but the blood of the first earl runs strongly in my veins and he was a wolf of a man. Earldoms are won by predators: men with ambition, men who take what they want. And so yes, Miss Travis, you were right: I *am* anything but a gentleman. But Windham . . . Windham is something much worse.'

She nodded. 'I sensed something devious about him,' she said. 'Underhand.'

'Windham is a vicious man.'

A vicious man. Yes, there was something about him that had seemed vicious, in a cold and calculating way. And the questions he had asked her had been about Kit. Marianne sat down suddenly, as vague yet alarming possibilities forced their way into her mind. 'He is after my brother.'

He looked at her penetratingly. 'What makes you say that?' Then, as the sound of a distant door opening and closing reminded him they were alone in an out-of-the-way corner of the house, he said, 'No, don't tell me here. We must not stay or our absence may be remarked.' He gave an ironic smile. 'I am enough of a gentleman, you see, to protect your reputation: education has done something to civilize my instincts.'

She smiled, if a trifle worriedly, and stood up. 'You're right. We can't stay here.'

'I think it would be best if we returned to the supper-room. There is a chance we will be able to talk there undisturbed.'

The supper-room was, fortunately, almost empty. The only person there was Mrs Dalrymple, an elderly lady whose head was nodding on her breast.

Lord Ravensford helped himself to a dish of boiled fowl and, taking Marianne a dish of fruit, joined her at one side of the room. 'You said that Windham is after Kit?'

'Yes. I'm sure of it. The questions he asked, they were so very particular.'

'What did he want to know?'

'To begin with, whether I had any brothers and sisters, but then he started asking about Kit in a pointed way; whether he was here tonight, or if he was in London. It could have been polite conversation, but somehow it felt all wrong. And so I told him a lie. I told him that Kit was in London. But now I'm worried I've done the wrong thing.'

'How so?'

She shook her head with a worried frown. She did not want to speak ill of her brother, but she was concerned that she might have unwittingly caused him problems and she needed someone to talk to, someone who would understand the world of gambling and debtor's prisons, and someone who would not be shocked when she – a young lady – asked about them. But where to begin? She opened her fan and shut it again, then said, 'You know something of my brother. . . .'

'I do?' he asked.

'When I said that Windham was after my brother, you responded by saying that he was after Kit.'

Luke cursed himself for the mistake, at the same time respecting Marianne's intelligence for noticing it. 'I have met him once or twice in town, I believe,' he said cautiously.

'Then you must have heard of his disgrace.'

She spoke flatly, hiding her emotion.

'I . . . have heard something of it.'

'It's funny. I never thought I would be worried about Kit. It was always Kit who looked after me. There are only two years between us, and he taught me how to do so many things. He taught me how to climb trees, and he taught me how to swim.'

She smiled as she told him about her happy childhood.

Lord Ravensford smiled, too. It was a charming picture she painted, and he himself felt younger than he had done in years. As he listened to her talking about the fun she and Kit had had on their father's yacht, and how they had enjoyed swimming in the nearby sea, he thought what a pity it was that he could not invite her to go swimming with him when the weather improved. But such a thing was impossible. The sight of her delectable body rising from the waves was, alas, not one he would be allowed to see. 'It sounds as though you were very happy.'

'We were,' she said, warmed by his tone. 'At least for a time.' She sighed. 'But now I am worried. If Kit has been gambling again then he may well have fallen into debt, and I am afraid that Mr Windham has come here to find him and possibly throw him into prison.'

'Ah. So that is what you think.'

Marianne, preoccupied with her worries, did not hear his sigh of relief. 'If he *has* come to find Kit,' she said, following her own train of thought, 'then he will be disappointed. Kit hasn't been back to the Hall since he told my father of his disgrace. But Mr Windham does not seem to be the sort of man to give up. If he doesn't find Kit here, I'm afraid he will find him elsewhere, and if he finds him, what then?' She turned to face him, her eyes looking into his own. '*Will* he be thrown into prison? If he can't pay his debts?' She coloured, realizing she had gone further than she intended, but she had been led on by the fact that there was no one else she could ask. Her father would not hear Kit's name mentioned in the house and Tom and Trudie, though willing to help, had no knowledge of these kinds of things. Nor, she suspected, had Mr Cosgrove. He would bluster embarrassedly if she spoke to him, and assure her in a bluff and hearty way that everything would be all right. But she did not want to be reassured. She wanted to know the truth. And she felt sure that Lord Ravensford, with the hard edge she had witnessed in his character, would tell her that. 'It must seem strange to you, me asking you these things,' she began hesitantly, 'but—'

'No. It doesn't.' He seemed to understand her dilemma. 'It seems to me that I am the only person you can ask.' He paused, as if unsure of how much to say. 'Windham is a vicious man, and I would advise you to keep well away from him. But as for chasing Kit with regard to the payment of gambling debts – no, that's not his line.'

Marianne gave a sigh of relief 'Are you sure?'

'I am.'

'But then, why did he want to know about Kit?' she asked, speaking more to herself than to him. 'Unless it is simply that he was making conversation. If he is vicious, as you say, then that is enough to explain my aversion to him; and I don't see how his questions could have done any harm.'

'Did he ask any further questions?' asked Lord Ravensford carelessly. 'Anything more than where Kit was?'

'No. You came in before he could ask anything else.'

'Then I should put it out of your mind.' He finished his boiled fowl and carried his empty plate back to the table. 'We ought to return to the company. We don't want to give rise to gossip. You see, I am still careful of your reputation.' He gave her a warm smile. 'I suggest that you go back into the ballroom without me, and I will go back into the hall and return via the card-room. It will save your chaperon from feeling any alarm.'

It was the first time she had seen any warmth in him, she realized. Heat, yes; but this was something different. She felt herself flush, as though his warmth had brought forth an answering warmth of her own. He raised her hands to his lips and kissed them in a way totally different to the way he had kissed her hands before, then took his leave of her.

She waited a minute and then returned to the ballroom. As she rejoined the other guests she was pleased to find that Miss Stock was happily chatting to a group of older woman and had not noticed her absence.

'Did you find something good to eat?' asked Jennifer, bounding up to her.

Marianne responded to Jennifer's schoolgirl enthusiasm with an enthusiasm of her own, praising the lavish spread that had been put on for the guests.

'There was going to be black butter as well,' confided Jennifer, 'but Jem and I ate it this morning.'

'What, all of it?' laughed Marianne.

'Well, not quite. But almost!'

'And what did your mother say?' teased Marianne.

'Mama was not pleased!' said Jennifer with emphasis.

'Marianne! Dance with me!' said Jem, claiming her for the last dance of the evening. Marianne gave him her hand with a good grace and joined him on the floor to dance the *boulanger*. It was a rather complicated dance, and Jem, the undeniable possessor of two left feet, made rather a mull of it. Still, Marianne managed to get through to the end in one piece.

'Oh! How good it is to see the young people enjoying themselves!' exclaimed Miss Stock, as Marianne joined her once the dance was over. 'But now, my dear, it is growing late.'

61

'Of course. I'll send for our cloaks,' said Marianne.

The ball was beginning to break up. Several guests were thanking Mr and Mrs Cosgrove for a delightful evening and taking their leave.

'Thank you for a wonderful evening,' said Marianne to Mrs Cosgrove as she waited in the hall for Tom to bring the carriage round.

'My dear, we were just glad you could come.'

'Yes, thank you Elizabeth,' said Miss Stock, adding her thanks to Marianne's.

And then Tom arrived, and Marianne and Miss Stock went out of the house.

CHAPTER FOUR

'I hope you mayn't have taken cold at the Cosgroves' last night,' said her father querulously, as Marianne played chess with him the following morning. He picked up his bishop and moved it with shaking fingers across the board. 'Going out in the winter is a perilous thing to do.'

'No, Papa,' Marianne reassured him, as she deliberately overlooked the fact that he had exposed his knight. She picked up one of her own pawns and moved it harmlessly up the board. 'I'm sure I have not.'

'Young people are so thoughtless,' he complained, studying her move. 'They open windows and let in the night air. And if you take cold I don't know what is to become of us, for I am only a useless old man, you know.'

'You are not an old man, Papa. And you are far from useless. If you would only bestir yourself, you could do everything I do.' She put out her hand, resting it on his as she tried to recall him to the world. 'And you would do it so much better than me. You have years of experience, Papa, whereas I am all at sea. I am trying to run the estate, but. . . .'

She tailed away; she could see that it was no good. Instead of bestirring himself, her father shrank back in his chair. 'I?' he asked worriedly. 'Oh, no, my dear, I am too old for all of that now. Far too old. If only Christopher hadn't disgraced himself,' he said, his voice starting to tremble as he embarked on a familiar theme. 'It—'

Marianne sighed. Her efforts to rouse her papa out of his lethargy had been wasted, as they had been wasted so many times before. 'Yes, Papa,' she said soothingly, knowing that soothing him was now her only recourse: if she did not, he would only become more deeply embedded in his woes. Then, speaking brightly, she tried to turn the direction of his thoughts by saying, 'I believe it is your move.'

Bit by bit she managed to get him to focus his attention on the game once more, and when it was finished she left the stuffy room with a feeling akin to relief. It was a trial to her to see her father behaving as though he was in his dotage when he was in fact still a comparatively young man. And although she knew he had had a lot of trials to bear, she wished he could have made more of an efort, for her sake if not his own. After all, she had had the same trials to bear, and she had not become a recluse.

After spending an hour in the stuffy atmosphere she felt in need of some fresh air, and looking out of the window she decided to take a walk. The day was cold, but the clouds were breaking up and a gleam of sun shone through. She waited only long enough to fetch her cloak and muff before setting out for the seashore.

Seaton Hall was bordered by the sea at its southern edge. Marianne often walked there when the weather was fine, finding the fresh sea breezes beneficial in blowing away the gloomy air that surrounded her papa; a gloomy air that seemed to work its way into her skin whenever she was with him. A brisk walk took her to the beach and she stood there undecided as to what to do next, whether to go on, or whether to turn back. There were a number of things which needed her attention back at the Hall, and she had just decided that she should return when she caught sight of a figure standing on the rocks in the distance, gazing out to sea.

The many-caped greatcoat and three-cornered hat the gentleman was wearing could have been worn by anyone, but the height
and breadth of the figure, together with the powerful stance, told
her who it was at once: Lord Ravensford.

But what was he doing on the rocks, looking out to sea?

Whatever it was, it would have to come to a halt: the tide was
coming in.

She expected at any moment to see him turn and stride back to
the beach, but as he continued to look seaward she realized he did
not know the danger he was in. The rocks at that point would be
covered by the tide before another ten minutes had passed, and
with the cliff wall behind him he would be trapped.

She called to him, trying to attract his attention, but her voice
was carried away on the wind.

She began to walk across the beach, calling and waving every
minute or so as the water edged its way further up the rocks. Still
he did not see or hear her. She reached a spur of rock that jutted
out from the cliff and knew that this was the point at which she,
too, must turn back if she did not want to be trapped by the
incoming tide. She stopped and called, the wind whipping the
hood back from her face and blowing her cloak around her ankles.
But still she could not attract his attention. There was nothing for
it. She would have to climb across the rocks to him and lead him
to the one place that was still safe at high tide: the cave.

Using her hands to steady herself she made her way across the
rocks towards him. It was something she had done many times in
her childhood, and she was thankful now for her intimate knowledge of the rocks. Though they were wet with spray she moved
across them surely, her old kid boots, with their roughened soles,
giving her a good grip. She had almost reached him when he
turned and saw her. A deep frown crossed his face.

'What are you doing here?' he demanded.

She fought down her resentment at his tone and said, 'These

rocks will soon be under water. You can't stay here or you'll be caught by the tide. We're already cut off from the beach.'

He looked back along the beach and saw that what she said was true. 'Then why did you come here, you little fool?' he demanded, already looking up at the cliff as if assessing his chances of scaling it.

'There's a cave further along,' she replied. 'Kit and I used to play in it when we were children. The entrance is concealed, but it goes back a long way and rises as it does so. It is always dry, even at high tide. I have come to show you the way in.'

'And wouldn't it have been easier just to call to me?' he asked. He gave a sudden predatory smile, showing gleaming white teeth. 'Or did you just want the pleasure of my company?'

At his smile Marianne felt something wakening inside of her. Was it the wolf in him that called to her? she wondered. Was it the strength of his personality? Or was it the aura of danger that surrounded him, challenging her to rise and meet it?

'I have been calling to you for the last ten minutes, but I couldn't make you hear,' she replied.

As if to illustrate her words a sudden gust of wind almost whipped them away, so that he barely caught what she said. But catch it he did. Giving her a curt nod he stood aside. Moving past him, Marianne made her way surely over the rocks, moving in towards the cliff. The face of the cliff appeared to be sheer, but once past a group of boulders that lay, sleek and shining like a group of seals in the windblown spray, there was a slight crack. From the outside it looked to be nothing more than a fissure which widened into a bole at the bottom but Marianne knew what lay inside. She crouched down, turning to Lord Ravensford. 'This is the way in.'

He took one look at the small opening and raised his eyebrows. 'You expect me to crawl through there?'

'Either that, or be washed into the sea,' she returned.

'Miss Travis, you have a streak as hard as my own,' he said with a mocking smile.

'My streak is practical, not hard,' she informed him. 'Kit always managed to get through the hole, even when fully grown. You are a little taller than him, and a little broader, but not enough to make any difference. It might be best to take your coat off before you try, though,' she added thoughtfully, looking at the many capes which broadened his already broad shoulders. 'I will go first and you can pass it through to me.'

'A woman after my own heart. I have always admired enterprise.'

Marianne pulled her cloak tightly round her and crawled through the crack, standing up inside a large, deep cave. A moment later the coat was pushed through to her and Lord Ravensford followed, standing up beside her and looking round in surprise.

'Who would have thought it?' he murmured.

Marianne handed him his coat. As he took it his fingers grazed the back of her hand, searing it with a burning heat. She gasped, letting go of the coat more quickly than she had intended.

He caught it as she dropped it, giving her a wicked look as though reading what was in her mind.

Why did he seem able to do that? she thought, finding it intimate and disturbing. He had no right to know what she was thinking; especially as her thoughts these days seemed to be all about him.

'If we go to the back, we'll be above the tide,' she said, picking up the hem of her cloak and leading him towards the back of the cave.

Natural light came from a hole in the cliff top, lighting a strip down the centre of the cave and casting shadows into the rocky recesses. The floor of the cave was covered in sand; dark and damp by the opening, and light and dry towards the back.

'We used to keep candles and a tinder box here,' said Marianne, running her hands along a rocky shelf just above her eye level when she reached the back of the cave.

Lord Ravensford, being taller than she was by some six inches, saw what she was searching for and fastened his fingers around the box just as her hand discovered it. The contact burned her like a brand.

'Why aren't you married, Marianne?' he asked suddenly, his eyes glowing gold in the shaft of sunlight and his fingers remaining closed round her own.

'I . . . I hardly think that's a proper question,' she gasped, her heart drumming in her chest.

'Of course it isn't.' He gave a wolfish smile. 'Proper questions don't interest me. But you should be married,' he said, his look suddenly intensifying. 'A woman of your passionate nature shouldn't be condemned to the single life.'

'Passionate?' She felt her eyes lock on to his, as though he was holding them there by some magnetic force, a force from which she could not break free. She made a determined effort and drew her eyes shudderingly away. 'I am not a passionate woman,' she said, trying to inject a note of normality into her voice.

'Oh, but you are.'

'That's preposterous.' She retreated into being Miss Travis, taking a step back and using a dismissive tone to hold him at a distance, or at least, to try.

But she had not stepped back far enough, and for answer he ran the back of his hand over her cheek. 'Can you deny the way this makes you feel?' he asked softly. 'Can you pretend it doesn't make you burn inside?'

'Lord Ravensford.' She tried to keep her voice level, attempting to fight down the tide of sensations and emotions that were rising inside her. 'Are you trying to seduce me?' Her words were intended to shock him back into polite conversation but they did nothing of the kind.

'If I was trying to seduce you, you would already be . . .' *on your back by now*, he almost finished. But his hand, grazing her cheek and then pushing back her vibrant black hair, revealed a pearl ear-ring, an ear-ring he himself had helped Kit choose. With a flash he remembered that she was his friend's sister, and that he was here to help her, not to taunt her with her passionate nature, a nature which he himself had unforgivably roused, making her body throb with forbidden desire. He had forgotten how to behave in polite company, it seemed.

He took his hand away from her face and, reaching up, took down the candles and tinder box. Within a few seconds he had managed to get one of the candles to light. The others, their wicks dampened by the air, took longer, but at last burst into flame. Letting a little of the molten wax drop on to a rock shelf at shoulder level he stuck the candles securely to the rock.

'How long will it take the tide to go down?' he asked, returning the conversation into more normal channels.

'Enough for us to be able to get back? A little over an hour.'

'Will you not be missed?'

'No. I told Trudie I was going for a walk. I am often gone for an hour or more, when I can spare the time.'

'Good. I'm glad your life is not all work. Will you not sit down?' He swirled his coat down onto the sand, making a soft, dry blanket for her to sit on.

She sighed; and then smiled. 'So am I!' She settled herself on the greatcoat, sitting down with her knees pulled up to her chest. 'But tell me,' she said, eager to turn the conversation away from the unsettling paths it had so far seemed inclined to follow, 'what were you doing on the seashore anyway?'

He gave a wry smile. 'I, too, was taking a walk.' As he spoke he sat down on a boulder, one foot raised on a smaller stone. 'It's just lucky for me that you saw me when you did. I wouldn't have liked to have tried to swim against the tide.'

'It's dangerous here,' she acknowledged. 'There are a number of treacherous undercurrents. We were both frightened of them – Kit and I, that is – on the day we discovered the cave.'

'You were cut off?'

She nodded. 'Kit at the time was only twelve and I was ten. To make matters worse, we hadn't told anyone where we were going. But then we discovered the crack and found the cave behind it. After that, we came here regularly. I did wonder—'

'Yes?'

She gave a twisted smile. 'I did wonder, when he disappeared shortly after Christmas, if Kit had come down here. It was a favourite haunt when either of us was in trouble of any kind. I came to look for him as soon as I thought of it, but there was no sign of him. That's when I accepted he'd really gone.' She wrapped her arms round her knees, hugging them to her. Her cloak fell in loose folds round her, the swansdown lining not only helping to keep her warm but also helping to keep her dry. 'But I'm still worried about him. And still concerned about Mr Windham.'

He frowned, leaning one elbow on his raised knee.

She had the feeling that he could say more about Mr Windham if he had a mind to, but at the moment he was keeping silent.

'You said Mr Windham was vicious, and I felt it, too,' she said. 'But if he is not in the pay of the money-lenders, then who is he?'

He sat up straight, looking at her appraisingly, as if wondering what to tell her. Then he seemed to come to a decision. He threw down the piece of sea grass he had been toying with and looked her directly in her gentian-blue eyes. 'Tell me, Miss Travis,' he asked her, 'what do you know about the Jacobins?'

Marianne looked startled. 'The Jacobins? What do they have to do with this?'

'You have heard of them?'

'Yes, indeed. It is the Jacobins who are behind the troubles in

70

France. I know about them because my mother's governess was French,' she explained. 'Marie-Anne taught my mama for many years. As Mama grew older the two of them became good friends. So that when Marie-Anne unexpectedly inherited a fortune and returned to France the two of them stayed in touch.'

'Marie-Anne,' said Lord Ravensford thoughtfully. 'Are you named after her?'

Marianne nodded. 'Yes, I am'

'I did not know that.'

She looked at him curiously. 'How could you?'

'As you say,' he remarked, cursing himself for almost giving his knowledge of her family away. 'How could I? And so they stayed in touch?'

'Yes. Mama and Papa used to visit Marie-Anne, and in time her new husband, the Comte de Trevourny, and their daughter Adèle. And when Kit and I were old enough, Mama and Papa took us on their visits as well. When Mama died we did not go to France for a while, but the *comte* and Marie-Anne persuaded Papa that it would be good for us if the visits continued: there is nothing like spending holidays in France for picking up an authentic French accent, they said. Kit and I enjoyed the visits. Kit always loved playing with Adèle. She was – is, I hope – a very pretty girl. I often used to think . . . but that is all beside the point. The point is that I know all about the Jacobins, and unfortunately at first hand.'

'You came across them when you were in France?'

She nodded. 'It was in the summer of 1788, the last time we visited France. It was a strange summer for weather. There were hailstorms and drought and the harvest was spoiled. There was a lot of unrest. The poor people were suffering from rising bread prices, and they knew the bad harvest would make the problem worse over the winter. It was then the Jacobins began to meddle, whipping up feelings and stirring up trouble.'

71

'The Jacobins wanted to further their own political ends,' nodded Luke. 'They wanted to overthrow the ruling classes and take power into their own hands. And they were happy to use the poor to further their own cause.'

'Even so, things weren't so bad at the time. It was more a case of the Jacobins whipping up feeling than actually causing harm, but the atmosphere in the countryside was unpleasant, and the *comte* warned us not to venture off the estate. After that, we returned to England, but we heard from Marie-Anne that things were growing worse. There were violent riots throughout the winter and before long the country was in a state of upheaval.'

Marianne fell silent for a minute. Then she sighed and continued, 'It is such a shame. We hoped the trouble might have blown over by the following summer, but Papa received a letter from Marie-Anne telling him it would not be safe for us to visit them. There were riots everywhere, and the peasants were attacking the nobility, burning property and killing animals.'

'Encouraged by the Jacobins,' nodded Luke. 'They are vicious people. Devious, underhand and evil.'

Marianne nodded. 'Marie-Anne met one of the worst of them, a fastidious and ambitious man: Robespierre. She told us about him in her letters – that is, before her letters stopped. We were all very worried about her and her family. Then came the *Grand Peur*, the Great Fear. So many members of the nobility were killed or injured during that time. Many of them brought it upon themselves, but Marie-Anne's family were decent people and it seemed unfair they should be in danger when they had done no harm. But fortunately they came through unscathed. After that, we hoped that affairs in France would soon settle down.'

'But instead they got worse,' said Luke.

Marianne nodded. 'And now we have not heard from Marie-Anne and her family for over six months. At first we thought they were just having trouble getting a letter through, but since the execution of King Louis. . . .' She shivered.

He put his hand over hers. To her surprise his touch was reassuring instead of searing. It seemed that he could control the effect he had on her; something which made her feel even more vulnerable. But for now she drew comfort from his touch.

'Your hands are like ice.'

He took them between his own. His warmth flowed into her.

'But why did you ask what I knew about the Jacobins?' she asked, drawing her attention away from his firm, strong hands and trying to concentrate on their conversation.

'Because,' he said, 'that is what Windham is.'

She looked at him in horror. 'A Jacobin?'

'Yes. His real name is not Windham, but Rouget. Philippe Rouget.'

'But . . . what is he doing over here?'

She saw Luke looking at her intently. She had the curious feeling he was on the verge of telling her something important, but then he seemed to change his mind. 'He's trying to drum up support for the Jacobin cause.'

'And why was he asking about Kit?' She drew her hands out of his. 'Does he suspect Kit – my family – of harbouring *émigrés*? French nobles who have fled to England? Is that what his questions were all about? Or is he after Henri?'

So those were the conclusions she had drawn. They were intelligent. But he was relieved that her guesses were wide of the mark. He did not want to worry her by telling her that Windham had been fishing for information. Knowing that Kit was missing and that he had friends in France, Windham had scented a mystery and had been trying to find out whether that mystery had had anything to do with a rescue attempt from France: the Jacobins were determined to make sure that the nobles did not escape. But Windham knew nothing definite. Luke suspected that he had simply decided to question Marianne in the hope that he might discover something of interest. Marianne's innocent lie about Kit being in London, however, had, it was to be hoped, put Windham off the scent.

'No,' Luke said, answering her question. 'Windham isn't after Henri. Henri is just a peasant. The Jacobins aren't interested in people like him. And I don't believe Windham suspects your family of harbouring *émigrés*. His questions were merely idle curiosity; something with which to pass the time whilst he is over here trying to drum up support for the Jacobin cause. You have nothing to fear.'

She felt a weight lift from her shoulders. 'That's a relief.'

'With any luck he will soon be leaving the neighbourhood. Over the next few months the Jacobins will be doing everything they can to further their goal to rule France. Let us hope that Windham wants to return to his homeland to share in their glory.' There was a bitter twist to his mouth as he said this, and heavy irony on his use of the word *glory*. 'But enough of this,' he said. 'The Jacobins are on the other side of the Channel – at least, most of them are. Let's forget about them.'

He smiled, and she felt an answering smile rise to her own lips. 'Agreed.'

She stood up. 'I think I'll take a turn round the cave.'

'A good idea.'

The sun had moved round a little, and the strip of brightness that ran along the centre of the cave had moved with it. Marianne stood up and walked up and down in the patch of sunlight. Before long it began to warm her through.

The cave was one she had always liked. Although there were other caves along the seashore, there were few with holes in the roof. They were dank and dark, but this one, with its access to sunlight and fresh air, was always pleasant. It held the tang of the sea, of salt and seaweed, without having a fishy smell. Its sandy floor was clean, and there was often some kind of life – a gull that had waddled in through the crack and would leave by flying through the roof, or, as today, a crab that scuttled across the floor, sending the dry sand flying as it hurried along with its curious sideways gait.

But as she walked around the cave she was aware of Luke's eyes following her, and was conscious of the harsh and disturbing admiration in his gaze. It was predatory; devouring. No gentleman had ever looked at her in that way – but then, Lord Ravensford was not a gentleman. It made her uncomfortable and restless. It also made her tingle from head to foot.

She fought down her disturbing sensations. But she could not stop herself from being very aware of Lord Ravensford. He reminded her strongly of a wolf. A ruthless predator who threatened her long-held beliefs. Men, she had thought, were one thing or the other: kind-hearted if bumbling like Jem; good company like her brother; or cold and frightening like Mr Windham. But Lord Ravensford was a disturbing mixture of parts; of light and dark, sun and shade. Dangerous and mocking on the one hand, but absorbing and compelling on the other. He was alarming and perplexing and difficult to understand. But when he looked at her as he was looking at her now, he was utterly magnetic.

'I think I should see how far the tide has turned,' she said, making an excuse to remove herself from a situation she was finding it hard to understand. She stood up and went down to the mouth of the cave, bending down to go through the small opening and standing up straight on the other side. The sea had receded, and most of the rocks were now above water, with only a trail of seaweed and a stranded starfish to show where it had been. It would not be long before they could leave, and she could retreat to the haven of Seaton Hall – away from Lord Ravensford; away from his lazy smiles and disturbing manner; away from the searing intensity of his glances and the burning heat of his touch; away from the dangerous air that surrounded him – and immerse herself once again in the safe, if boring, details of running her father's estate.

'She should 'ave been back long ago. Why 'ave you not sent Tom out looking for 'er?'

These were the words that Marianne overheard as she arrived back at the Hall. They were flowing out of the open kitchen door.

'Why, bless you,' came Trudie's voice in answer to Henri's worried questions, 'Miss Marianne's often gone an hour or more when she's out for a walk. There's no need to fret.'

'But she may 'ave been attacked, or 'ad an accident.'

'Marianne's not the type to go round having accidents, and as for being attacked, why who would want to attack her on her own estate?'

'There are bad people in the world,' said Henri. 'Me, I know it.'

'The English aren't like the French,' said Trudie comfortably. 'They don't go round chopping people's heads off. She'll be back again soon, never . . . why, here she is now,' she said as Marianne walked in at the door.

'*Alors*! There you are!' exclaimed Henri, neglecting to point out that the English had chopped off their own king's head in the seventeenth century, in his delight to see Marianne safely home again. He hobbled over to her and kissed her on both cheeks, a Gallic gesture which brought a look of horror to Trudie's face.

'There's no call for that,' she said.

Whereupon Marianne smiled. 'It's all right, Trudie.'

'Oh, is it now?' demanded Trudie. 'You're forgetting your place, my girl. Being kissed on the cheek by a servant indeed!'

'A thousand apologies,' said Henri. 'I was just – 'ow you say? – *overjoyed* to see Miss Marianne safely 'ome again.'

'I've only been down to the seashore,' said Marianne, taking off her damp cloak and hanging it on a chair in front of the fire.

'And so I told him. But would he listen? He was all for me sending Tom out after you. As if Tom didn't have enough to do!'

'Even so,' said Henri stubbornly, 'you 'ave been gone a long time, Miss Marianne. I worry!'

'Well, here I am, and in one piece,' said Marianne, touched at Henri's concern. Ever since he had discovered that her papa kept to his room he had seemed to take on the role of her protector, looking after her and trying to make life easier for her.

'Now you *are* back, the butcher's been pressing for his bill to be paid,' said Trudie. 'I don't like to worry you but—'

'No. You're quite right to mention it, Trudie. I'll deal with it at once.'

'*Non*. Not until you 'ave 'ad something to eat. You are cold. Sit 'ere, and Henri will pour you some good 'ot soup.'

He was as good as his word, and placed a steaming hot bowl of soup in front of Marianne. She ate it gratefully, and the appetizing bread that went with it, thinking again how fortunate they had been to find Henri: a piece of good fortune for all concerned.

'How is your leg today?' she asked, when she pushed the empty bowl away.

Henri pulled a face. 'It gives me no trouble, but to walk far – *non*, it is not possible.'

'Don't worry. I wasn't going to suggest you made the trip to London,' said Marianne, adding teasingly, 'I am beginning to think we will not be able to part with you when your leg finally mends.'

'Ah!' Henri gave a satisfied sigh. 'The good chef, 'e is 'ard to replace, *non*? *Mademoiselle* you make me proud.'

Marianne laughed and then, much refreshed, set about seeing to the accounts. But as she did so, Lord Ravensford was never far from her mind. What had been the meaning of his behaviour in the cave; half predatory, half protective? And what had he meant to say when he had stopped himself halfway through the sentence: If I was trying to seduce you, you'd already be. . . ?

She didn't know. But she had a feeling it would be exhilarating as well as dangerous to find out.

CHAPTER FIVE

*T*he weather turned colder overnight. Frost sparkled from the trees and ice glinted in the ditches. Marianne, having played her morning game of chess with her papa, was busily cleaning the morning-room when she saw Jem Cosgrove riding up to the house. Hastily she took off her apron – although the neighbours knew the Travis's means were straitened, they did not know that Marianne often helped out with the cleaning – and ran upstairs, changing out of her plain woollen dress and into something more suitable for receiving guests.

'A good thing you saw him coming, Miss Marianne,' said Trudie, fastening the wide green sash that girdled Marianne's trim waist and giving a last brush to the glossy ringlets that fell down her back. 'It's bad enough for the neighbours to see you go visiting in a horse and trap; you'll never hold your head up again if they know you do the dusting as well.'

Slipping her feet into a pair of satin slippers – a dark green, to match the colour of her dress – Marianne ran downstairs, and was sitting elegantly on the *chaise-longue* in the drawing-room when Jem was shown in, just as though she had been sitting there all morning, with nothing better to do than to browse through the latest edition of *The Lady's Magazine*.

'Raw weather!' Jem greeted her cheerfully as he came stamping
and blowing into the drawing-room. 'Cold enough to. . . .' His face
fell, as he remembered that he was in a lady's drawing-room and
not a gentleman's club. 'That is to say, cold enough to make a man
feel cold,' he ended rather lamely.

Marianne smiled. Jem, though good-hearted, had never had a
way with words. 'Won't you sit down?' she asked, indicating the
sofa.

'Yes. Rather. Raw weather,' he said again. He looked round the
room once he had planted himself on the sofa. 'Trudie not about?'
he said.

Marianne shook her head. Trudie usually joined her when she
had visitors, sitting and sewing discreetly in the background, but a
problem with one of the maids had called her away and as Jem
was such an old family friend, not likely to do Marianne or her
reputation any harm, Trudie had been prepared to leave her alone
with him for a few minutes.

'Hem.' Jem went bright red and looked at the wall. 'I say,
Marianne,' he broke out a moment later, 'you shouldn't have to be
doing all this.'

'All what?' asked Marianne, wondering whether Jem could have
seen her dusting as he approached the house.

But Jem, obviously embarrassed, was being even less coherent
than usual. 'All this,' he said vaguely. 'At least, that's what
m'mother says. And I agree,' he added hastily.

Marianne, usually able to follow Jem's somewhat incoherent
speeches, was mystified.

'Looking after everything. Running the whole show,' he
explained suddenly. 'Need a man to do that kind of thing. Two
estates. Joining one another. Join at Nether Field. At the corners.
Can't say they don't. May not join anywhere else, but join at
Nether Field. Oh yes. So what d'you think?'

He looked at her hopefully.

Marianne was at a loss. Then the light dawned. 'You're offering me Bates,' she said. She was touched. Bates was the Cosgrove estate manager, and Jem, it seemed, had been sent to offer her his services.

'Bates? Good God. Can't mean to say you'd marry Bates?' asked Jem, amazed.

'Marry. . ?' asked Marianne, startled.

'Not the thing,' said Jem, shaking his head. 'Not the thing at all. Can't marry Bates, Marianne. Good man, I'll grant you. One of the best. But got a wife. And children. Any number of 'em. Ten, there were, at the last count. And still rising.'

Marianne smiled broadly. 'I wasn't thinking of marrying him; I thought you were offering me his services to help me manage the estate!'

'Oh!' Jem slapped his thigh and roared with laughter. 'You thought m'father meant to share Bates! Lord, no, Marianne! M'father would never share Bates.' He suddenly sobered. 'Don't mean *Marianne*. Mustn't call you *Marianne*. Got to call you Miss Travis. M'mother says so. M'mother's never wrong. Though why in Hades I should call you Miss Travis when I've known you since forever's beyond me. Still, better do what m'mother says.'

He paused, obviously having lost the thread of his conversation.

Marianne prompted him kindly. 'You said your father doesn't want to share Bates?'

'No, Marianne – Miss Travis – dash it, Marianne – that's right. M'father don't want to share Bates. He wants to share me. Well, not share me exactly . . . Lord, I'm making a mull of this,' said Jem, tugging at his cravat. 'Jennifer said I would. Looks like she's right. Damn fine girl Jennifer. Oh! dash it! Didn't mean to say damn! Told me to go down on one knee or some such thing. Don't half like. Look a fool. But the ladies like it.' And to Marianne's amusement he knelt down in front of her.

'Oh don't, Jem,' she said, much to his relief. 'Do get up, I beg of you. I'm very fond of you Jem, you know that, but if you mean to ask me to marry you I'm afraid I must refuse.'

'Thought you would,' said Jem, gratefully getting up off his knees. 'Not dashing like Ravensford. Don't know how to sweep a girl off her feet.'

'Oh, Jem, it isn't that,' said Marianne, whilst being uncomfortably aware that his words held far more than a grain of truth. 'It's just that we have been such good friends for so many years that it would be a shame to spoil our friendship. I like you very much, Jem, but I can't marry you. We just wouldn't suit.'

'Ah well, can't say I haven't tried,' he said philosophically. 'Pity, though, Marianne. Devilish pretty girl you know.'

'You'll find another devilish pretty girl, Jem. One who can love you in a way I can't.'

'Might have something there,' said Jem, whose feelings, whilst honest, did not run deep. 'Might find one at Ravensford's do.'

Marianne looked at him enquiringly.

'Got an ice yacht,' Jem explained.

'Who has?' Marianne asked, finding it difficult, as usual, to follow Jem's rambling speech.

'Lord Ravensford. Having a party. Sail the ice yacht on the lake. Frozen,' he explained helpfully. 'Got the invitation this morning. Reminds me. Got one for you.' He pulled a crumpled card out of his pocket and handed it to her. 'Servant came round with them. Said I'd bring yours. Coming here anyway. Save the man a trip.'

'Yes. Thank you.' She turned the card thoughtfully between her fingers. 'However, I'm not sure I shall be able to go.' Her feelings for Lord Ravensford were becoming deeper and more difficult to control, and she wasn't sure it was wise to see any more of him than was necessary, however tempting it might be.

Jem's face fell. 'Got to,' he said. 'M'family'll be there. Got to tell 'em I didn't make a mull of it. Otherwise m'mother'll tell me to offer for you again.'

'Oh dear, Jem, are you sure? I'm not a good match, you know. I don't have any dowry to speak of. Can't you persuade her it's better this way?'

Jem shook his head. 'Can't say it's not a good match. Old family, Marianne. Good stock. Good match without a dowry. Devilish pretty girl. Can't tell her it's not a good thing for you, either. Not much of a catch, but still, husband to take care of you. Make life easier. Use the carriage. No more horse and cart. Good thing all round. Or so m'mother will say. Likes the idea, don't you know?'

Marianne sighed. It seemed there was nothing for it. She would have to go to Lord Ravensford's gathering and convince the Cosgroves that Jem had done the thing properly, but that she had still refused to marry him.

'You'll come?' asked Jem hopefully.

Marianne nodded. 'Yes.'

'Good show. Should be interesting,' he said, by way of consolation. 'Don't have to spend the whole afternoon with m'mother. Just enough to convince her I did it right. Down on one knee, don't you know?'

Marianne smiled. 'You did it very well. And I'm grateful to you, Jem. Truly I am. You will make some young lady an admirable husband.'

Jem went pink. 'Pish,' he said, but nonetheless looked pleased. 'Well, must be off,' he said, obviously deciding that as his task had been done he should not trouble Marianne further. 'Tell Ravensford you'll come, shall I?'

'Yes, thank you.'

'Good. No, don't trouble,' he said, as Marianne accompanied him to the door of the drawing-room. 'See m'self out.'

'And what was all that about?' asked Trudie, coming in a minute later, having just seen Jem leave the house.

'He came to propose to me,' said Marianne with a sigh.

Trudie nodded sagely,

'Trudie, you can't say you were expecting it?'

'And why not? Jem's of an age to be married, and you should have been married long ago, Miss Marianne. If you're not careful you'll end up on the shelf.'

'I don't intend to get married just so that I won't end up a spinster,' Marianne returned with spirit.

'No. It's love or nothing for you, Miss Marianne,' said Trudie, looking worried. 'You turned down three offers in London at your come-out, and all of them from rich and handsome gentlemen, and now you're turning down Jem. But you can't go on turning down gentlemen for ever, or it *will* be nothing, Miss Marianne.'

Marianne sighed. She went over to the window and looked out at the gardens, which twinkled prettily under their coating of frost and ice. Love or nothing. Yes, it had always been that way with her. She had received a number of offers from unexceptionable gentlemen during her London Seasons – paid for by the kindness of her London aunt – but had turned them down. Why? she wondered. Perhaps it was *because* they were all unexceptionable gentlemen. They would never have wanted her to lend a hand in running her family estate, and they would have been horrified at the idea of her rescuing a man from a mantrap. And as for her bandaging his leg. . . ! No, it would never have done. She could not have accepted any of them. Because, as they were unexceptionable gentlemen, they would have expected her to be an unexceptionable lady. And whilst she was most assuredly a lady, she could never be a milk-and-water miss who would sit sketching and sewing all day long. She simply had too much spirit.

And now she had turned down Jem. Dear, sweet, bumbling Jem. But she had had no choice. She could never have accepted Jem, not even if he had proposed to her before she had met Lord Ravensford. And now . . . her thoughts went to the dark man who was never far from her thoughts. Now it was impossible.

*

The carriage bowled along the drive, making for Billingsdale Manor. When last she had come this way, Marianne had been travelling in a horse-drawn cart, but this time she was arriving in style. The carriage, scrubbed and polished, was pulled by a team of horses, their manes and tails plaited, their gleaming bodies beautifully groomed. The fact that the horses were usually used for pulling ploughs was one which Marianne hoped no one would remark.

The carriage pulled up before the door. The step was let down and Marianne tripped out, finding it impossible not to think of what had happened on her first visit to this same house. But this, time she was not left to wander in alone and unannounced. She was greeted at the door by Figgs, who led her through a hallway lined with footmen, to the drawing-room which, unlike her first visit, was full of the sound of chatter. Miss Stock had again kindly agreed to be her companion for the evening and act as her chaperon, and followed Marianne into the house.

Once divested of her cloak, Marianne was dressed in a simple yet becoming gown of gentian blue which matched the colour of her eyes, tied about the waist with a white satin sash. The neckline was square and fashionably, though decorously, low. The sleeves were long and close-fitting, and ornamented at the bottom with three little buttons of mother-of-pearl. A blue ribbon was threaded through her lustrous curls, setting off their glossy black.

She saw the Cosgroves straight away. There, too, were the Lentons, the three girls, Amelia, Cordelia and Lobelia, all giggling mightily at something Lord Ravensford had just said. And there was Lord Ravensford himself, leaning negligently against the Adam fireplace which was decorated with a line of nymphs.

It was the first time, apart from the Cosgroves' ball, that she had really seen him in company, Marianne realized. And it was the first time she had seen him playing host to a gathering in his

own – albeit leased – home. It came as something of a shock to her
to realize how at ease he seemed, particularly as he was almost
entirely surrounded by females. And it also came as a reminder
that she hardly knew him. It would not do for her to refine too
much on the time they had spent together, the things he had said
or the way he had behaved, she realized. She would be a fool if she
read anything more into it than the attentions of a man who was,
by his own admission, anything but a gentleman, and who probably forgot all about her the moment she was out of his sight.

'Miss Travis,' he said, coming towards her with his half-mocking
smile. 'I'm so glad you could come.' His eyes roamed over her,
lingering on the ribbon which accentuated the blue highlights in
her hair, and on the bodice of her dress, which, decorously filled
in with lace, sculpted the curve of her breasts.

'Lord Ravensford.' On guard against his undoubtedly wicked
charm, and against her own unruly feelings, she returned his greet-
ing with a politely formal manner.

He lifted his eyebrows, but made no remark on her cool air.
'And Miss Stock,' he said courteously, turning to her companion
and kissing the spinster's hand.

'Oh, Lord Ravensford, so very happy . . .' mumbled Miss Stock,
quite overcome.

But when he turned to Marianne she knew he had noticed her
coolness and that he was determined to make her pay, because the
kiss he bestowed on her hand burned her even through her long
white glove.

'We are to have an interesting afternoon as I understand it,' said
Miss Stock breathlessly, as he finally let go of Marianne's hand. 'An
ice yacht, I hear?'

'Yes,' he said, speaking to Miss Stock, drawing his eyes away
from Marianne's.

'And what is an ice yacht?' Marianne asked, wishing he would
not look at her as though he was undressing her with his eyes. It

had been bad enough when they were alone, but in a room full of people it was ten times more disturbing.

'Why, the same as any other yacht; or at least, the principle is the same. An ordinary yacht carries people over the water; an ice yacht carries them over the ice. Shall you like to sail in it?' he asked.

'I didn't know it would be big enough for a party,' she said, surprised; for although an ordinary yacht could take any number of people on board she had the feeling that an ice yacht, because of its limited use, would be much smaller.

'It isn't. But it is big enough for two.'

His wicked smile invited her to protest, but she refused to rise to his bait, and he turned back to her companion.

'Miss Stock. You would not object to a turn in the yacht, I'll be bound?' he asked.

'Well, I don't know,' began Miss Stock, not sure whether to be flattered or scandalized. Even at the age of fifty, the idea of being in an intimate situation with Lord Ravensford was not one she could contemplate with equanimity: Lord Ravensford was so undeniably *male*.

'Marianne!'

Jennifer's halloo fortunately saved the good Miss Stock from the tricky situation, as all eyes turned towards Jennifer.

'Marianne. Jem said you were coming. Did he really go down on one knee?'

'Not here, Jennifer,' said Marianne, feeling it would not be fair to expose poor Jem's proposal to Lord Ravensford's mocking, and yet surprisingly interested, eye.

'Can I go on the yacht?' asked Jennifer, young enough to flit from one topic to another, and gauche enough to find nothing wrong in it. Or in asking such outright questions.

'Perhaps,' said Lord Ravensford, with the air of one speaking to a child. 'We'll see.'

Mrs Cosgrove, following her bouncing daughter, crossed the room more sedately. 'Marianne, I'm so glad to see you, my dear. Jem said you intended to come.' Mrs Cosgrove, however, being more sophisticated than Jennifer, did not ask the question she was obviously wanting to ask, preferring to wait until later, when she could speak to Marianne alone.

They fell into general conversation and Lord Ravensford was quickly reclaimed by the Lenton girls, who had visibly pouted when he had given his attention to Marianne. But was he enjoying their company, or was he silently laughing at them? Marianne asked herself. A moment later asking herself why she cared.

She turned her attention to the new guests who were just arriving, the Pargeters and Kents, thinking how fortunate it was that, as the party was being hosted by Lord Ravensford, she need have no fear of Mr Windham being one of the guests.

The hubbub grew until at last everyone had arrived and Lord Ravensford announced that the ladies should claim their cloaks and the gentlemen their caped coats as they were about to walk down to the lake.

'And there is the yacht,' said Lord Ravensford, as they reached the side of the lake.

It was tied up to the jetty, lying innocently on the surface of the ice. Small and slender, it looked something like a canoe. A sail was tied to a tall mast and flapped in the breeze. 'It was invented by an American named Booth a few years ago,' said Lord Ravensford. 'I've made a few modifications to his original design.' He lifted his head, considering the weather. Waving trees gave sign of the breeze. 'It should sail well today. There's enough wind to power it, but not enough to capsize it.'

'Wouldn't mind a go on that myself, Ravensford,' said Henry Kent, who had idled along beside them and was now looking at the ice yacht with interest, walking round it and admiring its construction.

'Be my guest.'

'Marianne, my dear,' came Mrs Cosgrove's voice, seizing the opportunity to speak to Marianne as Mr Kent asked Lord Ravensford to explain the workings of the yacht. 'Tell me, how is your dear papa?'

She drew Marianne aside. Marianne, whilst knowing that Mrs Cosgrove's questions about her father's health were just a subterfuge to gain her attention, nevertheless answered with a good grace, and then allowed Mrs Cosgrove to turn the subject round to Jem. Marianne listened patiently whilst Mrs Cosgrove explained Jem's worth, and the value of a husband to a young woman with a reclusive father and a missing brother, but whilst agreeing with much of what she said, Marianne nevertheless left her in no doubt that, although she valued Jem as a neighbour and a friend, she could not marry him.

'He made a mull of it, I suppose,' said Mrs Cosgrove with a sigh.

'No, not a bit of it.' Marianne was loyal to her childhood friend. 'I just don't think of Jem in that way. I couldn't have accepted him, no matter how romantically he'd proposed.'

'Then it is no use him trying again?' asked Mrs Cosgrove.

Marianne knew she had to be firm 'None at all.'

'Ah! Well,' sighed Mrs Cosgrove. 'I suppose it's for the best. A good solid girl will probably be more suitable, after all. Tell me, what do you think about Susan Kent?'

Happy to praise the stolid young woman, Marianne listened to Mrs Cosgrove's hopes for her children and then, when Mrs Cosgrove departed, turned her attention back to the lake. Lord Ravensford was demonstrating the ice yacht to young Mr Kent, controlling the precarious-looking machine with skilled ease. As she watched him lying back and shifting his weight to control the yacht, Marianne smiled. He was obviously enjoying himself. He looked younger. Almost boyish! Her smile widened. It did her good to see him like this. It showed her another side of his personality.

Realizing her smiles were likely to give her away she pulled her cloak closer and determinedly fixed her attention on the yacht, instead of its owner. The yacht slid across the ice, leaving a wake of churned-up ice behind it.

The young men in the party were all eager to have a go, and after Lord Ravensford had demonstrated the workings of the yacht they took it in turns to sail across the lake. Once they had tried it out the ladies were offered a turn at being a passenger. There was little room on the craft, it being low and slim, but there was just enough room for a second person to sit beside the first. One by one, the bolder of the ladies took a turn, some with their husbands, others with their brothers. And then Lord Ravensford turned to Miss Stock. 'Miss Stock, you have not yet taken a turn on the yacht. As your brother is not here you will allow me, as your host, I hope, to display its virtues?'

Miss Stock, thus appealed to, could not resist, and when her trip was over, what more natural than that Lord Ravensford should offer the same politeness to Marianne? 'You can have no objection, I hope?' said Lord Ravensford smoothly to Miss Stock. 'As Miss Travis's father is unfortunately unable to join us, I will offer myself to take her round the lake.'

The smile he gave Miss Stock was so disarming that, although she fluttered how it was not quite the thing for a young lady, she went on to say that with so many people there, and all in plain view, and as poor dear Marianne must not be neglected . . . in short, she gave way before his undoubted charm and Marianne allowed herself to be escorted to the yacht.

'Do you always have your way with maiden ladies?' she asked him mischievously, arranging herself, not without difficulty, on the yacht.

He threw her a wicked smile which brought a blush rising to her cheeks and she realized that her words, innocently spoken, could have a different meaning. Then he took pity on her. 'Not always,' he said.

Once they were settled he pulled on a series of ropes and the yacht began to glide forward over the ice. It moved slowly to begin with, but as Lord Ravensford tacked to catch the wind it began to pick up speed. Marianne let out a gasp: the sensation was exhilarating. The wind caught her hair and blew it into confusion, stinging her cheeks and making them glow. Back and forth across the lake they went, the yacht leaving a trail of churned-up ice behind them, whilst ahead it was as smooth as glass.

At last the yacht began to slow. Lord Ravensford steered it in to the shore and brought it gliding to a halt. He secured the ropes, sprang out of the yacht, and offered Marianne his hand. She took it gratefully – the yacht was breathtaking, but getting in and out of it was precarious – and found herself once more on firm ground. She looked across the lake towards Miss Stock, who was busily chattering to Mrs Kent. Lord Ravensford had brought the yacht to rest at the far side of the lake, away from most of the guests, something Marianne suspected he had done on purpose. Whilst still being in full view, they were accorded some measure of privacy, and would retain it until they had walked round the lake.

'It's good to see you enjoying yourself,' he said, taking in her brilliant eyes and rosy cheeks.

She looked at him suspiciously, not sure whether he was mocking her or not, but for once he seemed to be serious.

'It can't be easy for you,' he continued, 'now that your father's become a recluse.'

'Sometimes . . .' she began.

'Yes?'

'Sometimes it would be nice to have someone to turn to.' She knew herself to be both intelligent and capable, but even so, there were times when she found it all getting too much for her.

He looked at her intently. 'You weren't tempted to accept Cosgrove's offer, then?' he asked, his hand drifting to her chin, which he lifted gently towards him. His eyes were searching as they probed her own.

She swallowed. 'No.'

'Life would be so much easier for you if you had a husband.'

Marianne felt the tension in him as he spoke, as though he was a coiled spring. 'I could hardly marry Jem for that reason,' she replied.

'Many women do marry for that reason.'

'And I do not blame them for it. But that is not for me.'

He looked at her searchingly for another minute and then, seeming satisfied, dropped her chin.

They walked on in silence, skirting the lake. 'I have to admit that Jem's proposal has changed things. It has made it much more difficult for me to ask Mr Cosgrove for advice,' she said.

'I have my own estate in Surrey. I am used to managing it. If you need any help I hope you will ask me.'

Marianne was surprised and yet relieved by the offer. It certainly would make her life easier if she had someone to turn to and, hard though Lord Ravensford undoubtedly was, he was also someone she instinctively felt she could trust.

'And as to this estate,' he said, as they walked on, 'I know you were concerned about trees being cut down and not replanted, so I have given orders that the woods are to be restocked.'

She turned to him, eyes wide.

'You're surprised?' he asked.

She nodded.

'Good. I'm glad to have surprised you. Because you, Miss Travis, are surprising me all the time.'

On this enigmatic note they rejoined the other guests.

'You've left the yacht on the other side of the lake, Ravensford,' protested Maurice Pargeter, who had been looking forward to taking the yacht out again.

'The ice has been weakened enough for now. The yacht churns

it up, and it becomes thinner with each crossing. But don't worry, if the weather holds it should be possible to take it out again another day.'

With the yachting over, the guests began to think about return-ing to the house. The weather, which had been pronounced fresh on the way down to the lake, was now being described as perish-ing. A brisk walk, however, revived everyone and it was a merry party that, divested of their cloaks and greatcoats, settled down in front of a roaring log fire.

Marianne was claimed by Maurice Pargeter, whilst Lord Ravensford, shrugging off the attentions of the Lenton girls, was claimed by their cousin, Mrs Violet Kilkenny.

Marianne found her attention wandering to Mrs Kilkenny.

Mrs Kilkenny was an outwardly respectable matron of some thirty years, but she was rarely seen with Mr Kilkenny, whose business kept him in London. She had a decided preference for male company and had begun the afternoon by talking to Mr Havers, a wealthy merchant who owned much of the land here-abouts; now she turned her attention to Lord Ravensford. She had allowed her young cousins to make fools of themselves by giggling all over him first and then began to converse with him in a beau-tifully modulated voice, thereby making her sense and maturity seem all the more alluring.

And she was alluring, Marianne had to admit – though why the idea should occur to her she did not know. Although decorously dressed, Mrs Kilkenny wore her amber crêpe gown with a subtle negligence that made it seem almost risqué. It hovered on the verge of revealing her shoulder, and although the bodice revealed no more of her breasts than was fashionable, her rope of pearls was of just such a length as to nestle invitingly between them. She leaned towards Lord Ravensford as she talked, and if Lord Ravensford's smiles were anything to go by he was enjoying every minute of it.

Marianne turned her attention firmly back to Mr Pargeter, reminding herself that Lord Ravensford's behaviour was none of her concern. If he chose to flirt with Mrs Kilkenny that was up to him. Even so, she was relieved when Figgs entered the room and announced that dinner was served.

There was a chorus of approval from those assembled. The hour was early, but in the country dinner was always served early, particularly during the winter months.

Mr Kent escorted Marianne into the dining-room, whilst Lord Ravensford gave his arm to Mrs Cosgrove; something that did little to alleviate Marianne's feelings, as Mrs Kilkenny sat at Lord Ravensford's left hand.

However, fighting down feelings that she refused to acknowledge as jealousy, Marianne gave her attention to her fellow guests.

The meal, whilst not being up to Henri's standards, was well cooked and enjoyable. Split pea soup was followed by turbot set in smelts, after which came a round of beef and, to finish off, a plum pudding.

'Good food, good wine. What more can anyone want?' asked Mr Cosgrove of the table at large, when the meal finally came to an end.

There was a murmur of agreement before the ladies withdrew, to be joined not long afterwards by the gentlemen.

'Splendid afternoon, Ravensford,' remarked Henry Kent, as he drank his coffee.

'I'm glad you enjoyed it; because I am hoping to soon repeat it. I have it in mind to host a weekend party, to liven up the dull winter days.'

'What an excellent idea,' said Mrs Kilkenny, leaning forwards slightly and somehow managing to make the commonplace words sound intimate and full of promise.

'What do you say, Miss Travis?' he asked, turning to Marianne. 'Is it an excellent idea?'

'I'm sure it is. Unfortunately, I don't believe I will be able to attend.' A weekend of watching Mrs Kilkenny throw herself at Lord Ravensford, whilst he apparently enjoyed every minute of it, did not appeal to her.

'Oh, but Marianne, I'm sure it can be arranged,' said Miss Stock, ever helpful. 'Why, if it runs from Friday to Sunday, as I think dear Lord Ravensford intends, your father will only have to do without you on the Saturday. Don't forget, you can have your customary game of chess with him on Friday morning, and then tell him all about the weekend on the Sunday evening. And as for the Saturday, I'm sure my brother would be delighted to sit with him for an hour or two, for Sebastian, too, enjoys a game of chess.'

Faced with this excess of friendliness and helpfulness, Marianne realized it would be churlish of her to refuse.

'Splendid,' said Lord Ravensford, throwing her the mocking look she knew so well. 'Then it is settled. I will arrange the details with my housekeeper before sending out the invitations, and I hope you will all do me the honour of attending.'

This new turn of events gave an added impetus to the conversation, and it was late in the evening when the party finally came to an end.

'A weekend party?' Figgs was scandalized. The guests had gone, and he was alone with Luke in the library. 'What the devil do you think you're doing, organizing a weekend party? Have you forgotten why we took this place? So that we could put out to sea, if necessary, without raising any suspicions, and so that if all goes well Kit can land here without being seen, and therefore without any Jacobin spies getting wind of it. You know as well as I do that the Jacobins are doing everything in their power to make sure that no one escapes from France.'

'I don't need you lecturing me on what we're doing here,' remarked Luke. 'But until we hear from Kit there's nothing we can do to help him. And the neighbours, meanwhile, will be less suspicious of my presence here if I am throwing parties and am clearly enjoying myself.'

'And what if word comes during your party?' Figgs enquired.

'That isn't very likely. And if it does, I'll deal with the situation when it arises.'

'And all because of a woman,' said Figgs, making an unflattering noise with his lips.

'Mrs Kilkenny has nothing to do with it.'

'I never said she did.' Figgs's remark was dry.

'Meaning?' Luke's voice was demanding, underpinned with just the faintest tinge of danger.

'Meaning I've seen the way you look at Marianne.'

'Ah.' Luke's expression was predatory. 'Who wouldn't? She's enough to drive a man to distraction.'

Figgs's gaze became speculative. 'Seems to me there's more to it than that. Seems to me she means more to you than just a lovely face and a tempting collection of curves.'

'Of course she means more to me than that.' Luke's tone was contemptuous. 'She's Kit's sister. And the next time you're tempted to comment on her curves I suggest you remember it,' he said warningly.

'So that's the interest?' asked Figgs mockingly. 'It's because she's Kit's sister? Once Kit's saved, it'll be back to London and bye bye Marianne?'

Luke glowered. 'Haven't you got anything better to do than stand there talking damned nonsense?'

'Such as?'

'Such as getting things ready for the weekend party.'

'You're determined, then?'

'Yes.'

'Then there's no more to be said. But be careful with her, Luke. Like you said, she's Kit's sister—'

'I don't need you lecturing me on my private affairs either.'

The look that accompanied this speech was so dangerous that Figgs withdrew from the lists. 'Have it your own way.' He stood up and crossed to the door. 'So it's Friday, is it? The party?'

'Friday to Sunday.'

Figgs gave an ironic bow, and in his best butlering voice, he said, 'Very good, My Lord.'

CHAPTER SIX

The first of March dawned bright and fair. It was a balmy day, unusually warm for the time of year. The ice had melted, leaving green fields and rushing streams in its wake, and a few early daffodils nestled in sheltered spots around the Travis estate.

Marianne carried a bunch of them in her arms as she rode towards the village churchyard after lunch. She was enjoying the unseasonably warm sunshine and the balmy air. Nature was bursting into life all around her and it made her cheerful, however sad her task might be.

She dismounted by the lych gate, using one of the stones as a block, and tethered her little grey mare, then went into the churchyard. The graves were all well kept, and there was an air of peace about the place. Marianne found it welcoming – since the coming of Lord Ravensford, peace in her life had seemed in short supply. She went over to the far side of the graveyard and set about arranging the daffodils in a silver vase. The vase was set in stone in between two graves. One was the grave of her mother, the other was Julian's grave. Her beloved younger brother had enjoyed the outdoor life, and had made their mother promise not to bury him in the family crypt; and when Mrs Travis's turn had come, she had asked to be laid by the side of her younger son.

After fetching water from the well to fill the vase Marianne knelt for a few minutes in silence, remembering her beloved mother and brother. It was a fever that had taken her brother, and a riding accident that had taken her mother, but it was not the sadness of their deaths that she remembered, but the happiness of their lives. She felt calm and at peace when laying flowers on their graves.

She was just about to rise to her feet when she became aware of someone standing close by. She looked round to see Lord Ravensford. He had an unusual look on his face, a look she had never seen there before. It was a look which, on the face of another man, a man who was not as hard as Lord Ravensford, she would almost have called tender.

'I'm sorry,' he said. 'I didn't meant to disturb you.'

His tone was so gentle that she felt strangely touched. 'You haven't.' She rose to her feet. 'I have done what I came to do.' She looked at the gravestones and felt a desire to talk about her family. 'I come here each week to pay my respects to my mother and my brother. Not Kit,' she said, seeing his look of surprise. 'My younger brother Julian.'

She did not know why she was confiding in him, especially on such a personal matter, but she had the instinctive feeling that he would understand. It came as a relief to her to speak about her mother and brother. There were times when she longed to talk about them, but her father could not hear their names mentioned without becoming fretful, and Trudie, meaning well, would say it was better not to talk of the dead. But she had loved her mother and brother, and felt a need to talk about them now and again.

She saw him look at the gravestone and read the words chiselled there: *In loving memory of Julian St John Travis, born 1773, died 1784. May he rest in peace.*

'I . . . did not know,' he said quietly.

'Julian was my younger brother, the baby of the family,' she

99

said, looking lovingly at his gravestone. 'He was just eleven when he died. That's why. . . .' She paused as she felt a sudden catch in her throat, but then went on, 'That's why my mother learnt how to deal with the illnesses and accidents that happened round the estate.'

'And why she taught you how to deal with them as well?' he asked.

She nodded. ' "It's no use trusting doctors," Mama used to tell me. "Doctors don't always get through". There was a storm on the night of Julian's death, you see, and Dr Moffat couldn't get through. There were floods and gales and it was quite impossible. By the time he reached us the next morning it was too late. Julian was dead. My mother decided then that she would learn the rudiments of medicine, so that if something like it happened again she would know what to do.'

'Your mother must have been a fine woman.'

'She was.' Marianne spoke simply. 'She made Dr Moffat tell her what she should do in cases of fever in the future. At first, he didn't want to help her. It wasn't a fit subject for ladies, he said. But because of Julian's death he relented, and in time he came to teach her much of what he knew. She decided to pass her knowledge on to me. It shocked Papa, and many of the people hereabouts, but it did not put her off. She had a strong character, and did what she believed to be right.'

'I wondered how you had managed to make such a good job of Henri's leg. And also how you had the courage to help him free it from the trap. It can't have been a pretty sight. Most young ladies would have had a fit of the vapours.'

'I have to confess, I almost felt like it,' she said. 'His leg was a terrible mess.'

'He told me. He told me, also, how you bandaged it.'

'And you were not shocked?' she asked, looking sideways at him as they left the graves and walked down to the lych gate.

He gave a wry smile. 'We are neither of us conventional, Miss Travis; neither you nor I. I am anything but a gentleman, as you so rightly told me, and whilst you are most definitely a lady, you don't allow that fact to stop you being yourself as well. That, I suspect, is why we get on so well together: we both have strong characters – too strong to let society stop us being ourselves. But to answer your question: no, I was not shocked when I learned that you bandaged Henri's leg. It seemed to me to be a very useful thing to be able to do. And why should I be shocked at someone being useful?'

'Many people are. Being useful is not generally considered to be desirable.'

'And being useless is?'

She laughed, picking up on the humour in his tone. But at the same time she could not help remembering the gentlemen who had courted her in London, and their horror when they had discovered she had tended an injured parlourmaid. 'There are those who think so.'

'I'm not one of them. Being useless is all very well for those who *are* useless, but is a sad waste of talents for those who are not. And now *I* have shocked *you*.'

She realized he was teasing her, and smiled. He was revealing another side of himself; one she had not previously suspected.

'But I came to find you on purpose this morning,' he said, as they reached the lych gate. He stopped and turned towards her, the spring sunshine lightening his face. 'I've put the final touches to the weekend party and I've come to deliver the invitation in person.'

'I'm not sure . . .' began Marianne.

'When you've all but promised Miss Stock?' he asked her innocently.

She laughed. 'I suppose, in that case, I have no choice.'

'No indeed. I think you'll find it entertaining. There'll be music and dancing, and a host of other activities – including riding, if you care to bring your horse.'

He looked at her mare, who was grazing contentedly just beyond the gate.

'I'll do that,' she said. She looked round for his horse but could not see it.

'I came on foot,' he said, in answer to her enquiring look. 'The day was fine and I decided to walk. It was by chance I saw you in the churchyard and made a detour. But now, I hope you'll let me see you home?'

'You are as bad as Henri!' laughed Marianne. 'He is always trying to look after me, and doesn't like me to go anywhere alone.'

'Very wise. Coming from France, he must have seen a lot of terrible things, and even here, although we are far away from those disturbances, there are still footpads,' said Lord Ravensford, looking down at her with a smile.

Marianne sighed. 'I suppose so. Of course, it won't be proper for you to see me home. I am unchaperoned: as I was only going to the church, which is practically on Travis land, I didn't bring my groom. But . . . yes, thank you, My Lord. I would be honoured if you would see me home.'

He smiled at her formality. He seemed younger today, here in the graveyard, and she realized that even when a tense and danger-ous energy was not crackling between them they shared a strong bond, a bond she was beginning to realize was friendship of a deep and sincere kind.

He made to help her mount, but she said, 'No, I think I, too, will walk.'

She untethered her mare and led the animal by the reins. Together they walked along the country lanes, companionably enjoying the warm, spring-like day. They were just approaching a bend when they heard the sound of hooves coming towards them. Instinctively they moved to one side, so that the rider could safely pass them, but when he came into view they both stiffened. The rider was Mr Windham.

On seeing them, he reined in his horse. 'Why, Miss Travis,' he said. 'And Lord Ravensford.' He looked around ostentatiously for Marianne's groom.

Marianne did not rise to the bait. If he thought she intended to make an excuse for not having Tom with her then he was mistaken.

'I'm glad to have seen you,' he said, when neither of them replied. 'I have already called on you at the Hall, Miss Travis, but was sorry to find you were out. I am leaving the neighbourhood, and called to wish you *adieu.*'

Marianne, initially surprised he should have called on her to bid her farewell when she had only met him once, felt a surge of relief at the knowledge he was leaving the neighbourhood. She had never liked the man, and had been half afraid of him ever since learning that he was a Jacobin. Although she had seen him so little, she would still be happier when there was no likelihood of meeting him at social gatherings. This being the case, she was able to put on a smile and bid him a polite farewell.

'And you, Somerville,' he said, sweeping off his hat and making Lord Ravensford a bow. 'I will wish you, too, goodbye.'

'Somerv—' began Marianne, looking in sudden surprise from one man to the other.

Mr Windham gave a wide smile. 'Why, yes. Luke Somerville, the fifth Earl of Ravensford. Did you not know? But now I must bid you farewell.'

And, smiling maliciously at the damage he had done, he spurred his horse and rode away, leaving Marianne fighting a turbulent range of emotions that were seething in her breast.

'You?' she demanded, looking at Lord Ravensford with a mixture of horror and disbelief '*You* are Luke Somerville?' No. It couldn't be. Could it? Lord Ravensford could not be the man who had led her brother into temptation and caused him to run up huge gambling debts. Could he?

'Marianne, it's not what you think,' he said, cursing Windham. under his breath whilst seeking to reassure her.

'Not what I *think*? Don't you mean, it's not what I *know*.' She could feel anger and contempt welling up inside her as he did not deny that he was Luke Somerville. They overwhelmed her horror and disbelief, and were then coupled with disillusionment and a surge of pain.

'Know?' he asked, his face darkening in response to her own anger, so that his next words were tinged with a contempt to match her own. 'What do you *know*?'

'I know that you destroyed my brother—'

'I did no such thing—'

'And then came here posing as Lord Ravensford—'

'I *am* Lord Ravensford,' he glowered.

'Concealing your identity, worming your way into—'

'I have never wormed my way into anything in my life.' His eyes were dangerous, but Marianne was too hurt and too incensed to pay them any heed.

'And with what intention?' she demanded, too angry to think about what she was saying. 'Did you mean to ruin the sister as you had ruined the brother, was that what you—'

'By God, that's going too far, Marianne.' His eyes were molten, and suddenly his hand was at the back of her head, tangling itself in her glistening curls. He pulled her head back and she was forced to look up at him, afraid and yet excited at the naked emotion she saw there. 'If you knew how hard I've had to fight *not* to ruin you. From the first moment I saw you I wanted nothing more than to take you to my bed, and if you'd been the lightskirt I'd thought you were I wouldn't have waited even for that, I'd have taken you on the drawing-room floor. When I found you were a lady – God help me, when I found you were Kit's sister – it cost me all my self-control to hold back. You're the most bewitching creature I've ever met, Marianne, intelligent, beautiful and desirable, but I've scarcely laid a finger on you. Though perhaps I should have done,' he said, adding cruelly, 'You need it.'

The good he had done with the first part of his speech, the understanding he had started to win from her, was completely destroyed by these final words, which did nothing but incense her. 'I don't need anything from you,' she flashed, jerking away from him.

'Oh, don't you?' he demanded. Then, pulling her roughly towards him, he kissed her.

I must resist, she told herself. He ruined Kit. I must resist. But her body was acting of its own volition, meeting him on an intuitive level which was set apart from anger and disillusionment, where against all reason she trusted him. And her body began to respond. Her lips parted, reacting to the passion in his kiss. Her senses swam. And when he took her face in his hands, tangling his fingers in her hair and moving his mouth insistently over hers, her whole body began to quiver. And then he was tumbling her to the ground, his mouth demanding hers, his tongue tracing the line of her lips before diving into the warm moistness of her mouth, arousing in her instincts and desires that went far beyond those she was experiencing. His hands were on her shoulders, pressing her down, and the line of his body was hard against her. Her whole body was on fire for him. Every part of her – parts she had never even known existed – were crying out for his touch. Never had she realized that anything could be so glorious, so all-consuming, so entirely devouring.

But I can't, she thought, suddenly frightened as his hand stroked up her thigh, taking her skirt with it.

No matter how deep and intuitive her feelings for him she was gently raised; and even if she had not been gently raised, she could not embark on such a perilous and life-changing journey with a

105

man whose feelings she did not understand. And how could she understand his feelings when she could not even understand her own?

Feeling her resistance he pushed himself on to his elbows, looking down into her face. His eyes were glittering with unsatisfied desire, his breathing was coming in short gasps. 'Damn it, Marianne, why did you have to be so goddamn lovely?' he demanded.

Shakily, Marianne sat up. The action pushed him away from her. He sat, one leg bent at the knee, some way away from her, watching her, as though he could not take his eyes away from her.

She felt the breeze on her cheek. It was cooling. Slowly her heartbeat began to resume its normal even pace. When she had calmed down sufficiently she stood up. Her legs were still a little shaky, but already they were gaining strength. She looked down at her riding habit. It was covered with grass. Brushing the stems from the soft blue cloth she retrieved her hat, which had fallen on to the ground, picking a final piece of grass from its plume.

She walked over to her mare, who was grazing nearby.

'I'll see you back to the Hall,' he said, rising to his feet.

'Thank you, but I prefer to ride.'

Gathering up the reins she led the animal a little further down the road to where a stile led into a field. Using the stile as a mounting block she settled herself in the saddle. Then, holding the reins softly in her light hands, she turned the mare's head for home.

Lord Ravensford did not follow her, but stood looking after her, his long lean body in an attitude of frustration; a frustration that was not entirely physical.

As Marianne followed the country road she saw almost nothing of the countryside around her. For once her thoughts were turned inward, and those thoughts were painful and confusing. Why had Lord Ravensford really come to Sussex? Why had he ruined her brother? And why had he then denied it? Why had he started to make love to her and then been prepared to stop, when stopping had cost him such an enormous effort, especially if he was really the wastrel and rake rumour painted him? Why had he been concerned for her reputation if he was so disreputable? But then again, if he was not disreputable, and if he was really concerned for her reputation, why had he kissed her in the first place? Was it possible that he, too, was driven by conflicting desires? And if so, what were they? Why had he been so callous towards Kit? And worse, when she knew him to have ruined her brother, why had she responded to his kisses? She couldn't possibly have feelings for the man who had ruined her brother – could she? No, of course not. And yet . . . whichever way she looked at it, it didn't make sense. None of it made any sense.

She shook her head in frustration. Her thoughts were far too confusing to dwell on and she turned them into other channels, forcing herself to concentrate on the spring that was burgeoning all around her. There was so much that was good in the world. She would be a fool to dwell on something that was both painful and perplexing.

Soon the Hall came into sight. She took her mare round to the stables and then went into the house. She was hoping she could get to her room unobserved. She did not feel equal to holding a conversation, and planned to spend a quiet half hour upstairs before getting on with the housekeeping. But to her dismay, Trudie greeted her as soon as she walked in the door.

'I've been getting a few things together for your weekend,' said Trudie with a pleased and satisfied air. Marianne had told her about the proposed party and, pleased that Marianne was going to have some fun, Trudie had spent the morning making preparations.

Marianne's shoulders drooped. 'There isn't going to be a weekend. At least, not one I want to attend.' If she hadn't been so emotionally drained she would not have said anything of the kind, but as it was she did not have the energy to pretend an enthusiasm she did not feel.

Trudie fixed her with a shrewd eye. 'Lord Ravensford hasn't. . . ? Because if he has, then, earl or no, he'll answer to me. Your papa may not know what's due to you, Miss Marianne, but there's others in this house who do.' There was a sympathy and concern behind the bravado that almost undid Marianne. She was lucky to have such a devoted protector.

'No, Trudie, nothing like that,' she said tiredly. 'It's just that I have too much to do here.'

'Oh, is it?' said Trudie, regarding her searchingly. But then, seeing the droop of Marianne's shoulders, she relented. 'Well, we'll say no more about it.'

Marianne went into the drawing-room and threw her hat on to a Sheraton chair before sinking wearily on to the *chaise-longue*. She ought to be changing out of her riding habit, but her energy had left her and she felt in need of a few minutes' peace.

She lay back and closed her eyes. It had all happened so quickly. . . .

But she did not want to think about it. It was too fresh, too raw.

After a minute or two she opened her eyes. The drawing-room was familiar, comforting. She began to feel more herself.

She had almost decided to go upstairs and change out of her habit when there came a scratching at the door and Henri came into the room. He was carrying a silver salver, with a silver teapot and a plate of warm scones.

'Trudie, she says you are tired, Miss Marianne,' he said with a kindly air. 'And so I say to 'er, "What can you expect, after being out riding this morning. Miss Marianne, she needs a – 'ow you say? – a smack?" '

'Snack,' said Marianne, smiling despite herself at his mistake. She suspected it had been deliberate, to make her laugh.

'Ah, yes,' said Henri comfortably. 'A snack.' As he spoke he poured out a refreshing cup of tea and set it down on the pie-crust table next to Marianne, then offered her a scone. 'They 'ave just come out the oven. See, the butter, it is melting, is it not? You 'ave one, Miss Marianne?'

Marianne hesitated.

'To please Henri?' he tempted her.

'Thank you, Henri,' said Marianne. She felt somewhat revived by the sight and scent of the tea and scones. 'That will be lovely. It was a lucky chance that brought you to us,' she remarked, as she took the scone he offered her, arranged appetizingly on a china plate. 'Not that it was lucky for you to get your leg caught in the trap, but—'

'I understand.'

He waited for her to eat the scone, then his eyes became more intelligent. He lost the look of a kindly servant and became more of a definite character. He stood up properly and his speech lost some of its obvious Frenchness. 'But you see, Miss Marianne, luck 'ad nothing to do with it.'

Marianne paused in the act of putting her plate back on the table. She looked at him curiously. 'Luck had nothing to do with it? Henri, what do you mean?'

'I mean, I was coming 'ere on purpose. That is, I was coming to Billingsdale Manor.'

'You know Mr Billingsdale?' asked Marianne in surprise, putting the plate down with a clatter.

'*Non, mademoiselle*. I do not know the good Mr Billingsdale. Or the bad Mr Billingsdale, I think I should call 'im, as 'e allows 'is manager to lay traps to catch men.'

Marianne wiped her fingers on her napkin and her eyes narrowed slightly in puzzlement.

'Tell me, *mademoiselle*,' asked Henri gently. 'When you came in just now you were upset. Yes?'

Marianne nodded, a slight frown on her forehead. 'Yes.'

'And it is because, I think, of Lord Ravensford?'

Marianne dropped the napkin on to her plate and leant back in her seat, rubbing her hand over her eyes. 'Henri, it isn't something you'd understand.'

'Oh, me, *mademoiselle*. I understand many things. I understand that you are 'urt and angry, and I understand that Mr Windham came here to bid you *adieu*. And when 'e didn't find you, I think 'e met you returning from the churchyard.'

Marianne was looking at Henri in perplexity. He had changed in the last few minutes. He was not the simple chef she had thought him to be.

'Tell me, Miss Marianne, what did 'e say? That Milord Ravensford is Luke Somerville? The man 'oo ruined your brother?'

'How could you know that?' asked Marianne, sitting upright, her tiredness vanished.

'Because me, I know Luke Somerville—'

'You know him?' Marianne's voice was incredulous; and then she remembered the feeling she had had when the two men had met in her drawing-room – that they already knew each other. 'You should have told me at once,' she said with a frown. 'He disgraced my brother and—'

'*Non*.' Henri's voice was definite. 'Luke, 'e disgraces no one, least of all your brother.'

'He led him into temptation, gambling—' began Marianne angrily.

'*Non*. Your brother 'as not been gambling, Miss Marianne. He 'as gone to France.'

'France?' Marianne looked at Henri in astonishment.

' 'E 'as gone to rescue Adèle.'

The sound of the clock ticking on the mantelpiece could be heard. A bird trilled just outside the window. Far off, Trudie dropped something in the kitchen.

And then, as Marianne took in what Henri had just said, everything began to fall into place: Kit's supposed gambling debts, when Kit had never gambled in his life; his unexplained absence; his apparent indifference over the fate of Adèle . . . yes, it all fell into place. 'But my father . . .' she asked curiously. 'Why did Kit tell him – *us* – that he had been gambling? It doesn't make sense.'

'*Oui, mademoiselle* it does. Because your father would not have given Kit the money 'e needed to mount an expedition if 'e 'ad told 'im what it was really for. 'E would not 'ave wanted 'is only son to risk 'is life.'

Marianne let out a long sigh. 'That's true. So Kit has gone to France. He hasn't lost a fortune in gambling and loose living. He has gone to rescue Adèle.'

Her face lit; and then fell. In a way, she wished he *had* been gambling. Because going to France was dangerous. . . .

Seeing her expression, Henri nodded. '*Oui*. It is dangerous, what Kit does, but—?' He gave a Gallic shrug. 'Your brother, 'e is in love.'

'I thought so.' Marianne sat deep in thought, trying to reconcile herself to what Kit had done. 'But. . . .' She looked up at Henri. 'That doesn't explain your place in all this.'

'Me, I 'elp Kit. And so does Kit's good friend Luke. We 'elp 'im to set up the expedition and then we come down 'ere, Luke renting the Billingsdale estate so that 'e can put out to sea if 'e needs to go over to France and 'elp Kit, and me pretending to be 'is chef – only, me, I get my leg caught in a mantrap, and Luke, 'e say, Miss Marianne, she needs 'elp with the estate. You stay with 'er, Henri. Watch over 'er. 'Elp 'er, until 'er brother is safe. So we watch and we wait, and when Kit 'e returns to England, we will 'elp 'im land unseen on Mr Billingsdale's beach.'

'So that's why Luke was on the rocks, looking out to sea.' Marianne nodded, as yet another piece of the puzzle fell into place.

111

'*Oui.* 'E waits for news from your brother, and whilst 'e waits, every day 'e looks out to sea.'

'So Luke . . .' said Marianne.

' 'E 'is 'ere to 'elp your brother; to 'elp 'im land safely, or to set out for France and look for 'im if 'e does not return.'

Marianne gazed deep into the fire, taking it all in.

'Then, the rumours about him leading Kit astray. . . .'

'Were just that. Rumours. They spend a lot of time together. Then it is given out that Kit 'as run up gambling debts. It is not like 'im, so the blame is put on Luke's shoulders.' He gave a wry smile. 'Luke, 'e is a good friend to Kit, but 'e 'as a wild reputation. And now, Miss Marianne, you 'ave another cup of tea? Henri, 'e pours it for you. You 'ave 'ad a shock.'

Marianne took the tea gratefully. But as she put the porcelain cup to her lips she could not help wondering what now would become of her relationship with Luke.

CHAPTER SEVEN

'Is that everything?' asked Marianne, as Trudie folded the last of her clothes into an old and battered trunk.

'It is. It's a pity you won't have any new frocks to wear,' said Trudie. 'Lord Ravensford's seen all of these.'

'And so has everyone else,' Marianne pointed out.

She was pleased that Trudie had not asked her too much about her change of plan regarding the weekend party. What conclusions Trudie had drawn she did not know, but fortunately the redoubtable housekeeper had for once decided that least said was soonest mended, and Marianne was soon in the coach and heading on her way. She had made arrangements for her father to be visited by the rector in her absence, and was confident that Papa would not miss her. He thought of little but his grievances these days; grievances that, had he but known it, were not real.

She had considered telling him the truth, that Kit had gone to France, but had decided against it. In his present state he would worry about it and, as he could not do anything about it, his worrying would be pointless. And so she had left him under the illusion that Kit had fled in disgrace; nonetheless hoping that, if all went well, she would soon be able to tell him the truth.

As the carriage bowled along the country roads she felt pleased with her decision to attend the party. Now that she knew Lord

Ravensford was a friend of her brother's it would have been churlish of her to stay away; even though spending two nights beneath
his roof, after what had passed between them in the country lane,
was going to be difficult.

What were his feelings for her? she wondered. There was a
strong streak of protectiveness, she now realized, but that was
most probably occasioned by the fact that she was Kit's sister.
That, no doubt, was why he had been so concerned about her
running the estate, and why he had offered to help her. But
beyond that, how far did his feelings go? She did not know. His
passion was real, that much she knew, but then, passion was no
more than the embodiment of physical attraction, and physical
attraction fell far short of the feelings Marianne was beginning to
realize she had for Luke.

The carriage made a detour to collect Miss Stock, and by the
time Marianne and the rector's sister arrived at the Manor the
party was already under way. Figgs looked surprised to see her; a
surprise that was echoed on Luke's face when Marianne was
announced and walked into the drawing-room. But nevertheless he
came forward to greet her, albeit with a quizzical look on his face.

'Miss Travis, how delightful you could come,' drawled Mrs
Kilkenny from her place by the mantelpiece. Her words dripped
with insincerity.

'Oh, yes,' said Jennifer Cosgrove enthusiastically. 'Lord
Ravensford wasn't sure whether you'd be coming or not. He said
he thought you might be having problems with your father. It's
such a shame your papa's health is so bad.'

'Dear me, yes,' said Miss Stock sympathetically. 'Such a trial for
him! And such a shame for dear Marianne. She cannot always call
her time her own.'

'But for the weekend it is ours,' said Lord Ravensford, looking
at her curiously.

Was he pleased to see her? She thought he was. His hands, as

114

they touched hers, conveyed an unmistakable warmth.

Accepting the explanation he had given to his guests for his doubts about her ability to attend – after their encounter in the country lane it seemed he had thought she would stay away – Marianne greeted everyone politely.

'We were just about to have some music,' said Mr Cosgrove enthusiastically. 'Mrs Kilkenny was going to sing for us.'

'I'm not sure . . .' Mrs Kilkenny began, with a shrewd look at Marianne, thinking, no doubt, that it might not be wise to retreat to the pianoforte now that Miss Travis had arrived.

'But I insist.' Lord Ravensford's voice was polite, but brooked no argument, and the guests, laughing and chattering, went through to the music-room.

'I believe you'll find it's a fine instrument,' said Lord Ravensford, as Mrs Kilkenny sat down to play.

If Mrs Kilkenny had been afraid of him neglecting her she need not have worried. Lord Ravensford was very attentive, turning over the pages of her music and standing slightly behind her with a look of rapt attention on his face.

Marianne did her best to appear composed, but she was finding it hard. So his feelings had, after all, been nothing more than a desire to protect her, laced with a passion which, being so profoundly masculine, he no doubt felt towards every female.

She felt her spirits sink. The evening dragged. Lord Ravensford laughed and flirted with the elegant Mrs Kilkenny, whilst Marianne did her best to take an interest in her fellow guests, but she was not sorry when it was time to retire. As she climbed the stairs to her bedchamber, her candle in hand, the last thing she heard was Mrs Kilkenny's musical laugh as Lord Ravensford charmed her yet again.

Was I wrong to come? Marianne asked herself the next morning, as, throwing back the green damask curtains, she saw Lord Ravensford walking along the terrace arm in arm with Mrs Kilkenny.

But no, it would have been childish of her to stay away. Now that she knew Lord Ravensford to be Kit's friend she could not be at outs with him and besides, it would have caused comment if she had failed to attend. Her father's querulous nature might have been given as an excuse, but her absence would have caused comment nonetheless.

Even so, it was going to be difficult for her to be in his company for the rest of the weekend, particularly as he was so blatantly pursuing Mrs Kilkenny.

It surprised her just how much it hurt. Of course, she had known all along that he was anything but a gentleman. Even Trudie, who had at first encouraged her to see him as a suitor, had said hesitantly to Marianne only the day before, 'Some men are best not taken seriously, Miss Marianne. They don't have it in them to be faithful; they like all women too much to settle for one.' But Marianne had still been surprised and hurt at how quickly he had taken up with Mrs Kilkenny, and how he seemed to be flaunting the woman in her face. She realized now that she had been a fool to think that what had passed between them in the country lane had been driven by anything but lust. She admitted to herself that, after everything that had happened between them, she had thought there had been more to it than that; that the episode had also been driven by the friendship and the strong rapport they shared; two unconventional people being drawn to each other by a compelling force. Certainly for her it had been the result of a much deeper feeling, an emotional attachment which, seeing his pursuit of Mrs Kilkenny, she dare not acknowledge. But to him it had been nothing more than the natural reaction of a lusty man and, if she had any sense, she would school herself to forget it.

But how to forget the most wonderful thing that had ever happened to her; the most exhilarating, disturbing and exciting moments of her life?

A knock at the door gave a welcome break from her thoughts and Nell, Mrs Cosgrove's maid, came in.

'Mrs Cosgrove's compliments, miss, and would you like some help to dress?'

Marianne thanked Nell, and with the help of the maid was soon ready to go downstairs. The morning was to be spent riding, and Marianne, in common with the rest of the guests, had her own mare at the Manor, brought over tethered to the carriage the previous day. The morning was bright, and Marianne was looking forward to the ride. At least out in the open she would be able to avoid Lord Ravensford without seeming to do so, and be spared the sight of him paying court to Mrs Kilkenny.

Hardly had the ride begun, however, when Lord Ravensford hung back on his black stallion and made the magnificent beast fall into step beside Marianne's mare. The other guests had found their own preferred surfaces and speed, and whilst some were cantering along the grass others were walking their horses at a sedate pace along the gravel paths.

'You decided to come,' said Lord Ravensford, looking magnificent in a green coat, snowy white stock and tight cream breeches. He gave her a sideways glance, the early morning shadows casting sharp angles on his face. 'I thought you wouldn't.'

'I . . . think I owe you an apology,' said Marianne quietly.

He looked at her enquiringly.

'Since I saw you last I have been speaking to Henri.'

He frowned, and his mouth tightened. 'Henri?'

'He told me everything. About you, and Kit, and—'

'He'd have done better to keep his mouth shut,' he snapped.

'And let me believe Kit was a gambler and you were the man who ruined him?' demanded Marianne.

'You believed what Henri told you, then?' asked Lord Ravensford obliquely.

Marianne nodded. 'Yes, I did. I'd always found it difficult to

117

accept that Kit would run up gambling debts. He didn't like games, for one thing, and was never interested in dice or cards. And he never did things to excess. Perhaps he might have lost a few sovereigns at a game of chance, that I could believe, but thousands of pounds? And then to ask my father to pay his debts? No. Kit would never have done that. He has too much pride. If he *had* run up gambling debts he would have taken great pains to make sure news of it never reached my father, and he would have found a way of paying them off himself. I never believed it – except that, as he told me of his debts himself, I felt I had no choice. Why else would he say it if it wasn't true?' She shook her head. 'Even then, somewhere underneath, I still didn't really accept it. So that when Henri said he had needed the money to go to France, things began to fall into place. In normal circumstances Kit would never have asked my father for money, but to rescue Adèle? Yes, I believe he would do anything for Adèle. And then again, going to France to search for her is exactly the sort of hot-headed thing he would do. He is not the kind to gamble, but risking everything for the sake of someone he loved? – Yes, that is the sort of thing he would do.'

'And was it only your knowledge of Kit's character that led you to believe Henri, or may I hope that it was in part an understanding of mine? That you realized I am not the sort of man to lead an innocent young person to perdition?'

A sudden tension filled the air. Marianne's thoughts went to their encounter in the lane, the feel of his mouth on hers, and the touch of his hand as he stroked her thigh.

She fought down her unruly thoughts and, forcing them to focus on his question, turned to look at him. Strong, dangerous and implacable as he was, she did not believe him to be capable of such a thing. 'No. I don't think you are.'

'As I have told you before,' he remarked, 'you are a good judge of character. And so, what do you think of Kit going over to France?'

Marianne frowned. 'I'm concerned for him. And afraid—'

'Which is why he didn't want to tell you.'

'—but I'm pleased that he's gone. I always suspected that he loved Adèle. I pray he finds her and brings her safely to Seaton Hall.'

'Amen to that.'

They had now fallen significantly behind the rest of the party. 'I think we had better join the others, My Lord,' she said.

He threw her a tempting smile. 'I think, now that you know who I am, instead of calling me "My Lord" you should call me Luke.'

'No, I couldn't do that,' she said, feeling a small shiver wash over her at the intimacy of his suggestion. 'Come, we are falling behind.'

She spurred her horse, putting the animal into a gallop. He followed suit and she thought he meant to ride beside her, but he reached over and caught hold of her bridle, forcing her mare to slow, until at last the animal came to a snorting halt. He swung his own horse out in front of her.

'I would like to hear my name on your lips,' he said, his eyes trailing across them with barely disguised longing.

'I . . . don't think it would be proper,' she said. His glance was having a profound effect on her, and her voice came out as a whisper.

'Nothing between us has ever been proper,' he said huskily. 'Why should this be any different?'

'I don't . . .' She felt a pulse beating in her throat.

'Marianne . . .'

'You shouldn't call me that.'

'But I am going to. I've been fighting it for long enough. Miss Travis and Lord Ravensford won't do for all we've been through.'

'And just what have we been through?' she asked, her voice throaty, trying to keep him at a distance.

'If you've forgotten, perhaps I should remind you.' The glance that roved over her face was burning.

'Why are you doing this?' she asked, her voice low, as she had a sudden memory of him walking arm in arm with Mrs Kilkenny.

'Why am I doing this?' he repeated softly. Murmuring, a moment later, 'Yes, why *am* I doing this?' as though speaking to himself.

She danced her mare back a step. 'I think, My Lord, we ought to join the others before Miss Stock begins to grow concerned.'

He gave her a searching look and then nodded. 'Of course, *Miss Travis.*' He moved his horse aside. 'Perhaps you would care to lead the way.'

It was with relief that Marianne found herself once again riding next to Miss Stock. With that kindly lady on one side of her and Jennifer Cosgrove on the other she had some measure of protection against Lord Ravensford, a protection she seemed to need. Because somehow their relationship had not been simplified by the removal of the secret that had, unbeknownst to her, stood between them. Indeed, it now seemed more complicated than ever.

'. . . warm for March,' Miss Stock was saying. 'I am truly enjoying the ride.'

The conversation was general, and Marianne willingly joined in, praising the early spring sun, the beauty of the grounds and the newly burgeoning blossom that was appearing on some of the ornamental trees – trying not to notice that Lord Ravensford had fallen in beside Mrs Kilkenny.

During luncheon, rain set in. It began as a drizzle and then became a downpour, lashing the trees and scattering the blossom so that it looked like falling snow. Far from dampening everyone's spirits, however, the rain made everyone feel pleasantly smug, for they had beaten the English weather on this occasion and had returned to the house before it started to rain.

120

'I know,' said Jennifer, when they were all assembled in the drawing-room after lunch was over and an air of lethargy had started to set in. 'We must play charades! Can we?' She turned appealingly to Lord Ravensford, who sat, dark and amused, in a Sheraton chair.

'Jennifer,' said her mother warningly.

'Why not?' asked Mrs Kilkenny, finding the idea stimulating. She turned to Lord Ravensford. 'It would be a good idea for a wet afternoon, would it not?'

He smiled lazily. 'If it pleases you.'

Mrs Kilkenny gave an arch smile. 'Indeed it does.'

'But what shall our charades be about? I know. Plays!' Jennifer burst out.

'Plays?' asked Jem, his enthusiasm caught. 'Dash it, Jenny, that's just the thing.'

'Why, yes, that is a good notion,' said Mrs Kilkenny. 'And do you know, I believe I already have an idea.' She turned to Lord Ravensford. 'I shall need your help, My Lord.'

His regarded her mockingly. 'I thought you might.'

Mrs Kilkenny chose to take this as a compliment and fluttered her fan. Then, turning with a show of kindness to Jennifer, she said, 'We shall need you, too, if you would be so good.'

Jennifer beamed mightily at having been chosen, and carried away with an excess of high spirits asked, 'Can we look in the attics, Lord Ravensford? For props, I mean?'

He gave her a look of amused tolerance. 'Are there any props in the attic?'

'There are sure to be,' said Jennifer confidently. 'All attics have props. And Figgs can bring them down for us.'

'Really, Jennifer, it isn't up to you to arrange Lord Ravensford's household,' said her mother reprovingly.

But Lord Ravensford was in a mood to humour his young guest. 'Figgs shall bring down anything you require.'

'We'll have to practise somewhere. I know, the music-room,' Jennifer said.

'The very place,' agreed Mrs Kilkenny. 'And Mr Kent, Mr Havers, may we have your help as well?'

'Delighted,' they agreed, caught up in the scheme.

'And we will make a second group,' said Marianne, seeing Jem's crestfallen face: he had always been fond of charades. 'That is, if everyone wishes to play?'

Jem's face lit up. Mr and Mrs Cosgrove expressed their willingness, as did Mr Pargeter and Miss Stock, and before long everything was bustle and confusion. Mrs Kilkenny's group retired and Marianne asked her own companions for suggestions. They settled in the end for *The Winter's Tale*, and began to think of the tableaux that would illustrate their choice.

It had been arranged that the gong would ring in an hour and everyone would partake of tea, after which the charades would begin. There was much laughter in Marianne's group as the tableaux were rehearsed, and after tea her group was the first to act out the title of their chosen play.

Lord Ravensford's group sat in a semi-circle around the performers and the charade began.

It opened with Jem and Maurice Pargeter sitting by the fire, rubbing their hands and puffing and blowing.

There was much conferring amongst the other group. Mrs Kilkenny's fair head was almost touching Lord Ravensford's dark one as she talked over with him the meaning of the scene. Marianne, watching from the side of the room, felt her spirits sink. Mrs Kilkenny was making an obvious play for his attention; something he was only too willing to give. Surely Mrs Kilkenny was too shallow for him? She gave a start as she realized that that was the complaint she had levelled at Lord Ravensford on their first meeting; that *he* was shallow. But she had learnt since that he was anything but. Anything but shallow, anything but a gentleman, anything but a man who should make her melt inside . . . and yet he did.

At last, after several vain tries, Mr Kent guessed the word was *winter*, and the second tableau began.

This one involved Mr Cosgrove senior, marvellously entering into the spirit of the thing, galloping around the room with a skein of Miss Stock's knitting yarn hanging from the back of his breeches. After much merriment, the word *tail* was guessed.

The final scene showed the whole word. Marianne took her place by the fire with a book on her lap. Mrs Cosgrove and Miss Stock sat on low stools at her feet, turning expectant faces towards her.

'I have no idea,' said Mrs Kilkenny to Lord Ravensford, wafting them both with her fan. 'What can it be?'

'It's perfectly clear,' said Lord Ravensford, his eyes tracing the bright highlights in Marianne's hair, painted there by the leaping light from the fire. 'It's *The Winter's Tale*.'

'Of course it is,' said Mrs Kilkenny. Adding, to display her learning, 'One of my favourite of Shakespeare's plays.'

There was a round of applause, and then the two groups swapped places. Jennifer eagerly tried to lift a desk, which had been brought down from the schoolroom by Figgs and was now standing against the wall, but Lord Ravensford took it from her and carried it into the centre of the room. He gave her an indulgent smile and Jennifer, delighted to be mixing with such handsome adult company, flushed scarlet before applying herself to her role. She seated herself at the desk and began scribbling away on a piece of paper. In front of her, Mr Havers turned a globe.

'Lessons,' shouted Jem.

Jennifer rolled her eyes in disgust, her expression saying clearly, Trust Jem to get it all wrong!

'Learning,' ventured Mr Cosgrove.

Jennifer sighed, then taking her piece of paper she scrunched it up and threw it at Miss Stock. Marianne laughed, remembering all Kit had told her of his schooldays. 'School!'

Jennifer curtsied, making the most of her part, and then ran to the side of the room, whereupon Mr Kent strolled into the middle of the floor and held up four fingers. Despite the simplicity of the scene, or perhaps, rather, because of it, it took some while for the audience to guess that in fact he did mean *four*, and then the final scene began.

Mrs Kilkenny, looking conscious, reclined elegantly on the *chaise-longue*. She held a handkerchief delicately to her nose. Then Lord Ravensford, looking suitably saturnine, appeared from behind the curtains and strode over to her, dropping to one knee beside her and taking her hand. He bent over it and kissed it, and at that moment Mr Kent strode into the scene. He started, looked horrified, and made a dumb show of hitting Lord Ravensford across the cheek with a glove.

'Duel' called Jem.

'Affair!' called Mr Cosgrove, forgetting that he was in family company, but remembering shamefacedly as soon as his wife tapped him with her fan. Then Mrs Cosgrove, who loved the theatre and had already guessed the charade, called out clearly, *scandal*. There was a ripple of light laughter, laughter Marianne felt unequal to sharing, and then the tableau for the whole title began. It was not long before *School for Scandal* was guessed, and the afternoon ended with much laughter and good cheer.

Except for Marianne. For her, the sight of Lord Ravensford acting the part of Mrs Kilkenny's lover had dampened her spirits. She was in no doubt that she would be a fool to think of him any further, after the clear message sent by the charade, and decided she must put him out of her mind.

But deciding what she must do, and being able to do it, were two very different things.

124

By the time she had dressed for dinner, Marianne found that her spirits had been restored, and she could look forward to the evening with composure. As Mrs Cosgrove had sent Nell to her before making use of the maid's services herself, Marianne was ready early. She sat in her room for a while but then, growing bored, decided to find a book to read until dinner time. She went downstairs, meaning to choose a book from the library, but as she drew near she heard voices: the library was already occupied. They were not the calm, polite voices she would have expected from her fellow guests if they, too, had been ready early. Instead, they were urgent. Realizing she would be intruding if she went through with her plan she turned back, but as she did so a name arrested her attention. It was *Kit*.

She stopped, torn between two courses of action. On the one hand she did not want to overhear a private conversation, but on the other she was concerned about her brother and felt that, if something had happened to him, she had a right to know.

As she stood uncertainly in the passageway, she heard something that made her determined to push good breeding to one side: a man's voice said, 'according to the letter, he's been badly hurt.' She went over to the door and resolutely turned the knob.

The scene which met her eyes as she opened the door was business-like. Lord Ravensford, Figgs and Henri were sitting round the library desk, looking at a selection of maps which were spread out in front of them. All three men were in their shirtsleeves. Marianne swallowed at the sight of Lord Ravensford. His superbly toned body, its hard muscles outlined beneath the lawn of his shirt, was lithe and alert. At the sound of the door opening he looked up. As he saw her his face darkened. 'Marianne. What the devil are you doing here?'

'I came to get a book—'

He held her with his gaze. Then, sitting back in his chair, he said, his eyes hard, 'Then take one and go.'

'—but then I heard Kit's name,' she said, not to be so easily dismissed.

The three men looked at each other.

'—and I heard that he's been hurt. Where is he? What's happened? Is he back in England? Is he still in France? How badly is he hurt?' she asked, the questions tumbling out of her in her concern over her brother.

There was silence. And then Henri said, 'You 'ad better tell 'er.'

'No.' Lord Ravensford's mouth was grim. He looked up at Marianne. 'All you need to know is that Kit is all right.'

Marianne felt her anger rising. 'No, that is not all I need to know,' she said, meeting his hard gaze. 'I need to know what's happened to him, where he is, what—'

'Marianne, we'll deal with this.'

'Kit is my brother—'

'And would not want you to get involved.' Lord Ravensford stood up in one lithe movement and crossed the room, taking her arm. 'Come, I'll take you through into the drawing-room. This isn't your concern.'

'I'm not a child, to be ordered about by you,' she said, shaking off his arm, driven to oppose him by her fear for Kit.

'So I believe you've told me.' His eyes and mouth were grim.

'If anything has happened I have a right to know.' She threw her shoulders back, facing him with chin raised.

Figgs, who had been sitting silently throughout their exchange, now spoke. 'She's right, Luke. She does have a right to know.'

'She will worry less, not more, if she knows, *mon ami*,' said Henri.

Lord Ravensford looked into Marianne's eyes as if trying to read her thoughts, and then gave a curt nod. 'Very well.' He glanced at the clock on the mantelpiece. 'We have twenty minutes before dinner. If you feel you can behave as though nothing has happened for the rest of the evening, once you know what has happened to Kit, then you can stay. I hardly need to remind you that if word of this gets out then Kit could be at risk. Sit down.'

His tone was curt, but Marianne realized that, hard though he sounded, he was actually paying her a compliment; instead of treating her like Miss Travis, he was treating her like an equal. With a minimum of fuss she sat down on the chair Henri had pulled forward. Lord Ravensford resumed his seat and the conversation continued. After a few minutes of studying the maps, the significance of which Marianne did not as yet understand, Lord Ravensford turned to her and gave her a brief overview of the situation.

'Kit has managed to find Adèle and get her to the French coast, but no further. He had arranged for a ship to bring them across the Channel, and had paid the captain accordingly, but the man was a rogue and betrayed him to the Jacobins.'

'But why. . . ?'

'Double the money,' said Lord Ravensford curtly. 'One payment from Kit and another from the Jacobins; together with considerable kudos for helping the Revolution.' He frowned, then resumed. 'Kit realized he'd been deceived just in time and when he was ambushed he managed to break free. But not before he was bayoneted. We think the wound is in his leg but we don't know for sure; the message we received was written on a scrap of paper and by the time it reached us it had been torn in half.'

'If Kit was able to send a message, then he can't be too badly hurt,' said Marianne.

'The message didn't come from Kit.'

Henri looked at him reproachfully but he said ruthlessly, 'If Marianne wants to know what's going on then it's best she should know the truth. Half-truths are no use to anyone.'

Marianne nodded. 'Yes. I want to know.'

There was a lessening of the severity of his expression, as

though her courage had impressed him. He continued a little less harshly, 'Adèle found a fisherman who agreed to get a message out of the country. Their situation is desperate. It cannot be long before their hiding place is discovered. We need to get over there and get them out.'

'I'm going, too.' Marianne's voice was resolute.

Lord Ravensford glowered at her. 'I said you could sit in on our discussion; I didn't say you could get involved.'

'I'm already involved. Kit's my brother. And besides, he's hurt. If I go with you I can look after him once he's on board ship.'

'Like hell you can.'

Figgs looked at Lord Ravensford evenly. 'She does have a point.'

'Whose side are you on?' he demanded.

Figgs's reply was simple. 'Kit's.'

The answer gave him pause, and Marianne seized her oportunity. 'I grew up around boats. My father used to own a small yacht before my mother died, and I'm a good sailor. I'm not proposing to go ashore – I know that I would be more of a hindrance than a help – but I will be safe enough on board, and it means I will be able to see to Kit's wound as soon as he joins the ship.'

'Once he's on board ship we'll have him home again in a matter of hours. There's no point you risking the sea voyage; you can tend him as soon as he's back home.'

'A few hours might make the difference between life and death,' she pointed out.

'She is right,' said Henri.

'No. It's too dangerous. This isn't a picnic we're going on. Even on the ship there'll be danger. We stand a good chance of being shot at, and there's a possibility we'll be boarded.' He gave Marianne a hard look. 'If you're taken prisoner the French won't spare you because you're a woman. In fact, quite the reverse.'

'I'm willing to take that chance,' said Marianne.

'But I'm not.'

'I—'

'No arguments. You're not going and that's final.'

'It isn't for you to decide,' said Marianne.

'I am the leader of this rescue attempt. The decision is mine.'

Marianne looked towards Figgs and Henri, to see if they were prepared to support her, but at Luke's mention of the fact that he was the leader of the rescue attempt she saw their expressions change. They might feel she should be allowed to join the rescue attempt, but they knew they needed to be disciplined in such a dangerous matter, and being disciplined they accepted that in all matters of note Luke had the final word.

'We will go tomorrow evening,' said Luke. 'Figgs, tell Captain Gringe we're going to need him and his ship after all. Tell him to be ready to sail with the evening tide. He's to bring the ship round to the estate, and we'll row out to it from here. The estate is large and private, and with any luck the rowing-boat won't be seen. Even with Rouget – Windham – gone, the less that gets out about this the better.'

Figgs nodded curtly and went out.

'And you, Henri, see to the guns and ammunition.'

Marianne shivered slightly. Mention of guns and ammunition brought home to her just how dangerous the venture was.

'And now,' he said, turning to Marianne as he shrugged himself into his coat, 'you will have to pretend you know nothing about this. I expect you to make small talk this evening as though nothing has happened.'

'You needn't concern yourself,' she said, throwing her head back. 'No one will learn of this venture from me.'

'I didn't expect you to announce it over the dinner-table,' he said harshly. 'Just make sure no one can tell by your face or by any fit of abstraction that something untoward has occurred. And now, we had better go out into the hall separately, or we will give rise to gossip of another kind. After you.'

She could have protested, but instead she decided to show him that she knew the value of co-operation when it was needed, and she preceded him out of the room.

CHAPTER EIGHT

*D*inner was a difficult meal for Marianne. Knowing that her brother was hurt she did not feel like eating, but she forced herself to do justice to the meal. Lord Ravensford was right: no one must suspect that anything untoward had happened. Even here in Sussex, Jacobins were not unknown, and although Mr Windham had gone it was better if no whisper of Kit's situation got out. Therefore she praised the turtle soup, did justice to the sole, forced down a helping of loin of mutton and finished off with a syllabub, all the while talking over the latest neighbourhood gossip with her fellow guests.

The tables were then set up for cards. Whilst her partners frowned and considered over their play, Marianne played by instinct. Unlike Kit, she had always been fond of games, and now that she was sitting down to whist she knew that she could afford to let her thoughts wander. She was so used to playing that she need pay only the most cursory attention to the game.

Although Lord Ravensford had forbidden her to join the rescue attempt, she was still uneasy. If Kit was hurt then she wanted to be on board the ship that put out for France: he might well have need of her medical skills before the ship returned to England. Although the return trip should take only a few hours, those hours could prove vital. And if the ship should be delayed, by storms,

131

say, it would be even more necessary for her to be on board. Whatever Lord Ravensford said, she was determined to be there. She still bore the emotional scars from losing one brother; she did not intend to lose a second.

'Beat that!' said Jennifer eagerly as she played the ace of clubs.

'Oh, I'm sorry, Jennifer,' said Miss Stock gaily, laying down the two of trumps. 'I believe the trick is mine.'

Marianne returned her attention to the game, playing well enough for her wandering thoughts to go unnoticed, but it was a relief when it was finally time for her to retire.

'You did that very well.' Lord Ravensford spoke to her softly as she waited for Figgs to bring a candle to light her to her bedchamber. 'No one would have suspected you had other things on your mind.'

'But not as well as you,' she remarked, hiding the pain she had felt at watching him hanging over Mrs Kilkenny all evening.

'Jealous, Marianne?' he asked.

It was the amusement in his voice which led her to make a sharp retort; one which hid her true feelings entirely. 'Not at all. I think you suit each other very well.'

'If I thought you meant that . . .' he said tightly.

But could say no more. Miss Stock was coming towards them, a smile on her kindly face.

'Lord Ravensford. I must add my thanks to Marianne's,' she said, mistakenly believing Marianne to be thanking him for a most enjoyable day. 'That was a wonderful evening. I have not enjoyed my cards so much for years.'

Lord Ravensford bowed graciously and the two ladies, lighted by candles which Figgs had now brought, made their way upstairs to bed.

'Such a charming man,' sighed Miss Stock happily as she bid Marianne goodnight.

Charming? thought Marianne, as she went into her own room.

Confusing was more the word she would have used. Having spent all evening deliberately courting Mrs Kilkenny, why had he then been so angry at her retort that they suited each other very well?

She gave a sigh and put the candlestick down on the little table next to her half-tester bed. Impossible to understand him, so better not to make the attempt. But try as she might she could not stop herself thinking about him. What were Lord Ravensford's feelings for her? Were they simply the protective feelings of a man for his friend's sister, coupled with a strong desire? Or were they something deeper? Something, perhaps, that matched her feelings for him?

Chiding herself for wishful thinking she rang for Nell and, once undressed, she blew out the candle and climbed into bed.

The party broke up after breakfast on the following morning. As Marianne waited for Tom to bring the carriage, Lord Ravensford managed to get a few minutes alone with her.

'Don't worry about Kit,' he said in an undertone, as Miss Stock admired the Billingsdale family portraits which hung in the hall. 'We'll get him out of France, I promise you.'

'I'm sure you will.'

Her voice was cool; her manner was composed; and he was surprised by her attitude. If he hadn't known better he would have thought she didn't care. 'You're taking this very calmly,' he said, perplexed.

'There is nothing to be gained by having a fit of the vapours,' she remarked blandly.

'True.' He frowned. 'Even so. . . .'

'I have perfect confidence in you,' she said.

He looked at her uncertainly, and she realized that for once the tables had been turned. It was usually he who was in control of the situation, but now he was the one who was perplexed.

'That's good,' he returned slowly. 'I don't know how long it will take. We should be in France by the early hours of tomorrow morning, but we're not sure what we'll find. When Adèle sent the message she and Kit were hidden in a farmhouse just south of Boulogne, but they might have been forced to move on.'

'I understand.'

He looked at her curiously, still uncertain as to what had caused her complaisant manner. If she had been an obedient, biddable young lady he would not have been surprised. But she was not. Marianne was a young lady with a mind of her own. Still, she must have realized that in this matter he knew best, and he could not deny that it made things easier.

'Oh, here is Tom now,' said Miss Stock, as she caught sight of the Travis carriage rolling past the window. 'Marianne. . . .'

'Just coming, Miss Stock.' Marianne turned to Lord Ravensford and said formally, 'Thank you for a delightful weekend, My Lord. It was most enjoyable.'

'Thank you for coming, Miss Travis,' he replied. Adding, 'Oh, by the way, I've been meaning to thank you for allowing me to borrow Henri. It was good of you to let him come over here last night and lend a hand with the dinner. Mrs Hill is an excellent cook, but it's the little French touches that lift a meal out of the ordinary, wouldn't you say?'

'Oh, quite,' breathed Miss Stock, remembering the excellent meal.

'Would you mind if I borrowed him for a few more days?' Lord Ravensford asked Marianne. 'I'd like him to teach Mrs Hill how to make some of my favourite French dishes.'

Realizing he needed an excuse to take Henri away from the Hall for the next few days so that the Frenchman could go with him to France, Marianne said, 'No, of course not.'

'Thank you.'

Their leave taken, Marianne led Miss Stock out of the house. Once Miss Stock had been safely returned to the rectory, Marianne had time to think over her plan. She didn't like deceiving anyone but her mind was made up. Julian had died because there had not been a doctor on hand when he had needed one, and Kit might be about to die for the same reason. But she did not intend to let that happen. She would have asked Dr Moffat to undertake the voyage if she had thought it would do any good, but she knew he would refuse; therefore she intended to go herself. She might not be a doctor, but she had a lot of experience in tending people who had had accidents on the estate, and had even seen a bullet removed when Tom had had an accident with his gun. She knew how to clean and bind serious wounds and, furthermore, there were some laudanum drops in the medicine chest which she could use to ease Kit's pain.

The carriage pulled up outside Seaton Hall.

'Thank you, Tom,' she said, sweeping into the house.

Now all she had to do was convince Trudie that she had been invited to visit the Cosgroves for a few days and her plan would begin to take shape.

'There you are, Miss Marianne,' said Trudie, coming towards her with a beaming face; she was eager to hear all about Marianne's enjoyable few days.

Marianne obliged her with an account of the party.

'And I dare say you saw Henri there?' asked Trudie. 'Lord Ravensford sent for him yesterday. But still, you know all about that, I expect.'

Marianne agreed, and Trudie was satisfied. She was so impressed with Henri's cooking herself that it did not seem strange to her that Lord Ravensford should want the chef to teach his cook how to make his favourite French meals; little suspecting that he had needed Henri to help him formulate a plan for Kit's rescue.

'How has Papa been?' asked Marianne.

'Oh! Well enough. To tell you the truth, I don't think he noticed you'd gone.'

Marianne gave a sigh.

'Now, don't you take on so,' said Trudie bracingly. 'Your papa is what he is. Well, your room's all ready for you,' she said more brightly, as Marianne took off her cloak and bonnet. 'After all the gaiety, you'll be wanting a rest.'

'Thank you, Trudie, but I won't be staying long.' Trudie looked at her in surprise, and she explained, 'The party was so successful that Mr and Mrs Cosgrove have decided to host a gathering at their house, and I have said I will go.'

'Ah!' nodded Trudie trustingly, causing Marianne a twinge of guilt at her lie. 'That's a good idea. Once people get to enjoying themselves, they don't want to stop. And why should they? You go, Miss Marianne. You've done enough work over the winter to run a colonel into the ground. You go and enjoy yourself. And don't you worry about your papa: if he asks for you, I'll tell him you'll be home by. . .?'

'By the end of the week.'

Trudie nodded in satisfaction, glad Marianne was going to have a few more days of enjoyment.

But if she had known what Marianne was really going to do, she would have been up in arms.

'Well, you'd better go and tidy yourself. Will you be wanting lunch, or are you going on to the Cosgroves' straight away?'

'I'll have something to eat first – just something simple – and then when I've packed a few things I'll be on my way.'

'I'd better tell Tom to keep the carriage out.'

'No, that won't be necessary,' said Marianne quickly. 'I think I'd rather ride. It's a lovely day, and as Mrs Cosgrove has kindly offered to lend me some of Susan's dresses, I won't need to take too many things – just a few personal items thrown into a small valise. I can take it with me, tied on to the saddle.'

Trudie nodded sagely. 'She's tired of seeing you in the same dresses day after day. You and Susan were always much of a size,'

136

she said, thinking of Susan, the Cosgroves' married daughter, who now lived in Bath. 'It will be the very thing.'

Marianne would rather not have compounded her large lie with a small one, but the stakes were so high that the lies, which at any other time would have troubled her, caused her no more than a moment's guilt. She was determined to be on the ship when it set sail to rescue Kit, and inventing a party at the Cosgrove estate gave her the necessary excuse for being away for a few days.

Relieved that the first part of her plan had gone so smoothly, she allowed herself an hour's rest and then, having had something to eat, she dressed in her riding habit and took a small valise out to her waiting mare.

'You enjoy yourself,' said Trudie as she waved Marianne off.

Marianne smiled, but as she rode away she said softly, under her breath, 'I doubt it.'

Now that the first hurdle had been successfully cleared she turned her thoughts to what lay ahead. Following the road to begin with, she soon turned off on to a beaten track that made its way through open countryside parallel to the coast. She rode quickly and confidently, sure of where she was heading.

As children she and Kit had loved to mess about on the water. Their father had been a keen amateur sailor and had owned his own small craft. They had spent a lot of time in the neighbouring coves and quays, and had come to know most of the ships and their crews: which is why, when Marianne had heard Lord Ravensford mention the name of Captain Gringe, she had begun to consider the possibility of stowing away on his ship. *The Returner* was a craft she knew very well, and there was a perfect place where she could hide – at least until the ship was safely on its way to France. But she had much to do before she could go on board.

Arriving at the small harbour, which lay some ten miles west of Seaton Hall, she proceeded to the blacksmith's. Jim Smith was hard at work, his hammer rising and falling as he shoed a cart-horse. Marianne dismounted, sliding to the ground herself – she had grown used to managing this somewhat difficult task alone since the servants at the Hall had become depleted – and stood patiently holding her mare's head until he had finished.

Jim wiped the sweat from his brow with the back of his arm, then turned towards her. 'Mornin', miss, what can I – why, if it isn't Miss Marianne!' His round face beamed as he saw her.

'Hello, Jim.' She smiled in return.

'It's a long time since we've seen you in these parts – we haven't seen you since . . . oo, not since your pa gave up the yacht.' His face fell as he realized he had been tactless: Mr Travis had given up the yacht shortly after his wife's death. 'What brings you here, Miss Marianne?'

Marianne hesitated. She could not tell Jim what had really brought her to the harbour, but she did not like lying. She had been forced to lie to Trudie, but with Jim she hoped to be able to get away with making a vague answer; he was not likely to think it his business to ask any awkward questions.

'I need to stable my mare until Friday,' she said. 'For reasons I can't go into, I can't leave her at the Hall.'

'Why, that's no problem. I can keep her here for you 'til then.'

'I was hoping you would say that, Jim. Thank you. And Jim. . . .'

'Yes, miss?'

'I'd rather no one else knew about this. From the Hall, I mean.'

Jim grinned. 'A surprise is it, Miss Marianne? Well, I don't know what you're planning, but your secret's safe with me.'

Relieved that Jim had assumed she was planning to surprise someone – to give them the mare as a present, perhaps – she gave him a handful of coins. 'To feed her,' she explained. 'And . . . there is one other thing. If by any chance I haven't come to claim her by Friday, can you see that this letter is delivered to the Hall?'

Jim wiped his hands down the front of his leather apron before taking it.

'The letter will make sure the mare is collected by someone else, if for any reason I can't come.'

'Just as you say, Miss Marianne. I'll get my boy to take it over Friday if you don't manage to get here yourself.'

'Thank you, Jim.'

With that task done, Marianne took a walk round the small town that clustered round the harbour. She purchased some basic items of food to take with her on to the ship and then retired to the church until it was dark.

Throughout the day she was plagued with doubts about what she had done. She knew that her plan to stow away was rash, but she also knew that her brother needed her, and Kit's need outweighed all other considerations. If the worst came to the worst – if for any reason she did not return – the letter she had written for Trudie and left with Jim explained everything. But she hoped it would never be delivered. If all went well, she should be back in England with Kit before Friday arrived.

Outside, the day was waning. The warmer weather had given a false idea of the time of year, but dusk fell early and, as soon as it was properly dark, Marianne left the church. She made her way down to the quay, where half-a-dozen ships were tied up, and, with a quick look over her shoulder to make sure that she was not being observed, went aboard *The Returner*. Knowing the ship as she did, she knew that the captain's cabin had a large cupboard at one end which was now almost empty. The captain had had it put in for the benefit of his wife, who had accompanied him on his shorter trips in years gone by, and had needed it for her clothes. But she was bedridden now, and the cupboard was unused. Or had been, last time Marianne had been on board.

She made her way into the cabin. Sure enough, the cupboard – which was made by partitioning off the end of the cabin – was still there, and apart from a tattered cloak, a broken telescope and dusty pile of ropes it was empty.

She knew it would not keep her hidden for long – on a ship of this size total concealment would be impossible – but if she could just escape detection until the ship was too far out to turn back then she would be satisfied.

She settled herself as comfortably as she could. Then there was nothing to do but wait.

It was shortly after ten o'clock that the crew came on board. Marianne heard a snatch of song and some ripe laughter as the men walked up the gangplank, and then she heard Captain Gringe calling out instructions as the men passed to and fro overhead, carrying out their allotted tasks.

It seemed to be an age before they finally cast off but at last, with a flapping of sails and a creaking of timber, the ship began to move. Marianne felt its rolling progress as it made headway, rounding the coast and heading towards the Billingsdale estate.

Once the ship was moving, Marianne's greatest fear was that Captain Gringe would retire to his cabin and by some mischance discover she had stowed away, but the night was fine, and he remained on deck.

So far, so good, she thought to herself.

It was not long before the ship's regular motion ceased. She felt a lurch, and knew that the anchor had been dropped. They were just off the Billingsdale estate then, and Lord Ravensford would soon be coming aboard.

As long as he, too, decided to remain on deck she should be safe from detection. Until she decided to make her presence known.

She had thought it through all day. Sooner or later she would have to let Lord Ravensford know that she was on board: she could hardly tend to Kit's wounds if no one knew she was there. But when to reveal herself? When they reached France? She shook her head. If she did that, Lord Ravensford's anger might well delay the rescue of her brother. It must be sooner, then: soon enough to let Lord Ravensford recover from the shock of finding her on board before he had to set out in the rowing-boat for France.

It would take all of her courage, but she knew that, as soon as it was too late for the ship to turn back, she must walk on to the deck. And be prepared to face the inevitable storm of disapproval that would greet her.

In the event, however, her hand was forced.

It was a still night, and after hearing Lord Ravensford's party climb on board Marianne felt the ship begin to move again. She resettled herself in the cupboard, and after a while risked opening the door a crack. It relieved some of the stuffiness, and gave her a little light. It was too early to reveal her presence, so she ate a little more of the bread and fruit she had bought in the village. She was just wiping the crumbs from her skirt when there was a scuttling noise and she started up in horror: there was a rat. She hated rats. She backed out of the cupboard, shuddering, just as one of the crew came into the cabin, holding a lantern aloft. In the strange and ghostly light he saw Marianne and let out a cry. Marianne jumped, the crewman swore under his breath, and then, grabbing her by the arm said, 'What the 'ell are you doing here?'

'What's taking you so long?' came the captain's voice from above.

Pushing Marianne roughly in front of him, the crewman forced her up the stairs and on to the deck.

The moon was up, large and round, and the sky was lit with stars.

'What the devil—' exclaimed Lord Ravensford.

'So.' Captain Gringe's voice was icily calm. It seems we have a stowaway.'

'Damn it, Marianne, I should have known you'd given in too easily,' swore Lord Ravensford. He glared at her; then, looking at the captain he said, 'Turn the ship around.'

But a half-smile had appeared on the captain's face. Marianne felt some of the tension leave her: Captain Gringe had recognized her.

'I said turn the ship around,' said Lord Ravensford again.

'I give the orders on my ship,' said Captain Gringe politely, but with a voice of steel. 'Now then, Miss Marianne, why don't you tell me what you're doing on *The Returner?* She hasn't seen you for many a year.'

Marianne smiled in relief. His tone was friendly, and it was clear he remembered her with affection; as she remembered him.

'You know where we are going?' she asked.

He nodded thoughtfully. 'I know where. But not why.'

'That's none of your business,' growled Lord Ravensford.

'If you want me to put Miss Marianne off the ship it is,' he replied calmly.

'We're going to rescue Kit.' Marianne's words were simple, but conveyed a deep feeling nonetheless.

'Ah.' Captain Gringe was thoughtful. 'So that's it.'

'These men are Kit's friends,' said Marianne. 'But Kit is hurt and he may need medical attention. Which is why I need to be here when he comes on board.'

The captain nodded thoughtfully.

'Turn the ship around,' said Lord Ravensford again. 'France is no place for Mari— Miss Travis.'

Captain Gringe looked at him evenly. 'I can't do that.'

'We've barely left England.'

'But if we go back we'll miss the tide.'

Marianne had the feeling that he was making an excuse, and that Captain Gringe was on her side. 'Damn it, Gringe—'

'Accept it, Luke,' said Henri from the bow of the ship.

'Like hell.' He turned to Marianne. 'You and I have some talking to do. But not here. Downstairs.'

Marianne almost refused. But then, knowing that an argument

142

was to follow, decided she would rather not have it in front of the crew. 'Very well.'

She turned and led the way down the wooden stairs and into the cabin. Lord Ravensford followed, hanging his lantern on the hook in the ceiling.

'What the devil do you think you are doing?' he demanded angrily. 'Sneaking on board, stowing away – this isn't some kind of game.'

'I know that,' she flashed.

'Oh, do you?' His face was grim.

She refused to answer him angrily. If she did that, the argument would escalate, and she didn't want that to happen, not with Captain Gringe and Henri and Figgs, to say nothing of the crew, only a few floorboards away. 'I haven't done this lightly,' she said with forced calm, 'but I had to do it. There was no other way you would have let me come on board.'

'With good reason. You were told to—'

'Told?' she demanded, her good resolutions in danger of flying out of the door. 'Told? My brother needs me. Do you seriously suppose that, in these circumstances, I am going to do as I am *told?*'

'Damn it, Marianne—'

'I love Kit,' she declared. 'I am not going to sit idly at home whilst he might be dying for need of medical care. If I could have sent a doctor on the expedition I would have done, but I don't know any doctor who would have been prepared to come. I might not be a doctor, but I have a lot of experience of dealing with accidents and illnesses. I know how to clean Kit's wounds if they have not already been properly cleaned, how to deal with fever, and how to build him up if he has lost a lot of blood. Can you really expect me to do as I'm *told?*'

He looked at her for long seconds, then the vehemence left his eyes and there was only tenderness there instead.

143

Somehow, she was afraid of his tenderness, and had a premonition of what he was going to say. She felt an inward shudder.

'Has it ever occurred to you,' he said softly, 'that Kit might already be dead?'

She closed her eyes, and her shoulders slumped. It had occurred to her, but she had refused to think about it. She could not afford to.

She felt his hand reaching out to her, strong and supportive. It gave her the courage to speak. 'Yes. It has occurred to me.'

His strong fingers stroked her cheek, trailing across her chin. 'I didn't want you to come with us because of the danger, but also because I wanted to spare you the possible sight of Kit's body.'

She swallowed. And then resolutely lifted her chin. 'If Kit is dead, then it will not be any harder for me to see his body here that it would be to see it at Seaton Hall. In fact, in a way it will be easier. Because I will at least know that I did everything I possibly could to help him – even if, in the end, I couldn't do anything.'

He nodded.

'I've seen one of my brothers buried,' she said, grateful to him for his understanding, 'I couldn't bear to bury another – not unless I know I've done everything in my power to prevent his death.'

She felt him push back one of her ringlets, which had come loose of its pins. She turned her head instinctively, rubbing her cheek against his hand.

'I'll bring him back, Marianne,' he said. 'If there's any way of doing it, I'll bring him safely home.'

As he looked deep into her eyes she felt a sense of oneness she had never known before. It was as if there was something joining them together, invisible and intangible, but nonetheless real for all that.

'We had better be going back on deck. That is, unless you would rather stay in the cabin?'

'No. I prefer to be out in the fresh air.'

He stood aside to let her pass. Then suddenly, on instinct, he caught hold of her as she passed him and pulled her roughly towards him. His eyes, full of an emotion she could not begin to fathom, looked down into her own, and then he kissed her.

The kiss was like nothing Marianne had experienced before. It was deeper, slower and far more sensuous than the kiss he had given her at their first meeting. That had been driven by physical desire; this was driven by something far more profound.

Her arms went round his neck and her fingers tangled themselves in his dark hair. So lightheaded did his kiss make her that it was only his strong arms around her, crushing her to him, that held her up. She never wanted the kiss to end. His tongue explored her mouth, slowly, caressingly, tracing the lines of her swollen lips. Then he kissed her mouth with a hundred tantalizing kisses; kissed her cheeks and her forehead, her eyelids and the tip of her nose, before cradling her head in his hands and plundering her mouth with his tongue once more.

At last he drew his mouth away from hers. His hands fell to his sides and, standing aside to let her pass, he followed her on to the deck.

CHAPTER NINE

*T*he crew were going about their business when Marianne emerged from below. They were now well into their journey. It should not be too long before they reached France.

Lord Ravensford joined Captain Gringe at the bottom of the main mast, and the two men were soon deep in conversation. Marianne walked towards the prow and stood looking out over the dark waters. Somewhere on the other side of the channel was Kit, possibly hurt, possibly . . . and what about Adèle?

Up until now she had scarcely thought of her friend. She had been too busy thinking of her brother to have any thought to spare for anyone else. But now that she had accomplished her goal of sailing to France she felt a mounting concern for Adèle.

She felt a presence behind her and, without turning, knew who it was.

'I've brought you a cloak from below.' Lord Ravensford put it round her shoulders. 'It isn't how I like to see you dressed,' he said, referring to its tattered state, 'but at least it will keep you warm. You are not dressed for a winter night.'

Marianne accepted the cloak gratefully; it was indeed a cold night.

'I thought of a cloak, but there was a limit to what I could bring.

146

It would have looked odd if I had ridden out from the Hall in a riding habit *and* a cloak.'

'Odd? Then you mean you didn't tell your father where you were going?'

'No. It would only have worried him.'

He gave a wry smile. 'And he might have forbidden the scheme. Mind you, I'm surprised Trudie didn't object. From what Henri has told me, I can't believe she let you embark on such a mission at all. I'd have thought she'd have thrown every obstacle in your way.'

'She doesn't know.' Marianne felt a twinge of guilt as she admitted it. 'I didn't want to deceive her, but there was no choice,' she explained. 'If I'd told her where I was going she'd have done everything in her power to make me stay. And when I'd overridden her, she'd have fretted until she saw me safely home again.'

'So you told her nothing?' he asked incredulously.

'No, of course not. I told her I was spending a few days with the Cosgroves.'

She felt him tense. 'Marianne, have you thought about what will happen if we don't return?'

'I've taken precautions.' She turned to face hm and explained that she had left her mare stabled with Jim Smith, and that Jim had promised to take her letter to the Hall if, by Friday, she had not returned. 'The letter explains everything,' she finished.

She turned back again to the ocean, and they stood silently for a few moments, each one of them unwillingly thinking of the possible consequences of the expedition.

Then Marianne said, 'I didn't hear everything when I overheard you, Henri and Figgs talking last night. I heard that it was Adèle who got a message out of France, but I didn't hear anything more about her. Is she all right? Or is she, too, hurt?'

'As far as we know, she's all right. But the message was brief and not very clear.'

147

'And her family? Her mother and father, Marie-Anne and the *comte*? Do you now anything about them?'

'No. They may be with Adèle and Kit. We've no way of knowing.'

'I hope they are.' Marianne shivered, and Lord Ravensford, standing behind her, wrapped his arms round her. She leaned back against him finding the warmth of his body comforting. 'Some terrible things have happened in France.'

He kissed her softly on the top of her head. 'We'll get them out of there; at least, we will if there's any chance.'

They stood together for some time, before Figgs coughed discreetly behind them. Lord Ravensford turned, his arms dropping to his sides. 'All right, Figgs.' To Marianne he said, 'We have to study the map and choose the best place to land. It will be impossible to take the ship too close to the shore – we don't want to run into any French patrols – so we'll be going the final part of the way in the rowing-boat.'

'Do you know how long you'll be?'

'If all goes well, and depending on where we are finally able to put into shore, we should be able to reach the farmhouse within an hour of setting foot on dry land. After that, it will take at least another hour back again – perhaps two, if Kit is badly hurt.'

She nodded. Then, as Lord Ravensford was about to go down to the cabin with Figgs, she caught his arm. 'Don't leave him. Even if he's dead.'

He put his hand reassuringly over her own. 'Don't worry. I won't.'

And then she was alone.

Wrapping the cloak more closely about her she stared out over the ocean swell. What did Lord Ravensford's tenderness mean? she wondered, remembering the comforting feel of his arms around her. Was it proof that his feelings ran deep, as his kiss had led her to suppose? Or was it simply that, going into a dangerous

148

situation, he had become unusually warm? She did not know, and until she was certain it would be better for her to keep her own feelings under control.

But she knew in her heart of hearts that it was too late for that. Too late by far.

It was still dark when the ship finally dropped anchor about a mile off the French coast. The winter night served them well; it would not be light for hours. With a minimum of fuss Lord Ravensford threw his leg over the side of the ship and, giving Marianne a last, wolfish smile, he climbed down to the rowing-boat; the same craft which had carried him out to the ship and which had then been lashed to its side. Figgs and two members of the crew followed, but no one else: Henri was still walking with a limp and would not go with them for fear of slowing them down, and besides, the hope of the expedition lay in discretion, for which a small group was best.

Knowing the best way to pass the time without falling prey to endless worries was to keep busy, Marianne sought out Captain Gringe. 'When my brother comes on board it is likely he will be badly hurt. May I fit up your cabin as a sick-room?'

Captain Gringe looked at her with respect. 'You may.' His face softened. 'I'm pleased to see you take after your mama, Miss Marianne. She was a great lady.'

Marianne nodded. 'Yes. She was.'

'She would be proud of you.'

His words touched her. She had had to endure a lot of prejudice concerning her medical skills over the years. There were many people who felt it was unladylike for a young woman to tend the sick, and it heartened her to know that not everyone was so blind.

Having secured Captain Gringe's permission to use his cabin, she took a lantern and went below deck once more, looking round with a practical eye. The beds – two bunks which had originally been used by Captain Gringe and his wife – were bolted to the floor. Marianne nodded in approval: they would not move, no matter how much the ship may roll. The scant furniture – a table and two chairs – was also bolted down and would be safe whatever the weather. Two trunks were stashed against the wall, secured with strong ropes. A small porthole gave on to the inky ocean and the dark night sky.

Marianne set about her work. First, she hung her lantern from the hook in the ceiling and then opened her bag, which she had left in the cupboard. In it she had her mother's few basic medical implements, the remains of the bandages that had been used on Henri's leg, some laudanum, and a dozen eggs together with two bottles of port. The eggs and port constituted a remedy used by Dr Moffat when his patients, for any reason, lost a great quantity of blood, and if Kit was in a weakened state she hoped it would help restore his strength.

Having checked that everything was in order, she inspected the linen on the bunks. Here she was in luck. Captain Gringe was a man of fastidious habits, and the linen on both bunks was clean: she need have no qualms about laying Kit on one, no matter how badly he was injured. She shivered at the thought, and then went back on to the deck.

The hours dragged by. One hour came and went, and then two. Three hours passed, and Marianne was becoming more and more anxious. Her ears were strained for the sound of the plash of the oars, and her eyes were strained for a sight of the rowing-boat returning to the ship.

After what seemed an endless time, at last she caught it: the sound of oars, and the sound of something else: shouts. As Marianne strained her eyes, she could dimly make out a second boat hard on the heels of the first. Flashes of light came from it periodically, and loud reports: there was another boat following Luke's, and the men in it were firing guns.

'Look lively!' called Captain Gringe. 'We're about to have company.' He turned to Marianne. 'There's a drawer underneath one of the bunks in my cabin – the one furthest from the door. It has a gun in it. If things go ill for us, go below deck. If you need the gun, then use it.'

'But I don't know how. . . .'

'You will. If the time comes, you'll work it out. And if you have to use it, then use it. You can worry about the rights and wrongs of it afterwards. Do you understand?'

Marianne nodded mutely. She had always known the expedition might turn out to be dangerous, but now that she was actually experiencing danger she found it more frightening than she had anticipated. Not that she wished she hadn't come: she knew she could not have stayed behind. But she felt the chill of fear and her hands were damp.

She made her way closer to the cabin access. If anything should happen. . . . She could see the rowing-boats clearly now. There was a woman sitting in the bow of the first; a young woman; Adèle? She caught a glint of dark hair in the moonlight. Yes! Adèle. And she was cradling something. Marianne's heart was in her mouth: Adèle had someone laid across her knee. A man. As the boat drew closer, Marianne saw it was Kit. But was he – no, he was moving. He was alive! And behind Adèle and Kit – he was there! Her heart leapt as she saw Lord Ravensford by the light of the moon, his muscles working as he pulled at the oars. Behind him the two crewmen shared a second pair of oars, whilst in the stern sat Figgs, levelling a pistol over his arm and firing at the second boat, which was now almost touching the first.

Captain Gringe strode the deck giving orders and the crew set to with a will, readying the ship so that as soon as Lord Ravensford's group was on board the ship could set sail. The rowing-boat reached them, and Marianne barely registered a splash as willing hands reached down to take Kit, who groaned as he was half-lifted, half-pulled on board. Adèle followed, with Figgs behind her and then the crewmen. Lord Ravensford lifted his own pistol and covered the others as they scrambled on to the ship, then he, too, swarmed up the rope ladder and the ship set sail as the second rowing-boat almost reached its side.

The sails bellied out in the wind and the ship began to move. Marianne's heart surged as she saw Lord Ravensford safely back on board and then a groan caught her attention and she was lost in her concern for Kit. She moved across the deck towards him and knelt down beside him. He was clutching his leg, around which was wrapped a blood-soaked bandage.

'How did it happen?' she asked quickly, her voice business-like: she could not afford to feel any emotion until she had dealt with Kit's wound.

'A . . . bayonet,' said Kit from between gritted teeth. 'Oh, God, I must be feverish,' he said to Adèle. 'I think I can see Marianne.'

'You can see me,' said Marianne, putting her hand soothingly to Kit's head. 'I came over with Lord Ravensford. I knew you'd been hurt. I'm here to help.'

'He . . . let you . . .' said Kit, struggling to sit up and his eyes sparking with anger despite his pain.

'I stowed away. He had no choice. Now lie still.'

Kit sank back. The effort of escaping had used up his last reserves of strength.

'He will be all right, yes?' asked Adèle anxiously, as she sat cradling Kit's head in her lap.

'I hope so,' said Marianne. It was too soon for her to tell, and besides, she was not a doctor. She did not want to give rise to false hope. 'But for now, we need to get him down to the cabin. I need to re-dress his wound, and he'll rest easier there. Figgs,' she called, turning her head, 'can you help Henri carry Kit down to the cabin?'

Figgs nodded, crossing the deck towards her. Marianne stood up – and then heard a cry: 'Marianne!'

She turned to see Lord Ravensford leaping between her and a swarthy Frenchman who had just appeared on the deck. She froze. So that was the meaning of the splash she had heard: one of the Frenchmen in the pursuing rowing-boat had jumped overboard, striking out for the ladder which still dangled from the side of the ship. He must have climbed it swiftly whilst the crew were occupied with sailing the ship, whilst the rescue party was absorbed in getting on board, and whilst she herself had been absorbed in Lord Ravensford and Kit. And now he was taking the pistol from between his teeth; levelling it; pointing it straight at her; and Lord Ravensford was throwing himself between her and the gun and it was going off. There was a flash of light and a loud report, and—

'Luke!' Forgetting everything else, Marianne ran over to him, her hair streaming in the wind, kneeling down beside him, hardly seeing him through sudden, useless, tears. She wiped them away angrily and looked at the red patch steadily growing on the arm of his shirt. 'Thank God,' she sobbed, as two of the crew overpowered the Frenchman. 'It's just his shoulder. Oh, thank God.'

Biting back her tears she set to work. 'The bullet's gone straight through, but he's losing a lot of blood.' She stanched it with her fichu, which she rapidly unfastened from around her neck, and then said, 'Carry him down to the cabin,' to Henri and Figgs.

They nodded and obeyed her, carrying him down to the cabin and laying him on one of the bunks.

'Luckily it's only a flesh wound,' said Marianne, examining his shoulder with deft hands. 'Here,' she said, giving him some drops of laudanum, 'this is for the pain.' Then, working quickly and efficiently, she cleaned the wound before binding it tightly.

Lord Ravensford, who had endured this with closed eyes, now opened them again. Despite his pain there was the ghost of a smile playing round his lips. She smiled in return, a smile of relief, and stroked his brow with her hand. 'I don't know what you have to smile about,' she said gently, hoping to make him feel better by treating the matter lightly and teasing him, although she was shaking inside in reaction to events.

'Don't you?' He looked straight into her eyes and gave a satisfied smile. 'You called me Luke.'

Their eyes locked, and there was a moment of complete understanding between them. It was as though all the barriers had been removed, and they communed on some deep level where words were of no importance. Then, leaning forward, she kissed him on his forehead.

'It seems you were right to come along,' he said, watching her with smiling eyes.

'Oh, Luke! If I hadn't come you wouldn't have been shot.'

'It was worth getting shot, just to hear you say my name.'

There was a discreet cough. Marianne turned to see Figgs. 'We've checked there's no one else on board – no one who shouldn't be here, that is.'

'And the Frenchman?' asked Luke.

'We've thrown him over the side.'

Luke nodded.

Marianne thought it wiser not to ask if he had been dead or alive.

'Kit'll be here any minute,' said Figgs. 'Captain Gringe is giving Henri a hand to bring him down.'

Luke turned to Marianne. 'See to your brother. I'm going to see if I can get some rest.'

She nodded, feeling admiration for the way he could think of her brother when he himself was injured. He closed his eyes and a minute later Henri, together with Captain Gringe, brought Kit into the cabin. Adèle followed close behind.

Henri and Captain Gringe laid Kit on the bunk and he sank back gratefully against the pillow.

'How's Luke?' Kit asked.

'It's only a flesh wound,' said Marianne. 'But I won't be happy until Dr Moffat has seen it. And now I want to have a look at you.' Her bedside manner suddenly evaporated and gave way to sisterly affection. 'Oh, Kit, I'm so glad you're alive.'

Kit smiled weakly. 'So am I.'

'And not too bad, by the look of things.' She looked at his thigh once again, which was bandaged with torn strips of shirt.

Kit's eyes went to Adèle, and his hands covered hers. 'Adèle bound me up.'

'All the same, Marianne, if you would have a look at it?' asked Adèle. Her voice was anxious, and Marianne realized for the first time how deeply her friend loved her brother.

'Of course.'

Fortifying Kit with a few drops of laudanum she gently undid the bandages and checked his thigh, but Adèle had cleaned it thoroughly. 'It's a pity you had to put yourself to such exertion. It looks like your wound had already started to heal, but I'm afraid all the activity has opened it up again. I'll bind it with fresh bandages for you—'

'Your sister, she is adept at bandaging the legs!' said Henri with a twinkle.

'And then you must get some rest,' said Marianne.

Kit took her hand. 'Thank you, Mari. And then you must tell me all about your escapades. I gather you have been busy whilst I've been away.'

'Not as busy as you,' she said. She shook her head. 'Kit, you've worried us all to death.' But she found she could not maintain her anger against him; she was too relieved to know that he was alive. Instead she turned to her friend. 'And you, Adèle. How are you?'

'I am well,' said Adèle, in prettily accented English. 'Tired, but well; and glad to 'ave escaped from France.'

Marianne took in Adèle's slight figure, and noticed how thin

Adèle was looking. But after all the troubles she must have been through in the last few months it was not surprising.

'But I think you have better things to do at the moment than talk to me, yes?' asked Adèle with a smile.

Marianne was about to protest, but instead she said ruefully, 'You know me too well.'

'Figgs, you stay with her,' said Kit. There was something half-teasing and half-serious about him. 'I want to make sure she has a chaperon, in case I fall asleep. I know what Luke's like!'

Marianne tried to make sense of his half-jesting words. Was he warning her against Luke? she wondered. Or telling her he knew of her feelings? Or implying that she and Luke had feelings for each other? She did not know, and in front of Henri and Figgs she did not want to ask.

She turned her thoughts back to the task in hand and went over to Luke's bunk. Mercifully he had fallen into a light sleep.

'It is the best thing for 'im,' said Henri.

Marianne nodded. She sat down beside him and did not leave his side as the ship sailed back to England.

CHAPTER TEN

'Kit's sleeping.' Dr Moffat spoke comfortingly, patting Marianne paternally on the arm. 'The wound's opened again with the journey, but it's clean and it won't be long until it mends. All your brother needs now is plenty of rest.'

'And Lord Ravensford?' Marianne tried to make her voice sound casual. It would not do to let Dr Moffat guess that she had feelings for the man who was lying behind the very door she was standing outside; the door of one of the guest rooms of Seaton Hall.

'Ah.' His face became grave. 'Now that's a different story. The wound's been cleaned and properly bound, but it isn't the flesh wound it appears to be.'

Marianne swallowed. 'That explains the fever.'

'Yes. The bullet went through the shoulder, but unfortunately it grazed the bone on its way out. A splinter remains inside. It goes without saying that it will have to be removed.' He hesitated. 'Miss Travis, I know this is a lot to ask, but if I send for an assistant it could be an hour or more before one arrives, and the splinter needs to come out now.'

Marianne spoke calmly, though her face was white. 'I will assist you.'

'Thank you.'

Trudie, who had been standing beside the doctor with her hands on her hips all this while, shook her head, saying darkly, 'Oh, no you don't, Miss Marianne. An unmarried lady in a gentleman's bedroom? Your mama would turn in her grave.'

'Mama would understand,' returned Marianne, her concern for Luke making her speak sharply.

'But will anyone else?' argued Trudie. 'You're well liked in the neighbourhood, Miss Marianne, but it doesn't do to try people too far. If anyone finds out you've been—'

'No one will ever hear of it from my lips, I assure you,' said Dr Moffat, 'and I am sure no one will hear of it from yours. But I do need help, and I need it now.'

He turned back to Marianne. It had not escaped his notice that she was unnaturally calm, and he guessed from her white face and rigid demeanour that she was holding back some unusually strong emotion. As an intelligent man it did not take him long to work out what that emotion could be. Under the circumstances, he knew Marianne would want to be the one to help him in his task.

'Well, I don't like it,' said Trudie, shaking her head; but knowing that Lord Ravensford was badly injured, and had been injured in the course of rescuing Master Kit, she allowed herself to be over-ruled. 'Well, if it must be, it must. I'll fetch you some hot water.'

'Thank you, Trudie.'

Trudie bustled away and Dr Moffat entered Luke's room, followed by Marianne.

The next few minutes were painful ones for all concerned. Marianne had to bite her lip as she assisted the doctor in removing the splinter from the wound, and Luke mercifully lost consciousness, only coming round when the deed was done.

'Now, if you can just hold this pad to his shoulder,' said the doctor, as he administered some laudanum to Luke for the pain. 'And then if you can help me to bind it. . . .'

Ten minutes later, Luke was laid back against the pillows, and

Marianne saw with relief that he already seemed to be resting a little easier.

'You made a good job of it the first time round,' said Dr Moffat conversationally, 'but now that you have seen me remove a splinter of bone you will know what to look for if you should have to deal with a shooting incident again.'

Marianne flushed.

'Come, child. You didn't think I would fail to recognize your handiwork – or your bandages.' He smiled. 'I don't know how you were on hand to do it, nor is it my business to ask, but it's lucky for Lord Ravensford you were there: he could have bled to death otherwise. Now, all you have to do is to make sure that these two young men get plenty of rest, and then I see no reason why they should not both make a full recovery. As for you, young lady,' he said, standing up and surveying her professionally, 'you, too, need rest. And no, don't argue with me. You can do nothing to help either your brother or your – neighbour – if you are falling asleep on your feet. Let Trudie watch over them tonight, and then you can take over in the morning.'

Marianne was about to protest, but she swayed as she stood up and was forced to acknowledge that the doctor was right. She was of no use to anyone in her exhausted state, and she needed to be fresh if she was to nurse Luke – and Kit – back to health.

'Thank you,' she said. 'And thank you for not asking what Lord Ravensford is doing here.'

'My dear Marianne,' he said, taking the liberty of using her name as he had known her since the day of her birth, 'when one young man takes it into his head to go on a hot-headed expedition to rescue the woman he loves and another gentleman decides to help him, then nothing that follows would surprise me. But have no fear. No one will learn of anything I have seen or heard tonight. A doctor is used to being discreet.' He closed his bag. 'I will come back and see my patients in the morning.'

Marianne nodded and wearily showed him out. She returned to Luke's room once more, to reassure herself that he was still resting easily, and then returned to her own room where, as soon as she had undressed herself and laid down in the four-poster bed, she was asleep.

The following morning, Marianne felt much refreshed. She was just about to ring for Trudie when the housekeeper bustled into the room, carrying a tray of steaming chocolate and freshly baked rolls.

'Here you are, Miss Marianne. I've had the whole story from Henri, and after all you've been through in the last two days I'm not letting you out of that bed until you've eaten these rolls and drunk this chocolate.'

'I would have told you,' said Marianne sheepishly, 'but when we got home I was so tired . . .' She was sorry that Trudie should have heard the truth from Henri, instead of from her own lips, but in a way it made things easier for her, now that Trudie knew everything that had happened.

'Tired?' snorted Trudie. 'Is it any wonder? You and Master Kit! You haven't changed! Still getting into scrapes.' She gave an exasperated sigh. 'You're two of a kind, Miss Marianne – you're both as bad as each other!' With her hands on her hips she shook her head despairingly, exactly as she had done when Marianne and Kit had been children, and involved in a childhood prank. 'What your papa will say when he finds out I dread to think.'

'Do you know,' said Marianne, sipping her chocolate, 'I think it will be the making of him.'

'Let's hope so,' said Trudie, throwing back the drapes. 'Though Dr Moffat says your papa's not to be told at once. Your father's valet's getting him used to the idea, telling him there's a rumour abroad that Kit isn't a gambler, but that he's gone off to France to rescue Miss Adèle. Then, when your papa's used to the idea, he'll be told that Master Kit is safe and well.'

'Yes.' Marianne nodded as she took a delicious roll. 'It will be less of a shock that way.' She tried to eat the roll, but as she put it to her lips she shook her head. It was no good. She could not eat anything until she knew how Luke was. 'Did he . . .' she began hesitantly. 'Did he pass a peaceful night?'

'If you mean Master Kit, then yes, he passed an untroubled night,' said Trudie. 'And if you mean Lord Ravensford,' she said, giving Marianne a hard look, 'then yes, he did the same.'

Marianne heaved a sigh of relief. As long as the fever didn't return then, provided he got a lot of rest, Luke should make a full recovery. It would take time, and careful nursing, but she meant to see he had plenty of both. 'I will look in on him as soon as I am dressed.'

'The doctor's with him,' said Trudie with satisfaction. She did not approve of her young mistress nursing an eligible gentleman, and was happy to confound Marianne, who, she knew, now that the danger was past, would not wish to intrude on the doctor.

'Then I will sit with Kit until he leaves.'

And as soon as she was up and dressed, Marianne did just that.

'So, you've decided to keep me company,' said Kit cheerfully as his sister opened the door and went into the drawing-room.

'I have been looking for you all over,' she said in surprise. 'I was expecting to find you in your room, not down here. You should be in bed.'

'Not so!' Kit smiled. 'Doctor Moffat's pronounced me fit to take my ease downstairs.'

'Well, as long as you remain on the *chaise-longue*, I suppose it will be all right,' said Marianne doubtfully. 'But woe betide you if I see you walking around!'

She sat down next to him, on an elegant Sheraton chair, and looked at him with affection. His hard features seemed to have softened since the last time she had seen him, and there was an air of contentment about him that she had never witnessed before. 'I was coming in here to scold you, but I see you are irrepressible, and I will just be wasting my time. So now, instead, I will hug you,' she said, suiting her actions to her words. 'And thank God you are home.'

Kit stroked her hair, his arms around her, and then suddenly ruffled the raven ringlets and punched her playfully on the shoulder. Marianne laughed, and their habitual camaraderie was restored.

'So, you were going to scold me, were you?' asked Kit, with a humorous quirk at the corner of his mouth. 'You have no idea what I intended to say to *you*! Stowing away on a ship, coming over to France, frightening the life out of Trudie—'

'I didn't mean to do that,' said Marianne, suddenly contrite. 'I would have liked to have given her some warning of our arrival, instead of turning up on the doorstep when she thought I was at the Cosgroves', particularly as I had a party of men in tow, but it was just not possible.'

'Has she scolded you yet?' he asked with a gleam in his eye.

'Yes,' she admitted, with a quirk at the corner of her own mouth.

'Good! Then you have been told off for your exploits, and I have been told off for mine. It is quite like being children again, isn't it, Mari?'

She laughed. 'In a way. But children don't tell their families they have run up a fortune in gambling debts, and then go to rescue people from the Revolution,' she remarked with raised eyebrows.

Kit sighed, and shifted his injured leg. 'Now that was not well done of me. I confess I almost didn't go through with it. But I could think of no other way. It seemed better in the end to let you think I was a wastrel than to have you worrying I might be dead.'

Marianne nodded. 'I hate to admit it, but I think you were right.

If I'd known you'd gone to rescue Adèle, I wouldn't have had one peaceful night's sleep until you were safely back. But it has been very bad for Papa.'

Kit sombred. 'Yes. I've heard. Tom told me he's become a recluse. Is it true, Mari?'

Marianne sighed. 'Yes. He took to his room several months ago. It was with a cold, at first, and I thought he would be up and about again in no time, but his lowness of spirits persisted even when his cold had gone. I called Dr Moffat, who said he just needed time to recover his strength, but somehow it never came back. And alone in his room he brooded, so that his spirits became lower all the time. It was a vicious circle in the end – the more he brooded, the more despondent he became, and the more despondent he became the more incapable he became of leaving his room: and the more he stayed in his room, the more he brooded. . . .'

Kit frowned. 'I'm sorry for it. I really didn't think it would hit him that hard.'

'I think, for Papa, it would have been better if he had known the truth. He would have worried, and he would have forbidden you to go, but he would not have lost hope when you had left. It broke his spirit to know – or think – that his son and heir was a gambler.'

Kit nodded. 'What I did, I did for the best, but even so. . . . However, there's no point dwelling on the past. What's done is done. And besides, when Papa learns the truth I hope to find it will restore his health.'

'I think it will,' said Marianne. 'Especially,' she said with an innocent look, 'when you tell him that you are to marry Adèle.'

Kit's eyebrows rose. 'And what makes you think that?'

She twinkled at him. 'Are you trying to deny it?'

He laughed, warmly and happily. 'Not I. But there remains a formality. In all the confusion I have not had an opportunity to ask her yet. Once my leg is better I mean to take her out to our tree house and ask her to be my wife.'

'The tree house. Where we all used to play as children. That's a good idea.'

'I want to make our betrothal unique,' agreed Kit. 'So, no more talk of this until we are safely engaged.'

Marianne put her finger to her mouth in a gesture from their childhood. 'My lips are sealed.'

'But I am not the only one to be teased on such a subject,' he said with mock innocence. 'It seems to me you have a secret of your own.'

She suddenly sobered. 'I . . . I don't know what you mean,' she said hesitantly.

'You and Luke. No, don't deny it. I saw your face when he was shot. You're in love with him, aren't you, Mari? Or if you're not, you should be. Luke's a bit rough around the edges, perhaps, but all the more exciting for that. Or so most young ladies think,' he teased.

'Don't,' she said, a shadow crossing her face.

He looked at her curiously. 'I'm not wrong, am I, Mari?' he asked, worried.

'Yes . . . no . . . that is. . . . You go too fast. I have not said that I am in love with Luke, and even if I was, I would not know whether he loves me. . . .'

'Men don't jump in front of bullets for women they don't love,' said Kit perceptively. 'But if you wish me to say nothing more, then I won't mention it again. At least, not until you give me leave.'

Marianne gave a twisted smile. 'I can't keep anything from you, can I?'

'No, little sister.'

The door opened, and Adèle tripped in.

'Adèle. My love.' Kit's face lit up as he saw his pretty *amour*.

The petite brunette blushed charmingly and went over to Kit's side, taking his proffered hand. 'Kit. Trudie told me you were out of bed. But should you be down 'ere? What did the doctor say?'

'He said that I may take my ease downstairs provided I don't tire myself,' said Kit, repeating the words he had said to Marianne, but this time with an unmistakably lover-like warmth.

It did Marianne's heart good to see it. Kit's love for Adèle, and Adèle's for him, was lovely to see.

'Ah. *Bon.* Then I will 'ave to sit with you and make sure you follow 'is instructions,' smiled Adèle.

'For as long as Trudie allows it,' said Kit, plainly having forgotten Marianne's existence in his happiness at being with Adèle. 'She read me a lecture this morning about compromising you, and told me we must be chaperoned whenever we want to sit together.'

'Ah! But me, I told 'er we 'ave crossed 'alf of France with only a skin-and-bones 'orse as our chaperon,' said Adèle, similarly oblivious of Marianne's presence.

'And what did she say to that?'

'She told me that nothing that 'appened in such a barbarous country would surprise her, but that we are in England now!'

Marianne smiled happily to hear Kit and Adèle's banter: after all they had been through, it did her good to know that they could finally be together. Then, knowing that they were engaged – or would be, just as soon as Kit had found the right moment to propose – she ignored Trudie's feelings on chaperonage and discreetly slipped out of the room.

Kit and Adèle's happy laughter receded as she made her way along the corridor and upstairs, and her own happy thoughts receded with it: she was still anxious about Luke. Although Dr Moffat had said he should make a full recovery, and although her own knowledge and experience told her that this should be the case, until he was actually up and about again she would not rest easy.

The doctor was still in Luke's bedroom however, and so she waited patiently until he came out.

165

'Ah! Miss Travis! Just the person I wanted to see.'

'How is he?' she asked.

'He is resting now. His fever has gone and I have given him strict instructions to get some sleep. He should get as much rest as possible over the next few days. Then, as long as there is no return of the fever, he should be able to get up.'

Marianne thanked the doctor, and when he had gone, slipped into Luke's room.

It was bathed in darkness. The heavy drapes were drawn across the window, and no candles were lit. But by and by, as Marianne's eyes grew used to the darkness, she began to be able to see. To her right was the Adam fireplace; the fire, banked down, glowed in the hearth. On the wall ahead of her were the windows, covered with heavy damask curtains, and the bed was set against the wall to her left. It was a four poster, and the curtains which surrounded it were tied back. Under the coverlet was a figure lying quietly: Luke.

She moved into the room, gently shutting the door. She was determined not to disturb him, but she wanted to see for herself that he was resting peacefully. A little daylight was coming in through chinks in the curtains, and by this light she could make out his sleeping face. It was peaceful. There was no sign of the fever that had plagued him the day before. His features were relaxed, and she realized that she had never seen him like this before – he was usually such a strong and active man.

Her eyes lingered on his face: his smooth brow, his almond-shaped eyes, and his cheekbones, which were beautifully moulded. It seemed strange to think of a man as beautiful, but as she saw him like this, in repose, she realized that his face was indeed beautifully shaped. The high cheekbones and strong jawline were in perfect proportion and gave a fine structure to his face. With his face relaxed, however, he seemed younger than normal, and strangely vulnerable. The vulnerability touched her,

166

and made her insides ache. Her strong Luke, brave, fearless, looked almost boyish. She shivered, realizing that this vulnerable and disarming side of him would be one his wife would see every night – if he ever took a wife.

She moved further into the room. Although he was sleeping peacefully she wanted to reassure herself that his fever had indeed gone, and when she reached the side of the bed she put out her hand, resting it on his forehead. His skin felt cool and dry.

She was just about to remove her hand when his own rose, catching her by the wrist, and a smile crossed his lips.

'You're awake!' she exclaimed.

He opened his eyes, and there was a flash, faint but unmistakable, of wickedness in them. 'And glad to see you. More glad than I can say.'

'Oh, Luke, I was so worried about you. . . .'

'Were you?' His eyes were searching and his good hand, the hand that led from his undamaged shoulder, as it rubbed hers, was strong and firm.

'The fever . . .' she began hesitantly.

'The fever's gone now.'

'I . . . shouldn't be here,' she said falteringly. 'I should let you rest.'

'You will do me more good than any amount of rest. I was hoping you would come.'

'I had to see you. When we brought you home last night you were so ill—'

'Why *did* you bring me home?' he asked curiously. 'To the Hall?' He patted the bed beside him. 'Sit down and tell me all about it.'

Marianne hesitated and then did as he said. As she settled herself beside him she could not help noticing that his white lawn night-shirt set off his olive complexion most attractively, revealing as it did an inch or two of masculine chest. . . .

She gathered her straying thoughts. 'In the end, we had no

choice. In all the confusion, when the French were chasing you, no one gave any thought to the rowing-boat. It was only later, when Figgs went to look for it and could not find it that we realized no one had lashed it to the side. So Captain Gringe had to take us all into the harbour. It was daylight when we arrived, and he thought it better to wait until it was almost dark before smuggling us off the ship.'

Luke nodded in agreement. 'That makes sense. In the daytime, people would have been curious and would have talked about what they had seen. Two young ladies, two injured men and a couple of ruffians, coming down the gangplank, would have set the harbour buzzing.'

'Though I don't think Henri and Figgs would take kindly to being called a couple of ruffians,' laughed Marianne mischievously. 'Captain Gringe sent for his carriage as soon as dark began to fall, and gave the coachman instructions to bring us all here. Figgs would have taken you on to the Manor, but by that time you were feverish and I insisted you were brought inside.'

He lifted his hand and brushed her cheek. Even in his weakened state his touch was redolent of virility. 'It seems I have much to thank you for,' he said, his eyes looking deeply into her own.

'You can thank me by getting well again,' she remarked, suddenly feeling vulnerable at being so close to him and resorting to the manner of a nurse. She pulled up the coverlet around his shoulders as if to emphasize the point.

'I intend to.' He was unperturbed by her ministrations. 'Someone needs to keep an eye on you, and make sure you don't go stowing away on any more ships!'

'There's no fear of that. Once was enough. But now, I intend to go. You are still weak, and you need to rest. Dr Moffat has given strict instructions, and I mean to see that they are carried out.'

'Very well.' Then his good hand moved to the back of her head and he pulled her face towards his, kissing her deeply and sensuously, with such a firm movement that she had no time to resist – even if she had wanted to, which she did not. And then he let her go.

He heart pounding and her cheeks still flushed from his kiss she headed towards the door, unable to resist one final look back at him before she went out into the corridor, closing the door gently behind her.

The next week passed quickly. Despite her fears that the days would drag, Marianne found she had plenty to do. She was kept busy with nursing Luke and Kit, and in between she found time to send Tom to the harbour to bring back her mare from Jim Smith's, and to comfort Adèle, for the pretty Frenchwoman was anxious about the fate of her beloved parents.

The fate of the *comte* and Marie-Anne concerned Marianne as well. The *comte* was her godfather, and Marie-Anne had been almost like a second mother to her, so that she was almost as anxious as Adèle.

'We were separated as we tried to leave France,' said Adèle in her prettily accented English. 'Ah! Marianne. I 'ave tried to put on a brave face before Kit – 'e is injured, and I want 'im to get well – but it is difficult. I worry so much. Where are they, my parents? I 'ad 'oped I would 'ear word of them when I reached England. I 'ad 'oped they, too 'ad escaped.'

'They may well have done,' said Marianne.

'*Non.* If they 'ad escaped, they would have come 'ere.'

'Not necessarily. If they had wanted to mount a rescue attempt to save you I think they would have gone to London first. It would be much easier to arrange something from there.'

Adèle looked a little more hopeful. 'Ah! You 'ave something there. *Mais oui.* It is possible.' She nodded to herself '*C'est possible.*'

'Do you know anyone in London? Anyone they might turn to for help?'

Adèle thought. 'My father, 'e 'as a cousin, a Lord Dublaine, in Brook Street. Per'aps they 'ave gone there.'

'Why not write?' suggested Marianne.

Adèle, her face alight with hope again, nodded. '*Mais oui*. I will write at once, before tea. And 'opefully soon we will 'ave news.'

Marianne left Adèle to compose her letter. In all the danger and excitement of the preceding week there had been no time for her to attend to the estate, and she knew that there would be many things that needed her attention. She left the room, meaning to go to the stables and ride out towards the orchards, but just as she was crossing the hall she saw Luke coming down the stairs.

He looked paler than usual, and thinner, but still he looked magnificent. His long, lean body, encased in a cutaway coat, knee-breeches and boots, showed no sign of his recent injury, unless it was in the way he had one hand folded across his chest. His dark hair framed his masculine face, which was lean, angular and alert. And Marianne's heart did somersaults in her chest.

Even so, she was concerned.

'You shouldn't be up,' she said, taking a step towards him. 'Dr Moffat says—'

'Dr Moffat is a fine man, but he is used to dealing with invalids, not strong men who heal quickly.' He crossed the hall towards her and stood so closely to her that he could have touched her. 'Don't worry, I have been injured often enough to know what my body can and cannot stand,' he said, his eyes seeking her own. 'In more ways than one,' he added wolfishly.

Marianne tingled. But forcing herself to concentrate on his recent injury she gave a reluctant nod. She knew from Kit that Luke had been involved in other rescues before this one, and had to concede that he knew best as far as his own limits were concerned.

'And now that I'm up, I must be returning to the Manor.' He put out his good hand and brushed her cheek. 'I was going to wait for the right time and the right place to say this, but I don't want to wait any longer. Marianne, I have something to ask you. Something of great importance. Will you—?'

The sound of someone noisily clearing their throat interrupted him and he uttered an oath, but Trudie, who had followed him down the stairs, ignored his *sotto voce* Damn! as she ignored his darkling look.

'You were just going into the drawing-room to take your leave of Master Kit, if I remember rightly,' she said blandly; nevertheless looking pointedly at the barest inch of space that separated Lord Ravensford from her beloved Miss Marianne. 'He's just gone into the drawing-room.'

He looked as though he would have liked to curse even more, but mastering his temper he instead gave a wry smile and made the housekeeper a polite bow. 'You are a good watchdog, Trudie. You are also right. I am just going in to see Kit. Miss Travis?'

He offered Marianne his arm and they went into the drawing-room. Kit and Adèle were just approaching the French windows from the garden, which had been thrown open on account of the fineness of the day.

'Luke! Marianne! You can be the first to congratulate us!' said Kit, as he and Adèle walked into the room arm in arm. 'Adèle has just done me the very great honour of agreeing to become my wife.'

'Oh, Kit, that's wonderful,' said Marianne, running forward to give her brother a hug, before kissing Adèle.

'My heartiest congratulations,' said Luke with a genuine warmth; a warmth in which there was now no trace of envy.

Adèle blushed prettily and Kit beamed at her with obvious pride.

Trudie, who had followed Luke and Marianne into the drawing-room, smiled as much as any of them, adding her own congratulations before bustling off to fetch the tea.

She soon brought it into the drawing-room. The silver teapot was gleaming on the silver tray. Porcelain cups and saucers were set beside it, and the sugar was neatly displayed in a silver dish.

Once the tea had been poured, Luke turned to Kit. 'I hope you will bring your fiancée over to the Manor tomorrow afternoon, Kit, and take tea with me: I would like to repay at least some of the hospitality I have been shown over the last week. And Miss Travis,' he said, turning to Marianne with a meaningful look, 'I hope I can prevail on you to join your brother, too.'

'Splendid!' said Kit, beaming happily at his sister and his best friend.

And Marianne, with a warm glance at Luke, and thinking she knew in her heart what his important question was going to be, happily agreed.

CHAPTER ELEVEN

Sun streamed in at the windows. Marianne was awake early the following morning, roused by the sound of the birds. She threw back the covers. Today she was going to visit Luke. . . .

She sprang out of bed and rang for Trudie.

'You look remarkably cheerful this morning,' remarked Marianne, as Trudie entered the room. 'Still delighted at the thought of Kit and Adèle?'

Trudie shook her head. 'No, it isn't that, Miss Marianne, though that's wonderful enough. But something else has happened.'

She would say no more, remarking only that Marianne would find out for herself when she went downstairs.

Curious, Marianne dressed quickly and went down to breakfast, wondering what could have set Trudie smiling so.

As she opened the door to the dining-room she knew at once. There, sitting at the breakfast-table as though he had never taken to his room, was her papa!

'Ah! Marianne,' he said, pausing in the act of slitting open a letter with a silver paper knife, 'there you are. Did you sleep well?'

Marianne cast an amazed glance at Kit, who gave her a quirky smile as he tucked into a plate of ham and eggs, and then Adèle, who beamed at her happily from behind her chocolate cup. Then she turned her attention back to her father, who seemed to have recovered all his lost vitality overnight.

'What will you have?' asked her Papa conversationally. 'The eggs are very good.'

'Yes. Eggs,' she said in a daze.

'Good. And after you have breakfasted, be so good as to join me in my study. I want to know about everything that has been happening on the estate.'

Marianne gave him another amazed look and then, beaming from ear to ear, applied herself to her breakfast.

'Come in, my dear.' Her father's words were welcoming as she went into his study some twenty minutes later.

Marianne went into the room and closed the door behind her.

'Sit down.'

Going over to a Sheraton chair, Marianne perched on the edge of her seat. She still could not quite believe that her beloved papa was restored to her.

'Now, then, Marianne, I want to talk to you about the estate. This is splendid news, is it not? That Kit is going to marry Adèle? So I want to put everything in order. If we are to have tiny feet pattering up and down the corridors, I want to make sure they won't be rained on through a leaking roof. But I didn't want to set the repairs in motion before I had explained to you what I intend to do. I know you love the estate – and I must say how well you have looked after it during my . . . illness, perhaps we should call it . . . but now it is time for us to move on. And so I am intending to sell a hundred acres of land.'

'No, Papa!' Marianne sprang to her feet.

'I know your feelings about the estate, my dear, and I respect you for them. But whilst the past is important, the future is even more so.'

'But if we sell off the land—'

He gave her a smile; the kind of smile he used to give her when he had taught her mathematics as a child – when he had just explained some particularly difficult problem and was waiting for her to understand. 'That's what land is for, you know, my dear: we buy it in good times so that we may sell it in bad.'

Marianne was surprised, and then frowned, and then said, 'I'd never thought of it like that.'

'I know. Which is why I wanted to explain it to you before I took any action. I wanted you to understand.'

'I . . . think I do.'

'It has happened before, you know,' her father reassured her. 'My father sold off a lot of land fifty years ago to help the Stuart cause. But then, when he failed to help put a Stuart king on the throne, he gradually recouped his losses and bought the land back again. And that is what we must do now: sell some land and then hope that, in the future, we may be able to buy it back again. Not to finance some lost cause this time, but to set the estate in order, and to give Kit and Adèle a splendid wedding – a wedding worthy of the Travis heir.'

'Yes,' Marianne breathed. 'That would be lovely. And so good for Adèle.'

Her father nodded. 'It will help her take her mind off other things. She is still worried about her parents, particularly as she has not yet had a reply from Lord Dublaine, but choosing her bride clothes will give her something happy to think about. And you, Marianne, will need to choose your own gown. You are to be Adèle's attendant, I understand—'

Marianne nodded, delighted to be attending her friend as she married her brother.

'—and you will need something elegant to wear. And you must order a few new dresses whilst you're about it, my dear. I have neglected you for long enough.'

Her father opened his arms to her and she gave him a hug.

175

'Oh, Papa, it's so good to have you back with us.'

He held her close. 'My dear, it is good to be well again.'

She stepped back, hardly able to contain her happiness. Her papa was restored to her, Kit was to marry Adèle, and Luke – oh, Luke! She could hardly wait for the afternoon to arrive!

'I have sent a message to Madame LaTour, asking her to call on us this morning.' He paused. 'She is still the best *modiste* in these parts?'

'Yes, Papa.'

'Good. Then you and Adèle will select your style of gowns – oh, and make sure you select yourselves something for the engagement ball as well. It is to be a proper ball, mind, not the sort of country affair we are used to. There will be no informality; everything will be done in the first style. The ladies will have cards, the dances will be elegant – we are going to celebrate Kit's betrothal and wedding with splendour. It isn't every day I have my son restored to me, and then discover he is to marry my god-daughter, after all! But you will not be forgotten, my dear. Once Kit and Adèle are safely married I mean to take you to London. We will catch the end of the Season and indulge ourselves with visits to the museums and the theatres. What do you say?'

Marianne could say nothing, for she believed those plans would have to be altered, but at the moment she was not at liberty to speak, and said only, 'That would be delightful.'

'Good. Good. Well, now, Marianne, off you go, my dear.'

As she reached the door he said, 'You are to take tea with Lord Ravensford this afternoon, I hear?'

Marianne's heart sang. 'Yes, Papa.'

'Good. Then thank him from me for restoring my son to me, will you, my dear? And tell him that I will do myself the honour of calling on him to thank him myself just as soon as things are ship-shape here.'

Marianne promised to do so.

'And Marianne – do what you can to lift Adèle's spirits, will you, my dear? She seems rather low this morning. No letter came again in the post.'

Marianne nodded. 'I will.'

'Good. Then off you go. And mind, choose something truly elegant from Madame LaTour.'

With this happy injunction ringing in her ears, Marianne went to find Adèle.

Marianne was glad of Madame LaTour's visit, as it helped to pass the hours until it was time for her to go to Billingsdale Manor and take tea with Luke.

Madame LaTour was a splendid Frenchwoman of middle age. She had fled the troubles in France, like so many of her country-men and women, and set up her business in the neighbouring town, where she had relatives. She bustled into the Hall with a collection of journals and pocket books, and samples of silks and satins in the latest colours.

Settling herself down in the morning-room, she proceeded to cover the desk, and then the floor, with drawings, engravings and fabric samples, entreating Marianne and Adèle to 'see the cut of this gown, *mademoiselle*' or 'feel this piece of silk'.

Marianne and Adèle looked through the latest fashion journals, marvelling that a country in turmoil could still be producing such things.

'What can I say?' asked Madame LaTour with an expressive shrug. 'We French, we like our fashions, heh, *mademoiselle*? Not even revolution can change this about us.'

Marianne was about to ask Madame LaTour how she got her copies of the journals but forebore to ask. The Revolution had created all sorts of kinds of smuggling, and there were some things, Marianne decided, that it was better not to know. She looked through the latest editions of the *Journal de la Mode et du Goût*, noting that striped dresses were very popular, and decided on a blue-striped silk for her ballgown, whilst Adèle chose a white silk with a jonquil-striped bodice and sleeves.

'And so, at last we 'ave decided, *oui?*' asked Madame LaTour, making copious notes on the gowns the two young ladies had chosen. 'Very well. Your ball gowns, I will make sure they are ready in time for the ball. The bride clothes, they will take longer, but I 'ave some very good girls 'oo sew for me' – she wrinkled her nose, as though trying to remember the word 'extra . . . extra? . . . *in addition*,' she beamed, remembering the difficult phrase, 'to the other girls, when I 'ave the need.'

'Oh, Marianne, I am so 'appy!' said Adèle, when Madame LaTour had gone. 'And yet—'

Marianne knew she was thinking of her parents and gave her friend a hug. 'It will come right in the end, I'm sure of it, Adèle. We must just have faith.'

Lunchtime came at last, and then the afternoon – and then, just as Marianne was about to go upstairs and put her riding habit on, there came a blow. The Reverend Mr Stock called, with his sister, Miss Stock.

'I hope we're not intruding,' he said, 'But Minerva and I just happened to be passing, on our way back from Mr and Mrs Fanner's – yes, a boy, a fine, lusty chap, and both mother and baby doing well, thank you for asking – and I said to Minerva, "I think I'll just call in at the Hall and see if Mr Travis is ready to discuss any of the wedding arrangements".'

'An excellent idea,' said Mr Travis approvingly. 'And very kind.'

'As soon as I got your letter, I was delighted,' said the Reverend Mr Stock. ' "You will never guess", I said to Minerva – didn't I, Minerva? – "but Kit Travis is to be wed". I was delighted. We were both overjoyed.'

'Indeed,' beamed Miss Stock. 'Kit, Adèle, you must let me wish you joy.'

Mr Travis, too, beamed. 'This is a very special wedding, my only son to my god-daughter, and I can't thank you enough for coming, Reverend. I want to make sure everything is right.'

'It's very good of you,' said Kit politely. He turned to his father. 'You won't be needing us, though, will you, sir?'

Marianne gave Kit a quick glance, part grateful for his loyalty, but part concerned that he was preparing to forego his own important arrangements to help her.

'Not need you?' enquired Mr Travis, surprised. 'Of course we need you. You and Adèle are the two people we can't do without. And as the reverend's very kindly called on us I think it an excellent opportunity to make our plans.'

'You have forgotten, perhaps, that we are engaged to take tea with Lord Ravensford,' Kit said. 'We ought to be leaving in the next ten minutes or so.'

'You're right, Kit, I had, for the moment, forgotten.'

'I don't like breaking an appointment—' began Kit.

'No, no, of course not.' Mr Travis frowned. 'And yet the reverend is a busy man. We cannot make too many demands on his time.'

'If it means breaking an engagement . . .' said the reverend, looking worried.

'Unless, of course, Marianne went by herself,' suggested Kit with a happy inspiration. 'Then the engagement would not be broken, merely amended.'

'Of course! The very thing,' said Mr Travis. 'Marianne will still be able to convey my thanks to Lord Ravensford for all he has done for you, and we will be able to attend to the matter of the wedding.' Although he was delighted that his son was home safely, and to marry a beautiful young woman who was his god-daughter into the bargain, he did not want to neglect any courtesy towards the gentleman who had been responsible for rescuing his son from France. 'But you can't go without a chaperon,' he went on with a frown.

Marianne tried to hide her disappointment. She was delighted that Kit and Adèle were to have an opportunity to make the arrangements for their wedding, but the reverend's kindly visit was a sore blow to her nonetheless.

Miss Stock gave a nervous little cough. 'If I may be of any assistance. . . .'

'Perfect,' declared Mr Travis, seeing immediately what was in her mind.

'Would it not be too much trouble?' asked Marianne. The day had suddenly resumed its bright air, but she was determined not to take advantage of the kindly spinster.

'Not at all. I must confess I would enjoy it. Sebastian will be busy with your dear father, and of course your brother and future sister-in-law, for some time, and as I can have nothing to add to their deliberations I would like to make myself useful elsewhere.'

'And you will, of course, take Tom with you,' said Mr Travis. Concerned with Kit's impending marriage as he was, he did not forget that two unmarried ladies could not ride around the country without an escort.

'Tom has taken Hercules to the farrier's,' said Marianne.

'Then you must take Henri,' said Mr Travis, as the door opened and Henri entered the room with a tray of tea for the reverend and his sister. 'Henri, will you be so good as to accompany Miss Marianne and Miss Stock to Lord Ravensford's this afternoon?'

'*Mais oui, Monsieur* Travis,' said Henri putting down the tray. 'I am 'appy to oblige.'

'Then that's settled. You don't mind, do you, Marianne, my dear?'

'No. No, of course not.' Marianne said, her heart singing.

'Good. And now, Reverend,' said her father, turning his attention back to Kit's wedding, 'let us make our plans.'

Marianne left the room as Kit and Adèle began talking over the arrangements for their marriage ceremony. She changed quickly into her riding habit and then she, Miss Stock and Henri set off for Billingsdale Manor.

The day was cold but fine. The earlier, unseasonably warm weather had given way to the bright, breezy weather more typical of March. Marianne and Miss Stock rode side by side to begin with, but Marianne's horse was fresh and frisky whilst Miss Stock's mare was already tired from her earlier journey out to the Fanners' house.

'Don't dawdle on my account, Marianne,' said Miss Stock. 'Dapple's itching for a run. Give her her head, my dear, and wait for me outside the Manor.'

Marianne thanked Miss Stock for her thoughtfulness and gave Dapple a free rein. Since Tom had brought her back from Jim Smith's the mare had had little exercise, and she was champing at the bit.

Marianne enjoyed the ride. The wind whipped past her, and the exercise was exhilarating.

Henri rode behind her, keeping his position in between the two ladies, mindful of his duties as guardian to both.

They took the shortest route to the Manor, cutting across the fields instead of taking the lane. Approaching the house from the seaward side, they crossed the fields and orchards, and then drew near to the back of the imposing manor. As soon as the stately building was in sight Marianne began to rein Dapple in, slowing her gently and bringing her to a halt at the start of the formal gardens. There Marianne slipped from Dapple's back and, waiting only for Henri to take the mare from her, she walked on towards the house.

The library window was open. Marianne guessed that Lord Ravensford would be sitting there, waiting for his guests. She felt her heart beating more quickly as, at any minute, she expected him to turn round and see her. He would be surprised, of course, seeing that she was alone, and would no doubt take advantage of the few minutes they would have together before Miss Stock arrived to ask his important question. . . .

As she drew closer to the window, Marianne could see that he was indeed sitting there. His back was towards her, his wild dark hair combed into a semblance of tameness before being confined in a bow at the nape of his neck. His shoulders were straight and he sat erect, giving no indication that he had ever been injured. He was a strong man, and although it would take some time for his injury to heal fully, she was pleased to see that already it scarcely troubled him.

She had almost reached the house, and was just about to give way to an impetuous urge to call out to him, when she saw the door of the library open. . . .

Luke was sitting in the library, waiting for Marianne. He was impatient to see her. Ever since he had seen the Frenchman level a pistol at her; ever since he had flung himself between her and a bullet without even having to think about it, he had known that he was in love with her. He had found something he had thought he would never find: a woman he loved with a deepness and a sincerity he had never known existed. A woman he loved so much he would gladly risk his life for her. He smiled as he thought of Marianne. She was the most bewitching creature in every way. He could not wait to ask her to be his wife.

But he would have to wait, he thought ruefully as he glanced at the clock. He still had some ten minutes to wait before she was due to arrive. He could not pass the time in activity as, although almost recovered from his injury, he still needed to take things easy, and so he took out a book of maps.

The door opened. But before he could turn his head he heard a familiar and much-loved voice calling his name: 'Luke!'

He looked up in astonishment. But no, his ears had not deceived him. It was . . . yes, it really was . . . it was his beautiful young cousin who stood there, exactly as he had last seen her in revolutionary France. The same dark hair and velvety eyes; the same air and carriage, both being decidedly French; her head held high on her graceful neck and her gown, a simple yet elegant affair, revealing the only difference he could see in her – a sadly thinned body. But she was his Nicole for all that, his beloved cousin; the cousin he had thought he had lost to the guillotine. And she was safe.

He sprang out of his chair and strode across the room, taking her in his arms and joyfully crushing her to him, his arms wrapped tightly round her and his head buried in her hair. 'Nicole! Oh, what a joyous day this is, indeed!'

Outside the window, Marianne could not move. She had seen the young woman enter the room, seen Luke spring out of his chair and take the young woman in his arms. She had heard Luke's impassioned cry of *Nicole*! And it had left her devastated. She could not move; could not think; could only watch, as if mesmerized. Watch as Luke pulled away from Nicole, still holding her hands, and look her up and down. Watch as an unmistakable look of love spread over his face.

'Ah! What a beautiful sight, *n'est-ce-pas?*' came a voice at Marianne's shoulder.

Unbeknownst to her, Henri had handed the horses over to one of Luke's grooms and had joined her, standing just behind her.

'Young love; it is a beautiful sight,' sighed Henri. 'You 'ave feelings for Luke, Miss Marianne, I know, but you are too generous to grudge 'im this 'appiness: 'e thought 'e 'ad lost Nicole to the guillotine.'

Marianne could not reply. She could only stand there, frozen, watching Luke's love pour out over Nicole.

But then the thought of Miss Stock arriving stirred her.

She could not face an afternoon's tea with Luke. To make polite conversation, to congratulate him, perhaps. . . . She shuddered. No, it was something she could not do.

But she knew that if she did not act quickly she would be forced into it.

She scarcely knew how she managed to speak; nor how her voice managed to remain so calm. But somehow she managed it. 'As Lord Ravensford has other company, I think perhaps we should postpone our visit, and come back at another time.'

'*Mais oui*.' Henri, completely deceived by her manner, was quick to agree. 'I will go after the stable lad and retrieve the 'orses, and I will give 'im a message to send in to the 'ouse, that we are unable to keep the appointment. We will give Luke this time alone with Nicole.'

He disappeared, only to reappear a minute or two later with his own horse and Marianne's mare, and together they walked the horses down through the gardens.

'Miss Marianne . . .' said Henri thoughtfully. '*Mademoiselle*, if we tell Miss Stock the truth, it will be all round the neighbourhood before you know it, and Luke, 'e may not wish it to be known. It is a private matter, at least for now, so if you 'ave no objections, I will say Milord Ravensford sends 'is regrets, but 'e 'as some urgent business to attend to and cannot entertain visitors to tea.'

'Yes. Yes, Henri, whatever you think best.'

Marianne was not able to think clearly, and could do no more than listen with half an ear to the things Henri said. She was prepared to let him say whatever he thought best – indeed, she could not have stopped him even if she had wanted to, because she was too stunned with what she had just seen.

They reached the edge of the gardens and Henri cupped his hands together so that Marianne could mount. She moved awkwardly, but luckily Henri put her stiffness down to the cold. Another minute and they were riding back through the orchards to meet Miss Stock.

'Why, how unfortunate,' she exclaimed sympathetically, as Henri told her that Lord Ravensford was unavoidably engaged. 'But then, that is always the way with gentlemen. They have so many calls on their time. You are not too disappointed, I hope, my dear?' asked Miss Stock, turning to Marianne.

'No.' Marianne managed a semblance of a smile.

'Ah, well. It is a good thing your brother and future sister-in-law did not come after all.'

The ride back to Seaton Hall gave Marianne a chance to recover some of her composure. Miss Stock was not a natural horsewoman and made very little conversation whilst on horseback, a fact which allowed Marianne to restore herself to some semblance of calm. And calm was necessary. It was one thing to fool Henri and Miss Stock into thinking there was nothing wrong, but it would be quite another thing to try and fool Kit. Her brother had known her all her life, and was always able to tell when something was amiss. She would have to be extra vigilant during the rest of the afternoon and evening, to make sure he did not guess that she was disturbed. She did not want him to blame Luke for what had happened: Luke had done nothing wrong. No, all he had done was – what? What had he done?

Fallen in love with her? She had assumed so, but she had to acknowledge to herself that he had never said so.

Wanted to marry her? Again, she had assumed so, but he had never asked for her hand. She had thought he was going to declare himself the previous evening but she could not now even be sure of that. His important question could have been, 'Will you wish me happy on my marriage to Nicole?'

It must be, she told herself in her miserable state, that she had misread his feelings entirely, imagining that he was in love with her because she herself was so deeply in love with him.

In love with him.

Oh, yes, she was in love with him.

She had known it for some time.

He moved her in a way no other man had ever moved her. He matched her own unconventional nature with an unconventional nature of his own. He was anything but a gentleman, but then, she suspected she was anything but a lady. Oh, she was a lady in all the ways that truly mattered, she knew, but not in the superficial ways. She could not be meek or self-effacing. She could not stand by and pretend to be helpless when she was not. She could not flutter her eyelashes or pretend to be a simpleton. And Luke understood that. More, he admired her for it.

Or so she had thought.

But yes, she still thought it. He *did* admire her for her unconventional ways, she was sure of it.

It was just that admiration and love were two very different things.

Why, then, if he had not loved her, had he kissed her? she wondered, as they crossed the boundary between Billingsdale and Travis land. And not once, but so often?

But why shouldn't he? she thought, as she reminded herself again that he was anything but a gentleman. If he was not a gentleman, then how could she expect him to be governed by a gentleman's standards of behaviour? She couldn't. He was like the first earls he had openly admitted it. He saw what he wanted and he took it. And what he had wanted was her.

But wanting and loving were worlds apart.

The worst of it was that, although she had known from the first what he was, yet she still had not realized her danger. He *was* anything but a gentleman; she had told him so at their first meeting, and he had not disagreed; and she had suffered the consequences.

Even so, she thought, as they began the approach to the house, she had no one to blame but herself.

Dapple began to strain at the bit. She was nearing her stable and knew she was on the last leg of the ride. Marianne slackened the rein slightly, giving Dapple a little more freedom.

The one thing she was thankful for, she thought, as she clattered into the stable yard, was that she had told no one of her feelings, not even Kit – although she suspected he had guessed – and she still had her pride to sustain her, at least for the next few hours. After that, she could give way to her feelings. But not now. Not yet. Now, she must not think of it. For the rest of the day, however impossible it seemed, she must put it out of her mind.

And yet, how could she, when the image of him holding Nicole was playing itself endlessly before her? she wondered, as the stable lad helped her to dismount; alternating with the even more painful image of him looking at the Frenchwoman with an expression of pure love? Nicole, whom he must have known long before he had met Marianne; Nicole, whom he had thought he had lost to the guillotine.

It would have been a romantic story if it had not been so devastatingly painful, Marianne thought.

But she must not dwell on it. She must be able to offer Miss Stock a dish of tea when they went indoors as though nothing was wrong, and then listen to Kit and Adèle's plans for their wedding with interest, so as not to spoil a happy occasion for two of the people she cared about most in the world.

She felt her anguish imperceptibly lessen as she led the way into the Hall, soothed by her familiar surrounding. She had lost the terrible numbness that had gripped her, and felt equal to at least pretending to be calm. She invited Miss Stock into the drawing-room and soon afterwards they were joined by the Reverend Mr Stock, Mr Travis, Kit and Adèle.

'Marianne, you're back early,' said Kit, giving her a quizzical look.

'Yes, was it not a shame?' asked Miss Stock, fortunately saving Marianne from the necessity of speaking. 'Lord Ravensford had to attend to some urgent business, and our tea party had to be put off.'

'A good thing you didn't go, then,' said Mr Travis to his son. 'You'd have had a wasted journey, and so would the good reverend.' He turned to Miss Stock. 'Your brother has been giving us the benefit of his wisdom in arranging the order of service and in choosing the hymns,' he told her.

'Oh, good, Sebastian. I'm so glad you've been of use.'

'And then it'll be your turn, eh, miss?' said her father teasingly, turning to Marianne. 'With that new ball gown Madame LaTour's making for you, you'll soon find a husband, eh, Marianne?'

Her father's well-intentioned joviality could not have come at a worse time. She flushed, but fortunately her father took it for maidenly modesty and turned his attention back to the reverend.

'You'll stay for dinner, Reverend?' he asked. 'And Miss Stock, of course,' he said, making a courtly bow in Miss Stock's direction.

'Alas, no,' said the Reverend Mr Stock with genuine regret: the smells emanating from the kitchen were already making his mouth water. 'I'm afraid I am seeing Mr and Mrs Thwaite at seven and I mustn't disappoint them.'

'Another time, then,' said Mr Travis courteously.

He went out into the hall with the reverend and his sister, to see them on their way.

As soon as he had left the room, Kit went over to Marianne. 'Is anything wrong, Mari?' he asked.

She put a smile on her face. 'No. Of course not. What could be wrong? Now, if you'll excuse me, I must change out of my riding habit. I would have done it sooner, but I did not like to abandon Miss Stock.'

And with that she left the room.

Kit, puzzled, looked after her.

'What is it?' asked Adèle, going over to him and taking his arm.

'I don't know. It's just that, there seems to be something wrong with Marianne. I wonder if Luke was really out, or—'

'You cannot solve a lover's quarrel,' she said gently. 'If Marianne and Luke 'ave indeed 'ad a falling out, they must solve it on their own. You cannot do it for them, Kit – no matter 'ow much you might wish it.'

Kit sighed, covering her hand with his own. 'You're right, my love. We have had our fair share of problems, and our love is stronger because of them. Marianne and Luke must find their own way, too.'

CHAPTER TWELVE

*M*arianne found it very difficult to concentrate over the next, dragging, days. The time should have been enjoyable, consisting as it did of making preparations for the ball, and not just any ball, but a ball that was being held to celebrate her brother's betrothal. But she could not prevent her thoughts returning again and again to Luke. If only she could have disliked him it would have made it so much easier, giving her a vent for her turbulent emotions. But even now she could not dislike him, because he had never lied to her. He had never told her he loved her. He had never deceived her. The love, she now had to admit to herself, had been on her side only.

Or if only she could have disliked Nicole. But how could she dislike a beautiful young woman who had never intentionally done her any harm, and who had not only endured the terrors of revolutionary France but had also narrowly escaped the guillotine?

No; even in her pain she could not be so unreasonable.

The one thing which made it easier for her was the fact that she did not have to see Luke and Nicole together. In fact, she did not even have to see Luke. Kit was too preoccupied with his own concerns to visit his friend, and as Luke himself did not come to call she was spared the painful necessity of congratulating him on his happiness whilst she was suffering inside. She had been half-expecting it to begin with, jumping every time she heard the sound of a carriage and steeling herself to face the coming ordeal with calm. But he never came.

The reason for that, however, was soon explained: Miss Stock, visiting with the Reverend Mr Stock, revealed that Lord Ravensford had gone to London.

'Although what he can be doing there I'm sure I don't know,' said Miss Stock, who enjoyed a harmless gossip. 'Perhaps it is connected with the business that compelled him to cancel our tea party.'

Marianne's mind jumped to the most likely cause of his business, thinking that he must have gone to London in order to get a special licence so that he and Nicole could be married immediately.

She was numb.

'Per'aps you are mistaken,' said Adèle to Miss Stock, noticing that Marianne had gone suddenly pale.

'No, my dear, for I had it from my cook, who had it from Lord Ravensford's Mrs Hill. He has gone to London on some urgent business, my cook says. But never you mind, my dear Adèle: Mrs Hill says he will be back in time for your engagement ball.'

Excusing herself once the Stocks had left, saying she had a headache, Marianne sought her room, too distressed to be in company. It's for the best, she told herself resolutely, in the privacy of her own room. When he has the special licence they will be married, and then I can accustom myself to it. Once it is a *fait accompli* I must.

But her heart was dying inside her.

Lord Ravensford returned. No marriage took place.

Marianne did not know whether this made it easier or harder. In a way it made it easier because, although she kept telling herself that she would adjust to the situation once Luke was married, she knew it was not true; she knew she would never accustom herself

191

to it. But in a way it made it harder, too. The constant state of tension she was in was making her miserable. Every time she heard Luke's name mentioned she thought she was going to hear of his marriage and her heart started to pound; every time the word 'wedding' was mentioned – which, as her brother was shortly to be married, was at least a dozen times a day – she thought it was Luke's wedding she was going to be called upon to talk about.

But the days passed and no word of any wedding came.

It was a puzzle.

But perhaps he had decided not to marry at once, after all, she told herself. Perhaps he had decided he would rather wait until he could return to his own estate.

The idea gave her some relief. If he and Nicole married on his own estate she would not need to see them together, and would not even need to offer them her congratulations. And once he was out of the neighbourhood then Marianne felt there was at least a chance that, in time, she would be able to – if not forget him at least accept in some measure that he would never be a part of her life again.

She would have to.

In the meantime, she had to pretend, for her brother's sake, and for the sake of Adèle, that she was happy and contented. She would not spoil their happiness for all the world. But it was extremely hard.

'Ah! *Mademoiselle*! You look beautiful! Your 'usband-to-be is a lucky man, *n'est-ce-pa?*' said Madame LaTour to Adèle, a week after the abortive tea party, as she put the final touches to Adèle and Marianne's ball gowns.

Adèle swished from side to side, happily regarding herself in the cheval glass.

'What do you think?' Adèle asked Marianne. 'Will Kit like it?'

'He'll be enchanted,' said Marianne with a smile.

Adèle did indeed look lovely in her ballgown, the white silk skirt of which swished around her feet. The jonquil stripes on the bodice and sleeves suited her olive complexion.

'And you, *mademoiselle*, you like your gown too?' asked Madame LaTour.

'Yes. Yes, it's lovely,' said Marianne.

Her gown, with its delicate blue stripes, brought out the full beauty of her eyes, and flattered her figure in the most delightful way. The tight waist accentuated her slender figure and the scoop neckline revealed the most delectable morsel of creamy breast. But its delights were quite lost on her today.

'*Eh bien*, it suits you,' said Madame LaTour with her head on one side. 'But it is *un peu* too big. You 'ave lost weight since last time I saw you, I think.'

She adjusted the bodice slightly before sitting back on her heels with an air of satisfaction. 'Now, we need only a ribbon to trim it, like so' – she held a ribbon up against the gown – 'and then it will be complete.'

'It's so good of Godfather, to spend all this money on my clothes, and on the ball,' said Adèle to Marianne, as they changed back into their day dresses. 'I know, things, they 'ave not been easy for him.' She tried not to look at the peeling piece of wallpaper in the corner of the room as she spoke.

'What better to spend it on than your betrothal?' said Marianne. She looked out of the window. 'I used to be passionately devoted to the estate, and when I thought that Papa had had to sell off a large parcel of land to pay Kit's gambling debts I was angry. But when I discovered what the money had really been used for I was glad. And I am glad now that papa is to sell off another parcel of land so that he can restore the house to its former glory – or even better, for I'm sure he means you to take a hand.'

Adèle blushed prettily at the idea of furnishing and decorating her future home, and at Marianne's obvious belief that her natural taste would be an asset during the renovations.

'And he means to hire a full complement of servants, too,' went on Marianne, 'so you will be comfortable in your married life.'

'I am so grateful to 'im,' said Adèle simply. ' 'E is so good to me.'

'And so he should be. You are going to be his daughter, you know!'

Adèle gave a happy smile. 'Oh, Marianne, it is like a dream come true.' She hesitated. 'I 'ope, one day, you can be as 'appy.'

Marianne hesitated, then deciding it was better to avoid the painful subject she said, 'Come, let's go downstairs. We still need to help Henri finalize the plans for the ball supper. And then there are the musicians to arrange.'

Only one last effort, thought Marianne as she looked at herself in the cheval glass, and then the ball will be over and things will return to normal. I will not have to see Luke again.

She pinched her cheeks to put a little colour in them – her father had commented once or twice recently on how pale she was looking, and she did not want to give him any cause for concern – and then went downstairs.

Kit and Adèle were already waiting in the hall, together with her father, and as she reached the bottom of the stairs her father had just time to say, 'Marianne! You look lovely, my dear,' before the guests began to arrive.

The Cosgroves were the first to enter, wreathed in smiles. They greeted Marianne and her father warmly, then turned their attention to Kit and Adèle, delighted to hear how Kit had rescued his love from the jaws of revolutionary France. Jennifer, on her best behaviour because she had been allowed to attend the formal ball, was eager in her congratulations, and Jem clapped Kit on the back.

Then came the Stocks, and behind them the Pargeters and Kents; until soon the house was ringing with the lively chatter of dozens of guests.

'Well, my boy, I think it's time for you to lead your lovely young bride-to-be out to dance,' said Mr Travis, turning to Kit.

Marianne breathed a silent sigh of relief. Lord Ravensford had not arrived, and it seemed he did not mean to come. Although her heart sank, her courage rose. It would make it much easier for her to enjoy the evening if she did not have to see Luke with Nicole: that would have tested her to the limit, and been very hard to bear. But now she could relax, and put all her energies into making sure that Kit and Adèle had a night to remember.

Kit, however, seemed surprisingly reluctant to leave the foot of the stairs and formally open the dancing with his fiancée. Instead of falling in with his father's suggestion he fidgeted and looked at the door. 'Not just yet, Papa.'

'Not just yet?' asked Mr Travis in surprise, wondering why his son should be so reluctant to dance with Adèle, who was looking positively radiant.

'No. There's something . . . someone. . . . Ah!' He gave a sigh of satisfaction, his eyes riveted on the door.

Marianne, too, turned towards the door, which had opened one more time, to admit a party of four people, all beautifully dressed.

'Luke!' she breathed. Against all reason her heart leapt as she saw him, and then fell as she saw that, on his arm, was Nicole. But there were two more people with him . . . two people who looked. . . .

'Mama! Papa!' With a cry Adèle rushed forwards, and threw her arms round the necks of two middle-aged people who had run towards her.

Marianne, taking in the scene with joyful surprise, felt a surge of happiness for her friend; a surge which almost, but not quite, counteracted her pain at seeing Luke standing next to Nicole.

'You did it,' said Kit, with a catch in his throat, turning to Luke.

'Yes.' Luke's dark smile was genuine, with no trace of his usual mockery.

'*You* did this?' asked Marianne, turning towards him, all else forgotten in the joy of the moment. 'Oh, thank you, Luke!'

His eyes danced. 'You never suspected? I was sure you must have guessed what had been keeping me away.'

'No ... I ... that is ... no, I had no idea,' she said, with another delighted glance at Adèle, who was chattering away ten to the dozen in French and embracing her parents over and over again.

'Quite by chance, I discovered a possible lead to the *comte* and Marie- Anne's whereabouts and went up to town to see if I could find them.'

'So that's why you went,' she remarked in surprise.

'Yes, of course. Why did you think?'

'I— Never mind what I thought. But go on,' she said, determined not to lose the happiness of the moment by dwelling on more painful things. Her composure was not helped, however, by the way Luke's dark eyes were roving over her, drinking her in as though he had been parted from her for a year, instead of only weeks.

'That gown is new,' he said. His eyes dropped to her bare neck and throat and lingered on the delicate swell of her breasts, which could just be glimpsed before they disappeared decorously beneath her bodice. And then they dropped again, taking in the elegance of her figure which was accentuated by the gown's stylish cut.

She flushed, perplexed at his manner. She had expected him to be distant with her; brotherly, perhaps; but not like this. Not acting as though nothing had changed between them. 'Yes.' She replied to his comment, hoping to keep their conversation in practical channels. That way, she hoped, she would be able to talk to him without disgracing herself.

'It suits you,' he said, his eyes looking directly into her own. 'It makes you look even more beautiful.'

196

She flushed, and dropped her eyes. 'Don't.' The word came out huskily, and there was a catch in her throat.

'Why not?' He looked amused. 'Why should I not say what is true?'

'But you were telling me . . . about Adèle's parents.' She made a valiant effort to turn the subject back into less painful channels. She could not understand why he was complimenting her, and she felt confused. So that she wanted to talk of other things instead.

'Of course.' His eyes left hers with reluctance and went to the happy scene. 'Once in London, it was surprisingly easy to track them down. They had gone to London so that they could arrange for a rescue party to go after Adèle. They had already organized one fruitless search and were about to organize another, with the *comte* going himself, when I managed to find them. You can imagine their joy when they discovered that Adèle was safe and well. After that, it was easy to arrange the journey to Sussex. They would have been here days ago, but Adèle's mother had a slight indisposition and they had to delay their start. But now all is well: their family is back together again.'

'Yes, all is well,' said Marianne, watching her friend, forgetting in the joy of the moment that all was far from well with her.

Until there came a delicate cough, and looking round she saw Nicole.

If only she could have disliked the young Frenchwoman, she thought with a stab of pain. But Nicole had such a sweet expression that Marianne, knowing all she had been through, could not take against her.

'And now, Marianne, there is someone very special I would like to introduce to you,' said Luke. 'Marianne – Miss Travis – may I present Mademoiselle Fancheau – Nicole.'

'How do you do?' The polite words, calmly uttered, cost Marianne every ounce of self control.

Although they sounded completely unnatural to her own ears,

apparently they sounded perfectly all right to everyone else, because Nicole smiled prettily and said, 'Enchanted,' whilst Luke looked on with pride.

'Nicole is—' he began.

But he was interrupted by Jem Cosgrove's cry of relief 'Marianne! There you are! Quick, or we shall miss the start.'

Jem, Marianne's first partner for the evening, hurried into the hall looking harassed, and almost before Marianne had excused herself, he had whisked her into the ballroom and begun determinedly to dance.

As she caught sight of herself in one of the gilded mirrors that lined the ballroom, Marianne was relieved that he had done so. There were lines of strain around her mouth, and she felt that another minute of being polite to Nicole would have been more than she would have been able to stand. But now she could at least begin to recover herself. The steps of the dance were reassuring, the music soothing, and her strain began to gradually lessen. Now that she had been introduced to Nicole she would not have to speak to the young Frenchwoman again, she reasoned with herself. She need only avoid Nicole and Luke for the rest of the evening and all would be well.

Although that still did not explain Luke's attentive manner. . . .

Could it be, she wondered . . . but no. That was just wishful thinking. She had seen the look of love on his face when he had embraced Nicole, and Henri had seen it, too. 'Young love, it is beautiful,' he had said. She must not make too much of Luke's manner, which was most probably just the jubilant air of a man in love.

By the time the dance was over, she had recovered much of her composure, and a glass of punch gave her the strength she needed to move on to the next dance. Fortunately the ball was a formal one, and as she had deliberately filled in her card before the ball had begun she would not be forced to dance with Luke. Knowing him to be in love with Nicole, that would have been something she would have been unable to bear.

During the course of the evening she danced with almost every eligible young man in the neighbourhood, as well as many of the elderly gentlemen, and then with Jem again, She was about to dance with Lance Gutheridge when she saw him reeling towards the card room and realized with a sudden sinking feeling that the young fool had had too much to drink – which left her standing at the edge of the dance floor without a partner, and with Luke striding across the room towards her.

With an impoliteness born of desperation, she seized Jem, who happened to be passing by, and cajoled him into taking her on to the floor. It was highly irregular – she should not be dancing more than twice with any young man – but she had no choice: she could not bear to dance with Luke. To hear him speaking of Nicole, to listen to him telling her how happy he was – no, it was impossible.

She saw Luke's look of frustration, but he could do nothing about it and fell back as the music began.

Marianne tried to look as though she was enjoying herself. She smiled and made an effort to entertain Jem with her conversation, but all the time she was afraid of what would happen when the dance was over: there had been a determined look on Luke's face that told her she would not be able to avoid him for ever.

As the dance drew to an end she was relieved to see that Luke had been buttonholed by the *comte*. She herself had had no opportunity as yet to speak to him. She had wanted to greet him, for the *comte* was her godfather as her own Papa was godfather to Adèle, but she had generously held back so that Adèle could have her parents to herself for a while. Once she had the opportunity, though, she meant to hug him and hold him and hear all about his perils in getting out of France – as she wanted to talk to Marie-Anne.

But for now that would have to wait. The *comte* was busy with

Luke, and Marie-Anne was still chattering lovingly to Adèle.

Marianne, however, felt she could face no more company for a little while. Overcome by heat and fatigue, she decided to slip out of the ballroom. The musicians were tuning their instruments and she knew she would have a few minutes to catch her breath before the next dance began. The hall was cool, but it was also full of guests who were milling about with glasses in their hands, and Marianne felt a need for solitude – her exertions to appear lively and at ease had taken their toll. She made for the library and slipped inside, glad to find herself alone.

She walked over to the bookshelves and began idly running her fingers along the spines of the well-loved books. But after a minute or two she began to be aware that there was someone in the next room. The library adjoined her father's study, and the inter-connecting door between the two rooms was not properly closed. Not wanting to overhear a private conversation, she moved towards the door, meaning to close it fully, when her attention was caught by one of the voices. It belonged to her godfather, the *comte*. A minute later she heard Luke's voice. She stood, frozen, too surprised to move. Their conversation was becoming heated.

'You must marry 'er,' the *comte* was saying. 'By your own admission you 'ave compromised 'er—'

'The circumstances were difficult,' Luke was responding reasonably. 'The situation made it impossible for us to have a chaperon.'

'That is no excuse. If her father were 'ere 'e would tell you so 'imself. As 'e is not, I regard myself as taking 'is place. You must marry 'er. Your own conscience must tell you so.'

'I'm not going to marry a woman I don't love,' growled Luke. 'Particularly when I am in love with another—'

'Pah! You must give 'er up. You must do the honourable thing—'

Marianne could bear it no longer. Her frozenness having left her, she crept back from the door. She had been intending to close

200

it, but she feared she could not do so without drawing attention to herself, and in light of what she had just unwillingly overheard she could not face being discovered: her godfather, telling Luke he must marry her because he had compromised her. She could not bear it. Thank God, Luke had refused. If he had proposed to her out of love it would have fulfilled her most precious desires, but if he proposed to her out of duty, because he had compromised her on board ship – she could not bear to even think about it.

She went over to the library door, but the sound of conversation from the hall outside made her loath to leave the room. She had privacy and solitude in the library, and just at the moment she needed them. She could take a few minutes to master her emotions before going back out into company.

After a little while she felt she could face her father's guests again. She was about to return to the ballroom when the door opened abruptly and to her horror, standing framed in the doorway, was Luke.

'So this is where you are hiding,' he said with a smile.

'Lord . . . Lord Ravensford,' she said, trying to keep her voice even.

'Lord Ravensford?' he asked softly, coming into the room. 'Marianne, we have gone far beyond that.'

'Don't . . .' she said, stepping back as he approached her. Surely he had not given in? she wondered, confused by his manner. Surely he did not now intend to propose?

'Don't what?' he asked in surprise.

'Don't come any nearer.'

He halted, puzzled. 'Why not?'

'Because. . . .'

'Yes?'

'Because it would not be wise.'

'Wise?' He gave a wolfish smile and took a step towards her. 'When have we ever been wise?' The old, familiar seductive tone

201

was back in his voice. He took her hands and kissed them, and with the greatest of efforts Marianne wrenched them away.

'Don't,' she almost shouted at him.

He frowned. 'Marianne. . . .'

'No, Luke . . . Lord Ravensford . . . don't.' She took a shuddering breath to gather her thoughts and steady her nerve. If he proposed to her now she would break down, she knew she would. And so she said the first thing she could think of that would prevent it; at the same time leaving him to marry his real love – free to marry Nicole.

'Did . . . did you not wonder why I danced with Jem Cosgrove three times this evening?' she asked.

He gave a wry smile. 'I can't say I was counting.'

'There . . . there is a reason.' She hurried on before he had time to speak. 'It is not permissible for a young lady to dance more than twice with the same gentleman, but you see, there is a reason for it; Jem has asked me to marry him.'

'Old news,' said Luke with a predatory smile.

Marianne shook her head. 'I mean he has asked me again, this evening,' she lied. 'And . . . I said "yes".'

'You said . . . *what?*' The last word came out half amused, half incredulous. 'Marianne, you can't be serious. No, it must be a joke. Marry Jem Cosgrove? Throw away all your life and vitality on a bumbling creature like Jem – and no, don't upbraid me for saying it. I know he is a good young man; decent; honourable; and I admire him for it. But he is not the husband for you, and you know it. You are roasting me . . . unless you have had too much to drink?' he asked teasingly. 'The punch *is* rather overpowering.'

'Certainly not,' she retorted, wishing he would not make it so difficult for her, and wondering why indeed he wanted to. She had expected him to be delighted at this way out of his predicament. 'I fail to see why it is so impossible that I should marry Jem,' she said, lifting her chin. 'He is, as you say, decent and honourable. He also comes from a well-established family, and would make any young lady a good husband.'

'Dear God, you're serious. What has happened—?'

'Luke?' a musical voice came from the open doorway. 'It is nearly time for us to go into supper, *mon cousin.*'

Marianne was about to turn away when she caught Nicole's final words. *'Mon . . cousin?'*

'Yes, of course, *mon cousin,*' said Luke in surprise. 'You speak French, Marianne, you know what *mon cousin* means. . . .' His voice tailed away as he realized the implication of her words. 'But that's not what you thought, is it?' he asked incredulously. 'Dear Lord, you didn't think Nicole was my cousin, you thought . . . what exactly did you think?' he asked, his eyes becoming hard.

'I thought. . . .' She looked at him perplexedly, finding it too much to take in.

Nicole, all but forgotten by the doorway, realized that she had stumbled into an intimate conversation, and murmured, 'I will wait for you in the ballroom,' and discreetly left the room closing the door behind her.

'Yes?' he demanded, his eyes kindling. 'Just what the hell did you think?'

'You have no right to speak to me like that,' she said, her emotions a confused mix of relief, surprise, elation, and resentment, together with a whirl of other emotions that she could not begin to separate or understand.

'I have every right.' He was across the room in two strides, holding her by the arms, his eyes boring down into her own. 'We shared everything a man and woman can share, bar one – and even that we almost shared – and you tell me I have no right to be angry when you think I presented you to my whore?'

'I never said that,' she returned, pulling herself free and facing him, her own eyes kindling. 'I never even thought it.'

'Then what did you think?' he demanded.

'I saw your face, Luke,' she said, eyes flashing with anger at what she saw as his determination to put her in the wrong; not seeing the hurt that was all but consuming him because he thought the woman he loved – the woman he had thought loved him – did not trust him; and without trust, how could there be love? 'When I rode over to the Manor, when we were meant to be taking tea with you, I saw Nicole walk into the room; I saw you get up to greet her; I saw you hold her; I saw your face – I saw love in your face.'

'You thought I was *in love* with her?' he said, aghast.

'What else could I think?' she demanded.

'You thought that when I took you in my arms over the last few weeks I was in love with someone else?'

'Why not?' she demanded, driven on the defensive. 'You are anything but a gentleman. You told me so yourself.'

'By God, Marianne, I may not be a gentleman, but I'm not a cur! I don't go around seducing gently reared young ladies for my own perverted amusement. What do you take me for?' he demanded, his own hurt driving his anger.

'I never thought that. You're putting words into my mouth again!'

'Then what did you think?'

'I thought you were in love with her, but believed her to be dead. And then when she came back into your life . . . when you discovered that she had not gone to the guillotine, that she was safe . . . it was as Henri said, I couldn't—'

'Henri? What has he to do with all this?'

'He was with me when I saw you. He told me he knew I had feelings for you, but that young love was a beautiful thing and that I couldn't spoil your happiness . . . he said you thought you had lost Nicole to the guillotine—'

'And you really think I would have abandoned her, if I had been in love with her? That I would have forgotten her because I *thought* she had gone to the guillotine? That I wouldn't have gone over to France and found out for sure? That I would have been content to think that the woman I was in love with *might* be dead, and therefore I might as well forget her and move on to the next? My God, Marianne, what do you think I am?' His hurt was threatening to consume him.

'You're twisting things,' she declared. 'I thought. . . .'

'You thought I had so little loyalty in me that I would forget a woman I was in love with, who might or might not be dead, inside of three months, and make love to someone else – and then go back to the first – with never a word to the second – when I discovered quite by chance that she was still alive. Dear God, Marianne, it's lucky I didn't have a chance to ask you to marry me. With so little trust and understanding between us our marriage would have been a disaster.'

She was about to make a hot reply when the door opened and the drunken Lance Gutheridge wandered into the room. He stood by the doorway, clutching the knob for support, and looked at them with unfocused eyes.

'Shouldn't be here,' he said in slurred speech. 'Should be going into supper. Looking for you, Miss Travis. And you, too, Ravensford. You've been missed.'

'Pull yourself together, man. You're drunk,' said Luke in disgust.

'May be drunk, but at least I'm not having a lover's quarrel at the top of my voice. Surprised the whole house hasn't heard.'

'This lover's quarrel, as you refer to it, is at an end,' said Luke bitingly. And without so much as one last look at Marianne he strode from the room.

'Miss Travis?' enquired Mr Gutheridge with a hiccup. 'Time for supper. I'm to escort you in.'

Marianne, already seething with a deep sense of injustice, did not want to deal with her escort's drunkenness, but unless she wanted to risk him making a scene she had no choice but to accompany him. Once seated at the supper-table she knew he would not cause her any problems. She would be able to converse with her neighbours and leave the drunken Mr Gutheridge to the expert management of her father.

As she walked with him into the supper-room, doing her best to keep him upright so that he should not disgrace himself, she was still a prey to a turbulent mix of emotions. How could Luke have said such things? she asked herself angrily. The joy she had felt when she had discovered that he was not in love with Nicole – although the discovery left her perplexed as to the meaning of the conversation she had unwillingly overheard between Luke and her godfather – had given way to a sense of deep injustice. How could he have left the room before she had had a chance to defend herself? The fact that Mr Gutheridge had interrupted them was no excuse. He had accused her of a lack of trust, and had then walked out before she had had a chance to speak. If he had ever told her that he loved her it would have been different. Then he would have had a right to be angry; then he would have had a right to accuse her of a lack of trust. But not as things stood. Not when he had never told her he loved her. And he had not even told her now. Despite everything they had shared, no word of love had ever passed his lips. Even when he had been about to propose to her, she recalled, he had said nothing of love. How then could he blame her for having accepted the evidence of her own eyes? Especially when she thought of Henri's misleading words. And when she thought of the fact that Luke had done nothing in the intervening time to explain matters to her.

She felt a twinge of guilt as she realized that it was not fair of her to blame him for not having used the intervening time to explain: he had been looking for Adèle's parents – and finding them.

Even so, to blame her so unjustly for her natural fears and anxieties and, after she had witnessed the unmistakable look of love on his face when he held Nicole, to label them a lack of trust . . . it was something she found very hard to forgive.

She had by now entered the supper-room. The tables gleamed with damask cloths; the crystal sparkled; the silver shone. But despite the brilliance of the scene she was aware of only one thing: Luke's brooding presence at the other end of the table.

She tried hard to keep her mind on other things. She reminded herself that Tom and Trudie's arms had been aching from polishing all the silver, and that Henri had put all his ingenuity into devising a sumptuous meal. She told herself this was Kit and Adèle's evening, and that, no matter what her feelings, she must not show her distress. But no matter how lively the conversation around her, no matter how imaginative the soup or how succulent the rib of beef, she could think of nothing but Luke, and the estrangement that had grown up between them.

But there was nothing she could do about it. She could only laugh and smile, and pretend to be light-hearted and at ease; whilst all the while her smile was fixed and her stomach was tied in knots.

CHAPTER THIRTEEN

*M*arianne rose early. Despite the fact that she had only gone to bed six hours before she was not tired; rather she was filled with a restless energy that would not let her sleep. She had passed a troubled night. Spells of dozing had alternated with long periods of wakefulness, and whether waking or sleeping she had been plagued with memories of the perplexing conversation she had overheard between her godfather and Luke. What had been the meaning of it? she asked herself for what seemed like the hundredth time.

'You must marry 'er,' the *comte* had said. 'If 'er father were 'ere 'e would tell you so 'imself. As 'e is not, I regard myself as taking 'is place.'

And Luke's angry refusal – 'I'm not going to marry a woman I don't love. Particularly when I'm in love with another—'

It had all seemed so clear at the time: her godfather telling Luke to marry her because he had compromised her on the ship, where she had not had the benefit of a chaperon; and Luke refusing because he was in love with another woman. Yes, it had all seemed so obvious.

But that was when things had started to get out of hand.

Luke's coming into the library to ask her to marry him she had thought she understood – Luke had a strong character, but her godfather could be very persuasive. She had thought he had convinced Luke to offer for her in order to protect her reputation. But then Luke's frowns when she had told him she was engaged to Jem she had not been able to fathom. She had expected him to be pleased. It would have given him an easy way out of a difficult situation. But instead of being pleased he had first of all been incredulous and then extremely angry. He had berated her, and been angry with her for believing him to be in love with Nicole. But she had seen the look of love on his face as he had folded Nicole in his arms. How was she meant to have known that Nicole was his cousin? There was no way she could have known it.

But even with that part of the muddle sorted out she still could not understand the rest of it. He had behaved as though she meant everything to him, and how wonderful it would be if she did. But how could that be? If she really meant everything to him then he would not have refused to marry her when the *comte* had told him he must; and he would not have said, 'I'm in love with another.'

It was just too puzzling. She had tried to solve the riddle all night, but she had failed. And now she must do what she could to forget about it, before she drove herself mad.

At last, daylight broke through the crack in her drapes, and dressing herself quickly – a difficult task, since she did not want to disturb Trudie, and therefore had to manage her hooks and buttons alone, and dispense with her corset, which it was simply impossible for her to manage without help – she went downstairs, slipping out of the door into the grey morning. She felt too restless to stay inside, and longed for a ride. The fresh air and exercise would do her good, and perhaps help to soothe her troubled spirit.

Before long she was in the stables, and then, mounting Dapple, she set out for the seashore. Dapple was a little sluggish to begin with, but the mare soon began to enjoy herself, and by the time they had crossed the fields to the seashore both horse and rider were feeling better.

The beach was spread out before them, a vast expanse of dampened sand. The tide was almost out.

Marianne walked Dapple to the edge of the beach and then dismounted, using a boulder as a mounting block. She tethered the mare loosely so that the animal could wander about a little and nibble the coarse sea grass, before taking off her boots and stockings and walking across the sand towards the sea.

The sound of the waves was calming. She went right to the water's edge, letting it wash over her feet. It was cool and refreshing. The sun was up, and had a considerable amount of strength for the time of year. She stood there for some minutes, watching the receding mass of blue water, which was touched with patches that sparkled in the early morning sun.

Would she ever understand the events of last night? she wondered.

She shook her head, and then turned and walked slowly along the beach.

Luke was slouching in a wing-back chair in the library, his manner dark and brooding. He had not been to bed that night. By the time he had returned from the Travis's it was already after two o'clock and he had not felt like sleeping: he had had a hell of a night. He had finally had an opportunity to offer Marianne his hand, and what had happened? Had she agreed? Had she told him she wanted more than anything else in the world to be his wife? Had she melted into his arms, giving herself up to him with words of love and longing?

He gave a harsh bark of laughter. No indeed. Nothing could have been further from the truth.

She had first of all told him she was engaged to Jem Cosgrove – Jem Cosgrove! – and had then insulted him deeply by telling him she knew he was in love with Nicole. Nicole! His cousin, of all people! How could she have had so little faith in him? Had she really believed that he would go straight from the arms of one woman to another?

If he had not been in love, then yes, she might have been right – although never by taking advantage of a gently bred young lady. He was a man with all a man's instincts and appetites. But once he had fallen in love? Once he had given his heart and, but for an interruption, his hand?

How could she think it?

But underlying his anger was something far worse; a very real pain. He felt betrayed. He had believed in Marianne utterly – hadn't he laughed when she had told him she was engaged to Jem Cosgrove? – and yet she had not believed in him. She had thought he was in love with Nicole. And so he had stormed at her, telling her that, as she did not believe in him, it was a good thing they had not become betrothed.

But it wasn't. It wasn't a good thing at all. He loved her. God, how he loved her. Why had she not trusted him? At the very least given him the benefit of the doubt?

He had passed the night in an angry state of mind and, as the darkness finally gave way before the new day, he felt no better. After all they had shared, for him to find that Marianne had no faith in him, in his love for her; it hit him hard.

At last, he began to stir. The house was coming to life all around him and he felt he must rouse himself. The servants were already up and about, starting the new day. He went out into the hall – and there was Nicole, coming down the stairs, looking so fresh and innocent. Who would have believed she could be the cause of so much pain?

But it was not her fault. Nicole was the one good thing in his life at the moment, the one happiness. Her escape from France was his one source of unalloyed contentment.

He met her at the bottom of the stairs and went forward to greet her, putting his arms around her and embracing her as she

211

turned up her face trustingly to his and gave him a kiss on the cheek. As he held her close, he happened to catch sight of himself in one of the gilded mirrors that hung on the wall.

He froze.

This was the scene Marianne had witnessed. This was how she had seen him embracing Nicole.

What was it she had said to him? 'I saw love in your face.'

Yes, she had seen love. He was seeing it himself now, reflected back at him in the glass: his arms around Nicole and an expression on his face of love.

Good God! No wonder she had felt betrayed.

And he had blamed her for it, he thought with a twist of his mouth.

How could he have done anything so monstrous? he wondered, as he gently pushed Nicole away from him.

For the first time he saw their argument of the previous evening from Marianne's point of view. She had drawn an obvious conclusion from something she had seen, and what had he done? Explained it to her? Reassured her? Told her that Nicole was his cousin, and that although he loved the young Frenchwoman dearly he was not *in love* with her? That he could only ever be *in love* with Marianne?

No.

In fact, he had never told her he was in love with her at all.

The realization hit him with full force.

He had never once told her he loved her.

And yet he had railed at her; accused her of a lack of trust. He had told her that as there was so little understanding between them it was a good thing they were not to marry. He cursed himself. So little understanding! Of course there was so little understanding between them, he thought grimly. How could there be any understanding between them when he had never told her about his feelings for her? And when, realizing she had been shaken by something she had seen, he had refused to explain? When he had never told her anything about Nicole?

He had been a fool.

'I have to go out,' he said to Nicole. 'I shall be probably be gone for most of the morning.'

'*Ah! Bon,*' said Nicole. 'You wish to see Marianne? I understand.'

'Make yourself at home. Enjoy your morning. I hope I shall be back before lunch.'

'*Oui.*'

Taking his leave of her, Luke strode out to the stables and saddled his horse.

Marianne was walking along the beach. Shells and pieces of driftwood scattered the sand between low and high water marks, and here and there gulls stalked, looking for food. Finally she felt she had found a little peace. Until she saw, as yet far off, a horseman, and recognized him immediately as Luke.

He had had the same idea as her, it seemed, and had ridden down to the beach, was her first thought. But no. They were on Travis land. Had he ridden out here, then, specially to find her?

Seeing him dismount and stride towards her across the sand she was filled with a sudden awkwardness. Part of her wanted to run towards him, and part of her wanted to run away. . . .

With difficulty she fought down the urge to run and stood still, although filled with a strange restlessness, waiting for him to reach her. She must be cool; calm, no matter how much her heart felt to be in her throat.

'Marianne,' he said as he approached her.

'Lord Ravensford,' she replied.

There was a moment of awkwardness. He looked at her. She looked at him. And suddenly their misunderstandings meant nothing. Communing on a level where words were unnecessary, as they had done before, they instinctively knew that nothing else mattered; nothing except their love for each other.

Luke smiled, the old, wicked smile which set her pulse racing and made her legs turn weak. And then he swept her into his arms and kissed her as she had never been kissed before. It drove all thought out of her mind; all doubt; so that when he let her go—

'You love me,' she said, her face wreathed in smiles.

'Did you ever really doubt it? Yes, Marianne, I love you. I love you with all my heart and soul.' He looked down into her eyes with a wicked smile on his face. But beneath the wickedness was something warm and inviting; something deep and sincere.

'You're . . . you're not still angry?' she asked, although she could already tell by his expression that he was not.

'No, I'm not angry. How could I be, when the argument was all my fault?'

'Your fault?' She shook her head. Their argument seemed a million miles away, but still she could not let him take all the blame.

'Yes. My fault,' he said tenderly, stroking her windswept ringlets back from her face. 'Because I never told you what you needed to know. I never said the words you needed to hear. I never told you I loved you. But I am telling you now, so that there need be no more misunderstandings between us. I love you, Marianne, and I was a fool not to say so before now.'

'But . . . Nicole?' she asked, her mind in a whirl.

He shook his head. 'Marianne, I was such a fool last night. I was so taken aback by your ridiculous tale about being engaged to Jem Cosgrove – you're not, are you, by the way?' he asked, with a look that said if she was then it was no more than a minor irritation that he would easily sweep out of the way.

'No,' she admitted, smiling ruefully.

'I thought not. But I was so taken aback, and so hurt by what I saw as your lack of trust in me, that I didn't explain. Nicole is my cousin, my dearly beloved cousin, but nothing more. I love her, but I am not *in love* with her. I should have told you so last night. But I was angry with you. Angry with you for not knowing that I loved you, even though I had not said the words.'

'But I did know,' she said with a sigh. Her eyes went to his. 'It's just that, when I saw you with Nicole, the expression on your face – it didn't leave any room for doubt. It was obvious you loved her.'

He ran his eyes over her face; her smooth forehead, her raven ringlets, her gentian-blue eyes, her beautiful nose and enchantingly curved mouth, and smiled but tenderly this time. 'You're right. I do love Nicole, but not in the way I love you. Nicole is my beloved cousin. You are the love of my life.'

'Oh, Luke,' she said, leaning her head against his shoulder as they walked along the beach, too happy for the moment to think of anything else. But presently she asked, 'What changed your mind? What stopped you being angry and make you decide that I wasn't to blame?'

He held her closer. 'It was because I saw myself. This morning, when Nicole came downstairs, I embraced her, and as I did so I caught sight of myself in one of the hall mirrors. I saw what you had seen, and I saw that you had been right – there was an unmistakable expression of love on my face. And I knew that, at my first meeting with Nicole, it must have been even more pronounced. I thought I had lost her, you see – but then, Henri told you that.'

'Yes. He said you thought you had lost Nicole to the guillotine. He also said young love was a beautiful thing, and that he was sure I was too generous to begrudge you your happiness.' She sighed. 'I misunderstood.'

'It's hardly surprising. Henri's English is not very good. He can understand, and make himself understood. But when it comes to the finer points of the language—' He shrugged. 'He probably didn't even realize that his words could have another meaning; that they could imply that Nicole and I were lovers. He knew the truth; that we were cousins; of course. Even so, didn't your heart tell you that I was in love with you?'

'Yes, it did,' she admitted. 'But my reason told me that it was wishful thinking. If you had told me you loved me, then things would have been different, but you had never done so.'

'Because once I had discovered that fact for myself I had never had the chance. It was not until the Frenchman levelled his pistol at you, you see, that I knew for sure. It's strange, I had been envying Kit his love for Adèle when this whole situation began. I realized that he had found a woman he loved so much he would gladly risk his life for her, whilst I had found only shallow affairs. And I thought that I would never fall in love like that; that I would never find a woman I would willingly risk my life for because life without her would be meaningless and hollow. But when I saw you in danger, I knew with an all-consuming certainty that I was in love with you, and that nothing mattered except your safety. Because my life without you would be meaningless.'

He pressed her tightly to him and she felt a deep and profound sense of satisfaction at his words.

'There's still one thing I don't understand, though,' he said thoughtfully, as they walked along the beach. 'Why did you say you were going to marry Jem?'

She sighed. 'I overheard your conversation with my godfather. I didn't mean to, but I was in the library when you were in the adjoining room, and the door was not properly closed. I was going to close it, but once I overheard the *comte* saying you had compromised me and that you must marry me, I froze. And then I didn't like to close the door in case it made a noise: I did not want to draw attention to myself as the conversation had been about me.'

'You thought the conversation was about *you*?' asked Luke in surprise.

'Yes.' She was curious. 'Wasn't it?'

Luke burst out laughing. 'What a tangle!' he said. 'You thought

216

I was refusing to propose to *you*! Oh, Marianne, I was refusing to propose to Nicole!'

'Refusing to propose to Nicole?' she asked in astonishment.

'Yes. The *comte* felt protective of Nicole – they had escaped from France together, in fact that is how I managed to track him down – and he felt that, as she had stayed under my roof unchaperoned I should marry her. He said that, as her father was not here – her father was sadly killed – he must make me see my duty.'

Marianne gave a gurgle of laughter. 'So that's what he meant. I thought it was odd that he should say Papa wasn't there, but I assumed he meant that as Papa wasn't in the room he must make you see your duty himself!'

Luke threw back his head and laughed. Now that there was a perfect understanding between them he could afford to find Marianne's mistake a subject for mirth!

'But did you not hear the *comte* saying that I must marry her because I had compromised her?'

'I did. But I thought he was talking about you compromising me on our trip to France.'

Luke smiled. 'Nothing so dramatic. He did not even know about your – our – trip to France. He was talking about the fact that Nicole had been staying at the Manor without a chaperon. After all she has been through in France, worrying about a chaperon was the last thing on her mind.' He shook his head. 'But I couldn't possibly marry Nicole, even if she wasn't my cousin. She has always been very dear to me – I don't have any sisters, you see, and Nicole, as my closest cousin, filled that role – but as for offering her my hand in marriage? No. I love her, but only in the way Kit loves you; with a protective and caring love. But not as a man loves a woman – not as I love you. And so I told the *comte*. And when I had explained the situation fully he understood; it is just a pity that you didn't overhear the entire conversation. Besides, Nicole would not have had me even if she had not been my cousin, and even if I had asked her: she is shortly to be married herself.' He shook his head. 'She will be mortified if she learns that she nearly came between us. It is only because she wanted to meet you that she has stayed in Sussex so long. She is eager to return to Oxford, where her fiancé is waiting for her. She only came down here when she heard that I had been shot – news like that always seems to get out, no matter how hard one tries to prevent it – and once she had seen that I was all right she intended to return to Oxford straight away. But when she discovered that I was in love she did not want to go without meeting my intended bride.'

Marianne shook her head. 'What a tangle it's all been!'

'And all because Jem interrupted us when I was introducing you to Nicole. Another moment and I would have told you she was my cousin, saving us both a painful episode.'

'Poor Jem!' laughed Marianne. 'He was so determined not to miss the start of the dance!'

Marianne stepped over a piece of flotsam, holding up the skirt of her riding habit so that it would not get wet.

'But there is still one thing I don't understand,' said Marianne. 'How *did* you manage to find Adèle's parents? When Lord Dublaine hadn't heard anything of them we felt we had drawn a blank.'

Luke's hand stroked her waist and drifted down to her rounded buttocks in the most distracting way. 'It was Nicole,' he replied. 'She told me all about her escape from France, and mentioned that there had been other people who had escaped with her. When she told me of a *comte* and his wife who had become separated from their daughter, I wondered if they could be Adèle's parents. I didn't want to say anything in case I was wrong, but Nicole knew where they had been heading, and after that it was not hard for me to track them down. They had been staying in London with other *émigrés*, trying to organize an expedition to go and search for Adèle. Once I told them she was safe, and at Seaton Hall, they cancelled their search party and came on to Sussex – just in time for Kit and Adèle's engagement ball. The rest you know.'

They fell silent. The tangled situation was at last unravelling, and their tensions were ebbing away. Above them the sun was shining with the promise of spring, and the sand was damp under their feet.

'But why did you say you were going to marry Jem?' Luke asked at last.

Marianne sighed. 'I wanted to free you. I thought you were going to propose to me because you felt you had compromised me on our trip to France, and I could not bear it. I thought, you see, that my godfather had persuaded you to offer me your hand, and I wanted to free you from any feeling of obligation so that you could marry Nicole.'

'And had you told Jem?'

'That I would marry him? No. It was said on the spur of the moment.'

'Good. I don't want Mrs Cosgrove glaring at me over our wedding breakfast!'

'As to that, I'm sure I hope Mrs Kilkenny will not look too sour,' teased Marianne, matching his bantering tone.

'Mrs Kilkenny has already left the neighbourhood, as well you know,' he returned.

'And will you miss her?' asked Marianne, able to tease him about Mrs Kilkenny now that she was secure in his love.

'Hussy,' he said affectionately, giving her a playful squeeze.

'Why *did* you pay so much attention to her?' asked Marianne.

'To try and take my thoughts off you, of course. I was not meant to be falling in love with you, you see. I was meant to be looking after you because you were Kit's sister. But it did no good; nothing could take my thoughts off you. Every time I saw you I wanted to take you in my arms and do this. . . .'

He suited his actions to his words and turned towards her,

pressing his lips over hers, then gently parting them with his tongue, so that shivers ran through every part of her.

'And every time I saw you, I wanted you to,' she confessed.

'Did you?' he asked wickedly.

She smiled provocatively. 'Yes.'

And he kissed her again.

As his hands stroked her face he said to her, 'Why *had* you never married, Marianne? You had had a number of Seasons, and a number of offers – you see, even before I met you I had heard all about you from Kit.'

'Because I never fell in love,' she said simply. 'I met a lot of unexceptionable gentlemen. They were witty, charming, handsome – but they were also horrified by my unconventional nature. And even if they hadn't been, I could never have married any of them because none of them moved me in any way. I liked being with them, but forgot them as soon as they were no longer there. Whereas with you – from the moment I met you I knew I could never forget you, not for as long as I lived. You touched parts of me I had never known I possessed. When you kissed me I felt I was melting—'

'But then you had never been kissed before.'

'Not so. Lord – but I had better not mention his name. Suffice it to say that a young gentleman, carried away by the romance of a full moon, stole a kiss from me on the terrace of his London home. It was the last ball of the Season and I think he had decided that he must do something to try and show me that I would like to be married to him. But it didn't have that effect at all. In fact, it didn't have any effect. It seemed to me that if that was what kisses were like, I could very well manage without them.'

He raised one eyebrow. 'And do you feel that way still?'

'Not if the kisses are yours.'

He rewarded her with another.

And then, unclasping her hands from behind his neck and holding them in his own he said, 'Marianne, will you marry me?'

She smiled. 'Yes.'

'Even though I am anything but a gentleman?' he asked her teasingly.

'I think, perhaps, *because* you are anything but a gentleman,' she said honestly.

He nodded. 'A gentleman would stifle you, Marianne. We are both of us unconventional; we belong together, you and I. We will fit together – in every sense.'

She felt a shiver of anticipation as he drew her close, longing to be in his arms – and in his bed.

As if he could read her thoughts he gave a slow smile, then tilting up her face to his he kissed her with a languorous sensuality that made her buckle at the knees.

'I suggest we marry as soon as possible,' he said, as at last he released her.

And Marianne agreed.